SHADOWS OF THE MIND

A HORROR ANTHOLOGY

EDITED BY

LJ GASTINEAU, DORIS ROSS, & TRICIA SPARKS

TRINITY GATEWAYS LLC

SHADOWS OF THE MIND: A HORROR ANTHOLOGY

Trinity Gateways LLC
www.TrinityGateways.net

Cover Art & Interior Graphics by Henry L. Livingston
Cover Layout & Interior Design by Doris Ross

ISBN-10: 0988195194
ISBN-13: 9780988195196

CONTENTS

Contents

The Hunger

By Kevin Coryell

I woke up not remembering going to sleep. All was darkness. I didn't seem to be able to move. My brain felt sluggish as I tried to figure out where I was.

I remembered a hot summer day lounging by the pool with my wife Maria. I felt myself smile as I thought how beautiful she looked in her new bikini by the pool in our backyard, her foot trailing idly through the cool water as I cooked us some steaks on the barbeque.

The memory continued as I realized I could now move my hand. I clenched my fingers into a fist and for some reason slammed my hand upwards. After traveling only a few inches it hit solid wood which splintered with a crack. Particles of dirt started to drift down onto my chest.

The radio was playing an oldie, but goody when the song was suddenly replaced by an annoying noise; half beep and half squeal. The emergency signal blared for several seconds. I cursed aloud at the fact that they always tested the damned things during a song that I liked. Maria shushed me as the announcer came on the air instead of the song continuing. He started talking about some sort of attack in Orlando an hour away from us. We listened raptly as the news came in about hundreds being wounded and taken to the hospitals. Then he said a word that made us laugh- he said the Z word; Zombie! We both laughed and started discussing what we were going to do for Halloween the next month figuring that the broadcast was an elaborate hoax by one of the local theme parks to sell tickets for their upcoming haunted parks.

Again and again my hand smashed into the wood, moving over half an inch each time the wood cracked then fractured. After a time I started to pick at the bits that were smashed pulling them down, dropping them to my side. Small rivers of dirt came cascading down onto my chest and head each one getting larger as I removed more and more wood. I didn't care. I had to get out of there. I had to see Maria so I could let her know I was alright.

We had just sat down to eat the steaks I had cooked when we heard something that sounded like a car skidding out of control. It was soon followed by the sound of splintering wood as our front privacy fence was run down. We hurried out front there we saw an old Pontiac sitting half in our yard the hood having crumpled some when the car hit the concrete posts we had put in by the fence openings to prevent sagging. I told Maria to run inside and call 911. I sprinted to the car as I saw movement. I had to get the people out and make sure they weren't hurt!

I was out; somehow I was able to dig through the soft earth. I stood at the edge of my grave and stretched wondering how long I had been down there. I turned my eyes to the full moon above then looked around to gain my bearings. I lumbered towards the eastern gate of the cemetery my legs and knees were too stiff to walk normally. The family plot was not too very far from my house. Judging from the position of the moon I would be able to get home just before dawn. Wouldn't that be a great way for Maria to wake up; to find that I was still alive and it was all just a huge mistake of some sort?

I pulled both of the people out of the car. The driver was in bad shape having hit his head on the steering wheel when they crashed. He also had a huge tear out of his shoulder where it connected to his neck that almost looked like something had tried to tear a piece out of him with its teeth. I took off my shirt then tore a piece off. I pressed it to the wound using the rest of the shirt to tie an improvised tourniquet to keep the pressure on it while I looked at the other person.

I ended up walking for hours; I was just so stiff from laying in such cramped quarters for too long. Finally as the sun began to peek through the misty morning fog I saw my destination in front of me, I was home. I made my way through the broken portion of the fence up to the house to look through the front window. There she was, sleeping on the couch, my Maria. She had always told me that when I wasn't there due to business trips that she would sleep on the couch because the bed just felt too empty without me there.

When I knelt above the female passenger I could tell almost right away that they were both dead. Their eyes were pure white having rolled back into their head, their skin was a chalky gray. All up and down her body were places where she had been gashed open by the car wreck. It seemed she had taken her seatbelt off right before they had smashed into the post. Her right arm looked to be broken in several places probably from being caught half in the seat belt. I reached up to brush my hand over her face to close her eyes when she reached up and grabbed my arm. She pulled me down sinking her teeth into my forearm. Even as I cried out I reached over, snatched a piece of wood then slammed it into her head several times until she finally let go of me, collapsing to the ground with a large hole in the side of her head. Maria had come racing out at my cry asking if I was alright. I don't know why, but as I cradled my arm I made up a story about having fallen, the bloodied piece of wood somehow gashed open my arm. There was so much pain it felt as though it was on fire. The agonizing sensation was spreading.

I reached up above the front door trying to grab the spare key we had always kept there. My fingers could not seem to work well enough to get it, though. I fumbled for the key on the side of the door jamb and then dropped it to the ground. After several attempts at picking it up I finally gave up. I raised my arm then brought my hand down onto the door knocking hard. Again and again I knocked hoping to wake my love; desperately longing to see her smiling face once more. Within moments I heard movement inside so I stopped my pounding. Slowly the door opened upon the face of my lovely wife.

I saw once more in my mind's eye the first time I saw my wife, how the sun shone in her golden hair creating a brilliant glow.

I took a step forward, a deep moan escaping my throat as I tried to say her name. Her hands flew up to her mouth as she stumbled backwards.

I remembered the smell of her perfume on our first date, vanilla with a hint of sandalwood. We had eaten at an expensive steakhouse. I thought she had smelled better than any of the food we had been served.

The scent of her fear hit me and I found my mouth watering. Slowly I advanced on her as she backed up hitting the side of the couch.

I felt her soft skin against mine as we made love on the beach one night after a storm had blown through.

I grabbed her roughly pulling her up from the couch, towards myself. I felt my mouth opening. What was I doing? Why wasn't my body responding to me? All I wanted to do was hug her yet I seemed to be attacking her!

I remembered the taste of her kisses as we made out at the movies. The saltiness of her skin as I kissed her shoulders in the shower after an evening workout.

I couldn't stop myself, she smelled so good, so very delicious. I felt like I hadn't eaten in years. I struggled to stop, but my mouth opened wide then bit down hard on her shoulder. I pulled away a hunk of her flesh. It hung from my mouth as I swallowed. She had passed out in my arms. Oh, god, what am I doing?

The radio announcer had been right, there were Zombies. It seems I was now one of them. However, no one ever realized that while our bodies are driven by an instinctual need for food, our minds are trapped in the memories of who we used to be when we were alive. We see everything, we remember our lives in exact detail, but we are unable to affect the world around us. Who suffers the most from the curse of the zombie- the humans or the zombies themselves? That question is one that still remains yet to be answered.

Kevin Coryell is a jack-of-all-trades from Philadelphia who has called Florida his home since 1997. He has recently been published in the Anthology *Twisted Tales in 66 words* and *Zombie Writing!* and has his own E-book called *Twas the Zombie Attack Before Christmas*. You can follow his writing as well as finding other indie authors books at his blog:
http://promotewriters.wordpress.com/

Locker Number 51

By Bruce Memblatt

I did this every morning like clockwork because the numbers seemed to appear on my iPhone the same time every day. But today I was late for class. Mrs. Molnar had warned me if I was late one more time my grade for the year could drop a full point. I didn't like high school and Mrs. Molnar was fast approaching the number one spot on my shit list, presently held by gym teacher, Mr. Chet Chester.

Like practically each day I was sitting at my desk fidgeting and Mrs. Molnar was sitting at hers- fidgeting, then at the next desk over Joey Russo raised his hand. Naturally, he wanted to go to the restroom. One thing I could always count on was Joey would need to go to the restroom at the same time every day, and that the numbers would always appear- make that two things.

I imagined every morning Joey had an extra-large glass of orange juice. Then his bladder filled up just before he left his house, but for whatever reasons he never had time to relieve himself. So, by the time he got to class the pressure on his bladder must have been enormous. Joey was one of those kids that was out there. There was no mystery to Joey. He said exactly what was on his mind. Usually it was something he wanted. With Joey what you saw was what you got.

As far as the numbers went, at first I didn't know what they meant. I thought they were caused by a bug in my iPhone, until I saw the pattern. I wanted to look and see if the numbers were still there that morning. However, I didn't think I could take the risk of pulling out my phone. At least not with Mrs. Molnar watching; no doubt in rapt anticipation to find out if I did last night's reading assignment.

It was too late; Mrs. Molnar's quest had begun. Standing next to her desk, a piece of chalk dangling deftly from her right hand, she pointed to me then said, "Richard, Richard Piedmont..." (She always said my first name twice before she got to my last name. It was as if saying it twice would ensure I had heard her and no other Richard Piedmonts got confused with me then answered her question first.) "...in *To Kill a Mockingbird* what does Atticus Finch mean when he says, *the one thing that doesn't abide by majority rule is a person's conscience?*"

"That a person ought to stick to their guns no matter what anyone thinks."

"So, Mr. Piedmont, if you thought people should be hung for wearing red shoes, you should stick to your guns no matter how anyone advised you?"

"Well, I should be able to believe what I want to believe no matter what, but that is an extreme example, Mrs. Molnar."

"Nonetheless, Richard, according to Atticus Finch you would be correct, sticking to your guns, as you put it."

"Well, Atticus didn't say anything about right or wrong."

"Indeed, he didn't. His statement was morally neutral. He simply stated, *what goes on in a person's head when he faces just himself can't be determined by the will of the majority.* Very good, Mr. Piedmont, thank you," Mrs. Molnar praised as she smiled.

By that time Joey Russo had returned to his seat Mrs. Molnar was satisfied that I'd read last night's reading assignment, which I hadn't. Fortunately her question was so general it didn't matter. I had often wondered if she'd asked those general questions so she could tell herself her students were good, and she was a good teacher because her students had kept up with their assignments, rather than deal with the awful truth that most of us were just getting by. Regardless, she was in a better mood because I had effectively answered her question which meant it was a perfect time to ask her if I could excuse myself and go to the restroom because what I wanted to do most of all was to check my phone for the numbers.

The numbers worked like this: The first number was the locker number, I didn't get this part right away, but when I was sure the numbers that followed were the combinations to the lockers, the mystery behind the first number quickly fell into place. Every day through some mysterious burst of magic a new locker would open up to me. Soon I'd have the combination to every locker in the school. At first it didn't seem like much. You know, so what; you can open a bunch of high school students' lockers? Big deal! Why would a spirit or a force come all the way from the great beyond to transmit such insignificant information? I still hadn't figured that one out. But in the hands of a high school student this information wasn't all that insignificant.

Soon I discovered if I was careful I could have a good haul nearly every week. I'd find a dollar here a dollar there, a little grass, maybe some Vicodins. It was a nice little cushion to beef up my allowance before I grew up and went into the work force. Like I said, I was really careful, so no one would notice. I just took a little at a time. Some may argue that's how it starts, *just a little at a time*, but in my case it was true. I had no higher ambitions; this was just extra money and I was quite satisfied with it. I had no disillusions either. I knew what I was doing was wrong, there wasn't any moral neutrality here.

I had never been a wild kid. Sure, I'd smoke a little grass here and there. Overall I was pretty much down the line average. I didn't have teenage angst. I didn't even like teenagers with angst. Hell, I hadn't had sex yet. I figured everything in due time. I was pretty mellow.

Still the question of why this was happening to me seemed to always hang over my head like a rusty old pipe about ready to burst.

When I entered the boys' room it appeared empty. There was water dripping out of the faucet in the first sink, but it was always that way. Still, I ducked into a stall just in case anyone walked in. I lifted my phone from my pocket, tapped on it to bring it to life. I was relieved to see a new set of numbers on the screen fading in and out like they usually did. The locker number was 51 which meant it was located on the first floor, most likely in the closest hallway to the main entrance. The combination was 13-21-66. It was funny because it contained an unlucky number, a lucky number, and two thirds of the mark of the beast. Not that I believed in that shit.

As I walked out of class later that day I waved to Mrs. Molnar. She didn't seem to notice at first. I figured she was lost in thought contemplating tomorrow's lesson plan or maybe she was thinking about her shopping list. We spent most of our days with our teachers, but it was pretty amazing how little we knew about them. I guess the same was true vice versa; how little they knew about us. Mrs. Molnar gave a silent nod as the door closed behind me so I guessed she was still in teacher mode.

There was only one thing on my mind anyway; getting to locker number 51 to see what was inside. I was already salivating over what new goodies were going to be added to my haul. Usually I'd sit tight for a few minutes until everyone got where they were going and the halls were fairly empty, but I was anxious that afternoon. So I just trekked down the hallway. Mrs. Molnar's class was on the first floor; not far from where the locker was located. To my surprise just as I turned down the hall I saw Joey Russo standing in front of number 51. Shit, it was Joey's locker.

I kept walking past Joey as if I was just casually strolling down the hallway.

I waved my hand at him, "Hi, Joey."

He turned around then said (as only Joey would say,) "Didn't I just see you? Why are you saying *hi?*"

"I don't know. It's just a little hallway friendliness. Sorry, Joey."

Then he turned back around and closed his locker. I continued walking until I was satisfied that he was gone.

Joey had left. In fact the entire hallway appeared to be empty. I noticed the afternoon sun was still strong. The light poured through the windows down at the end of the hall reflecting against the long line of steel lockers causing a harsh glare. Fortunately, I could still make out the numbers. When I turned the wheel to the last digit in the combination (six,) I felt the click followed by the sweet release of the hinge as I pulled the door open. There was a strange odor and dust, something in dust, before I felt the blow to my head.

Who knew how much time had passed, but my eyes began struggling to open while my head felt like someone had trampled across it with steel boots. The most frightening thing I noticed as my eyes began to focus was seeing the back of Joey Russo's head. He was driving. I tried to move my hands and I felt rope tighten against my skin. My hands and feet were tied. It wasn't a joke. It wasn't a prank. It was serious. I tried to yell but found that I was also gagged. I realized I was wrong about Joey; there was more to him then met the eye. Unfortunately, what was hidden wasn't very good. Joey was crazy.

The car began gaining speed. From the back seat it was hard to tell where we were.

I heard him crying before he hit the gas harder. "What were you doing in my locker, you son of a bitch? Haven't you taken enough?"

How could I possibly respond? I was tied up, my mouth was gagged, and I was scared shitless. His car was moving fast. I tried to free my hands, but they wouldn't budge far. Joey didn't want a response anyway; his questions were rhetorical, and he was dangerous. I knew the only way out of this nightmare was to get him to take the gag out of my mouth allowing me a chance to convince him to let me go.

I wondered what he meant when he said I had taken too much. Could he possibly have known, or was it just a crazy rambling?

He called out, "You're going to pay for this, for everything!" Then he dug into the steering wheel as he made a sharp right turn.

My stomach felt like it tore out of my belly. The car started to bounce and jerk like it was a jackhammer. We were driving across a field. I was utterly lost. Matters seemed to be getting worse. Joey was becoming more belligerent. I didn't sense any easing up in sight.

The shiny blade of a knife in his hand crossed my view as the car came to a sudden stop.

How could my life change so dramatically, so quickly?

He turned his head. His eyes looked crazy, like glazed over; I couldn't see anything in them. I was searching for some kind of recognition. We weren't friends, but we saw each other every day. There had to be something inside Joey that would stop him from hurting me, but I saw nothing, except his arm moving toward me as the edge of the blade came closer. Tears formed in my eyes. I was going to cry because I realized I could actually die that day. For the first time ever, it became a palpable possibility in my mind.

He heard me sobbing and growled, "Shut the fuck up, bitch!" Then he took the knife and ripped the tape off my mouth.

I breathed in deep feeling relief. I thought, maybe I was wrong. Maybe I wasn't going to die, until he slapped me across the face and said, "You're not taking that too!"

He was sweating profusely. His face was red. Everything about him seemed out of control and sudden. I couldn't even begin to guess what he would do next. The sun appeared to be setting, but it was still strong enough to heat up the car.

I cried back. "Taking what, Joey? Taking what?"

"Don't play games with me, Richard. At first it seems simple, harmless, but then they get to you."

"Who gets to you? What are talking about?"

He slowly whispered, "They make you do stuff; stuff you would never do." His face was real close to mine, I could feel him breathe. His breath stank. I wondered if the *they* he was talking about were the spirits behind the numbers; it was a possibility, though he hadn't mentioned numbers. Maybe in some crazy way he was trying to warn me about them.

"Are you talking about the numbers?" I asked, searching for something in his eyes again, but I still saw nothing. All I could feel was the slap of his hand against my face.

Through my tears I sobbed, "Stop it! Stop it!"

He laughed. I saw my future disappear. He was getting farther away. I had to think of something to say to bring him back. I saw the handle of the door out of the corner of my eye. I wondered if I could possibly throw him off guard somehow and reach it. It must have been shut tight as a drum, but maybe in his mental state he forgot to lock it. It was a straw to grab onto. Then I remembered my hands and legs were tied. My stomach sank. Still I didn't think as I pushed my legs toward the door. They didn't budge far. Unfortunately, Joey saw them move.

He stopped laughing. He pressed his hands against the rope on my legs as he warned, "Don't try anything. You think you're a big shot, Richard. Think you're cool, but you don't know what you're doing, what you're playing with."

"Tell me. Tell me what I'm playing with. What am I playing with?" I was sweating. I knew there was no way he was going to open a window. We'd die like dogs left behind in a station wagon on a hot day before he'd open a window.

Then he did something strange; he reached into my pants. For second I thought he was going to rape me. I had no idea what he was capable of. My mind traveled to all kinds of horrible places. Instead he took my iPhone out of my pocket and set it down next to my face so I could see the screen. I knew he had to know about the numbers. That's what this was about. Maybe I could reason with him now. Since he knew about the numbers, this could be the way to get to him; they were something we had common.

I began to speak when his face seemed to calm. An expression came across his eyes that said he had reached some sort of peace. I'd finally seen something in his eyes; it was the wrong something.

He smiled, "It's too late."

Before I knew it he was gagging me again.

I pleaded, "Joey don't," but he wouldn't listen and I was silenced. I was too terrified to speak anyway. All hope vanished. I began to sob. He turned around. There was the back of his head again. I heard the key turn in the lock then the sound of the engine revving up. I thought, dear God, it was really happening. I glanced at the screen of my phone. There was nothing on it out of the ordinary, no numbers.

As he put the car in drive then we began to move I heard him say, "They want me to take you for a ride, Richard."

The car abruptly sped up. The ropes meant nothing anymore. Even if I weren't tied up; I'd be too terrified to move. The wheels jerked against the rocks and the grass. I couldn't speak. All I could do was pray for a miracle. The car continued to bounce then we picked up more speed. I was surely on my way to hell. I struggled for a breath. We were heading back towards the highway, and fast!

He called out, "They say it will be a short ride, Richard."

The car shook heavily. Turning back onto the road we slammed against the concrete border. Thankfully there was hardly any traffic, not that it mattered.

"I think they like you," he said. "They like me too. They like me billions."

We were flat on the highway again. The car rested at a standstill for a moment then he stomped his foot on the gas pedal and we took off.

I didn't think it was possible to drive so fast. We must have been going 150 if not more.

I heard him laugh, "They like you 150, Richard. Maybe 160."

And we went faster.

"How about 190?"

Just like Joey. I struggled to break free but it was no use. I saw him turn the wheel. My stomach was in outer space. Everything whizzed by so fast. Nothing was making any sense. Trees blended together, houses, signs, cars, my life; were all a blur.

I tried to cry out, "No, no!" This couldn't be real. It couldn't! But I wasn't able to speak. All I could do was listen to the sounds of the world disappearing. Joey was completely gone.

"1 99,300, 700, 973, 8000, 2200, 6, 13, 3000, 0000, 0000, 799, 2222, 666, 88888, 90, 0000, 5 4 3 2."

God, he just kept shouting out numbers! They had taken him over completely. Up ahead I could see the back of a gasoline truck. It was coming closer, fast as a rocket. The number zero flashed across the screen of my phone. I felt hot, very hot.

***

"No one can say what happened in that car yesterday. All we know is it was a horrible, tragic accident that took two of our finest classmates and friends from us; Richard Piedmont and Joey Russo. We pray they rest in peace. Like I said earlier, there are grief counselors on hand if any of you should need them."

"Mrs. Molnar. Mrs. Molnar!"

"Yes, Gwen, what's the matter?"

"Under Joey's desk I found a note. It says: *Richard Piedmont stole my magic.*"

Bruce Memblatt is a native New Yorker. He is a member of the Horror Writers Association. His stories have been featured in such publications as *Aphelion, The Horror Zine, Post Mortem Press, Dark Moon Books, Short Story Me!, Bewildering Stories, The Strange Weird and Wonderful Magazine Static Movement, Danse Macabre, SNM Horror Magazine,* and many more as well as in numerous anthologies.

PUTRID FRIENDS

BY INDY MCDANIEL

Andrew poked at the corpse with a stick.

It had become bloated and disgusting between the humid heat in the air and the swamp water it lay in. At one point, the body had been a woman. Probably not bad looking either. Now she was barely recognizable as human. All sorts of critters had come by to have a nibble. Some were nibbling on her still, as was clear by the squirming maggots festering in one of her eye sockets. As Andrew poked at her with the stick, there was a flutter of water as some unseen creature that had been taking refuge underneath the body fled in terror at the sudden prodding. Andrew took little notice of it, his eyes focusing on the body, mesmerized by it.

It wasn't the first time he'd seen a dead body. Hell, it wasn't even the first time he'd seen this specific dead body. After finding it about a week ago, he'd made a point to come by each day. He'd gotten the routine down so well that he almost arrived at the exact same time each day. Just as the sun was starting to set, he'd arrive and there she'd be, the unknown woman, waiting for him. He'd spend some time with her, sometimes talking to her, but mostly just poking her with the stick. When the sun set, he told her goodbye, got on his bike, and headed home for dinner. His mom wasn't too thrilled about the way his clothes smelled when he returned.

"Smells like you been rollin' in somethin' dead!" she'd exclaim, before demanding he change his clothes and wash up before dinner.

Andrew didn't much care about his mother complaining about the smell. He loved it. That wasn't to say he thought it was a particularly good smell. It wasn't pleasant, he knew that, but that was one of the reasons why he loved it so much. Each day, it got a bit stronger, filling his nostrils and making his eyes water. Each day, he studied her thoroughly, taking note of the transformation she was going through. He'd looked up the word for it in the dictionary.

Decomposing. Verb. To rot; putrefy.

It seemed to be a very fitting description. For the smell, especially. He thought that putrid was a very good way to describe it. Still, there was something about the smell that intrigued him. If he had to come up with a single reason why he kept coming back, he'd have to say the smell.

He wasn't really hugely interested in death or dying. Nor did he want to kill anyone or anything, not really. He might have gotten mad at his parents or at the bullies that picked on him at school, but his wishing physical harm upon them didn't last long, and it was never a hundred percent serious. Still, he seemed to have a nose for death. The nameless, mostly faceless, woman lying in the muck before him was the fourth corpse he'd stumbled across. It made him sad sometimes, to think that the people weren't being missed, that no one aside from him could find them. Three previous times, Andrew had watched the bodies decay until there was nothing left but bones.

Three times in as many years. Which meant he'd been about five the first time he'd seen a dead body. He hadn't been frightened or disgusted or traumatized into a mute state. He'd just been fascinated. At first, by the lack of life. That had been another woman. Her head had been smashed in and Andrew had seen her brain glistening through the split in her skull. He didn't understand exactly what the problem was. He understood the general concept of death, but being confronted with it so brutally for the first time, it just didn't click in his mind. He thought that maybe the woman was only sleeping, that she'd wake back up when her head finished healing. So he'd kept returning to check on her each day.

Andrew didn't notice her wounds healing, though. Instead, her body seemed to be going through some startling changes. He had become scared, because the woman seemed to be transforming into some kind of hideous monster. Still, he kept going back, if only to confirm that the monster was still where he left it. It always was, and more and more he began to figure out exactly what death was. It became more than just a concept for him then. It became a reality. He wasn't bothered by it. After all, the bodies he found weren't of children, so apparently, he had a quite a while before he had to worry about this 'Death' character himself.

The second body Andrew found had been further along already. The smell had drawn him in. He'd been walking through the woods behind his house when it struck him so he followed it back to the source. It had been a man the second time, stripped nude and shoved half under a dead tree limb. Andrew wasn't really all that sure on how the man had died. By the time he found him, he was already well into the transformation process. Being a lonely child of six, with few friends to play with, Andrew had decided to keep the man company during his transformation. He considered how he'd feel if he were dead and alone in the woods. He thought that it would be quite boring. He'd be very happy to have someone check in on him and keep him company for a while. So he'd started talking to the man, telling him about his days at school, how he hated broccoli and the bad dreams he had at night where he was being chased through long hallways by tall, lanky humanoid creatures with grey skin and black eyes.

The man never replied, but Andrew wasn't upset by the lack of response. On the contrary, it was nice to have someone to talk to who never told him to shut up, or go to his room, or told him he was stupid. It was nice to talk and have someone just listen to him, without them cutting in to talk about themselves. Yes, Andrew liked the second man quite a bit. By the time his body had been reduced to bones, he was actually very sad to see him go. He hoped that he'd be able to find another friend like the man. After that, Andrew explored the woods even more, in hopes of finding new friends to spend time with. It took almost another full year when he was about to give up, but then he'd found his third dead body.

Well, mostly...

The third body he found, Andrew wasn't too sure whether it was a man or a woman, because there really wasn't much body to it at all. It was an arm. Just an arm. Andrew looked around for any other pieces, but he couldn't find any. It looked as though the arm had simply fallen off, the edge smooth. Andrew wasn't sure what to make of it. He'd never found just an individual body part before; he actually found that stranger than a whole body. Who would just leave an arm lying around? Where had the rest of the person gotten off to? It bothered Andrew quite a bit. So he kept an eye on the arm, waiting to see if someone would come and claim it, or if maybe one day the rest of the body, like a last surprise gift at Christmas, would suddenly appear beside its missing limb.

There was no such luck, though, the arm was soon worn away rather quickly by the elements. Feeling even more disappointment, Andrew had given up his daily search for new friends. It hadn't been till a little over a year later that something had drawn him far into the woods, to the swampy marsh area. It felt as though some force was guiding him; he listened because he had nothing better to do plus it was quite persistent. And that's how he found his fourth dead body. The murky swamp water was making her body transform in even stranger ways than the others, which was one of the reasons why Andrew poked at her with the stick, to see what would happen. Another reason was to discourage any of those aquatic animals to take up residence in her. He considered what if he had been in the woman's place and thought that he really wouldn't much like having something living inside him. It was bad enough things were nibbling bits and pieces off of her, but to live inside her? That just seemed incredibly rude.

The sun had almost finished setting. Andrew would have to leave his friend for the night. But he'd be back the next day. He'd try to arrive even earlier. He could tell her transformation was nearing completion; he wanted to spend as much time with her as possible before it was. As Andrew set the stick aside, he told the woman goodnight. As he mounted his bike, he wondered where the bodies came from.

And why no one seemed to care that they were there.

Indy McDaniel lives in Florida and has been writing stories since he figured out how to scrawl letters into dead trees. He's had stories featured in a number of anthologies, including 'Leather, Denim & Silver', 'How the West Was Wicked', and 'Sinisterotica' (among others, all from Pill Hill Press), 'Bonded by Blood III' (from SNM Horror Magazine), & 'The Psyche Corrupted' (from Shade City Press). He's currently working on his first novel, *Nadya's Nights: An Action-Horror Tale'* . His Twitter handle is @steelcorpfilms.

Mountains Taunt

By Angela Trumbo

The cool windowpane offered little comfort to the forehead of the man who leaned against it watching the trees pass by, but only registered a blurry haze of evergreen. Hopelessness pulled at his mind offering pools of self-doubt and pity to drown in. So much easier to let go – give in to the beckoning depths of emptiness then slip under for the last time. His eyes closed in anticipation.

"Ryan?"

Damn. Ryan considered faking sleep, but decided to the hell with the effort so he opened his eyes.

"Good, you're awake." Gabrielle, Miss Bright Side of Life herself and wife to Ryan's best friend Jordan, sat down on the bus seat next to his beaming a cheerful smile in his direction. Everyone called her Gabby and the nickname fit her well for she gabbed more than anyone he knew. Inwardly he groaned. Through clinched teeth hidden behind closed lips, he acknowledged her greeting with a smile of his own.

"You okay?" Concern with a touch of sadness marked Gabby's features when Ryan didn't respond. His hands rested on his thighs. Gabby laid her hand atop one of his. "I'm sure you're still dealing with some unresolved feelings for Barb, but this hike will do you good."

The only unresolved feelings he harbored for Barb consisted of an intense desire to stab his ex-wife in her deceitful black heart, but he knew that wasn't what Gabby wanted to hear. Ryan growled in frustration. "Gabby-"

"Oh Ryan, it'll be fun. The mountains are beautiful this time of year. It is just the type of getaway you need right now to heal. You'll see." Gabby smiled patting his hand.

What he wanted to see was his ex-wife penniless and alone with a broken heart and dreams – or maybe just a broken neck. He would be most happy if she fell off the face of the earth or some high cliff with jagged rocks below.

Ryan rested the side of his head against the bus window, unfortunately his retreat into what he had hoped to be a dreamless sleep never happened for Gabby talked non-stop the entire trip. Her determination to lift his spirits made him want to jump out the window. This hiking trip with his friends would be the death of him for certain.

The bus stopped at the park entrance. Everyone rose to their feet in preparation to exit. Due to Gabby's persistent rambles, a line formed in the aisle long before either she or Ryan could leave their seats. Ryan spotted Jordan several spaces back in the line. When he eventually caught Jordan's eye; Ryan mouthed the words, "Thanks a lot."

Jordan grinned then mouthed back, "Had the best nap ever."

Ryan rolled his eyes and shot Jordan the middle finger.

They made their way off the bus headed towards the luggage which the driver had heaped into a stack. Gabby turned her attention to Jordan which left Ryan free to make a brief escape from the couple. He took his time to find his backpack in the pile while he enjoyed any peace available before he had to meet up with Jordan and Gabby.

With one strap slung over his shoulder, Ryan searched through the various groups of hikers scattered throughout the park. He inched closer to the trail entrance until Jordan called his name. He waved at him from a short distance away motioning for Ryan to join his group.

"Ryan! Nice to finally meet you." A tall man with sandy brown hair and a welcoming smile shook Ryan's hand. "I'm Andrew, the group leader." Andrew released Ryan's hand then placed his own hands on his hips.

"Mighty fine day to start an adventure, don't you think?" Andrew scanned the area before his gaze returned to Ryan before he added, "Especially for someone who needs a fresh new start."

Ryan shot a look at Jordan.

"Jordan has been a dear friend and told us all about your

misfortunes." Andrew placed an arm around Ryan's shoulders then gave him a friendly hug. "We're here to help you get through this. Later we can sit around an open campfire so you can talk about it."

Ryan shrugged Andrew's arm off, stepped back as he held up both hands. "Hey, man. It's cool. I'm good. I don't need to talk about anything."

Andrew exchanged glances with the other members of the group. "You don't have to go through this alone, Ryan. We can help if you let us."

"I don't need your help."

"Everyone could use a little from time to time."

"But I don't want your help."

Jordan came up behind Ryan and patted him on the back. "Come on, dude. They're just trying to be social. Give the guy a break."

Ryan closed his eyes then pinched the bridge of his nose where a headache brewed. "Okay. Fine. I'm sorry." His eyes opened. "I agreed to go on this hiking thing to get away from my problems, not be reminded of them."

No one said a word.

Ryan signed then, with head lowered, he dragged behind the members of the group as they entered the mountain trail. He kicked at the occasional rock muttering to himself. "All these blood-sucker bugs and other assorted crawlers on the ground hide waiting to reach out then attack the passer-by."

Ryan used his foot to shove a piece of fallen branch aside. "Even if the passer-by is minding his own business." He glanced up at the other hikers. "Like everything and everyone else should be," Ryan mumbled. "Until all of a sudden he gets knocked to the ground."

He kicked another rock. It flew off the path into a thicket of brush. "Then, as the poor bastard attempts to get up from his bone breaking and teeth jarring fall," Ryan's gaze rose to the sky, "The blazing hot sun burns its way through the treetops to scorch his eyes out. What a way to die — bruised, bloody, and no eyeballs."

"What the hell?" Ryan said after he plowed into the back of Jordan, bounced off, and came face to face with an expression of pure irritation. Before Jordan spoke, Gabby interceded.

"Come on, Ryan. Give it a chance." Gabby took a deep breath. "Let the mountain air cleanse your senses. Let nature's healing power soothe you. Everything will be okay. You'll see." She winked at him, giggling.

Ryan wanted to kill her. Strangle her in her sleep. No one could be *that* happy all the time. He gave Jordan a pitiful look and received a glare in return. To his dismay, Ryan found the attention of the group centered on him as well. Some had the decency to glance away once caught staring while others openly showed their displeasure with frowns or arms folded across their chests.

Ryan shrugged. "Fine. Sure. Whatever. I'm game."

With a little squeal, Gabby hugged Ryan. "Thanks, Ryan. Things will get better for you soon. I just know they will," Gabby said before she released Ryan then looped her arm with Jordan's. His friend bent down and kissed her. Ryan closed his eyes fighting back the pain for his own love lost. Even though Ryan sincerely hoped Gabby's prediction for him came true, he seriously doubted a favorable outcome to this trip. In a brooding silence, Ryan trailed behind the group.

A vision of who Ryan once considered his soul mate swam in his thoughts. Instead of dispelling the image as he had done so many times before, Ryan concentrated on the form letting it grow until his ex-wife shown as plain as if she stood before him. No tears came this time. Bitterness and hatred replaced what had once been sorrow. Sacred marital vows of 'for better or for worse, through sickness and in health, until death do we part' – nothing more than a load of crock. He often wondered why God didn't strike people dead – and especially *her* - for lying at the altar in front of a preacher, one of God's own chosen men for Christ's sake.

Ryan spat at his ex-wife's vision. The contents passed through the mirage landing close to Jordan's foot. His friend looked down then over his shoulder.

"Bug in my mouth," Ryan said with a lopsided grin. Jordan slowly shook his head then faced forward.

The day turned out longer and more brutal than Ryan had expected. While others marveled at the beauty of their surroundings, the sight of tree after tree grated on his nerves. For Gabby and Jordan's sake, Ryan pretended to enjoy the journey when he really wanted nothing more than to be left alone to lick his wounds and die in peace. They hiked for hours without a break. Even though Ryan ached all over, he refrained from complaints. Late in the evening the group stopped in a sparsely wooded area then prepared to make camp.

"What gives? Where's the little cabins ... shacks ... whatever they're called?" Ryan asked when members of the group pulled out their sleeping bags then placed them on the ground.

"Didn't I tell you that we do the rustic route?"

Ryan stared at Jordan. "Rustic route? What is that? What does that mean?"

"Means we don't use the park shelters." Jordan replied.

"What the hell? So what? We sleep on the ground with the bugs and shit?"

"Why do you think we told you to bring a sleeping bag?" Jordan countered.

"I don't know. Thought maybe we needed them to put on top of cots in case there weren't any sheets or something."

"It'll be fun," Gabby said as she bounced up next to Jordan. "Besides, if you see any bugs, just brush them away." She made a sweeping motion with her hand.

"They'll just crawl back and bite your ass for pissing them off."

"For the love of God, Ryan," Jordan said.

"Here, come with me and we'll find a place together," Gabby linked her arm around Ryan's then guided him further into the campsite.

Ryan mouthed "this is bullshit" as he passed Jordan to which Jordan shrugged and fell into place behind them.

Wrapped in a sleeping bag, Ryan tried to ignore the crevices poked into his back by the hard ground as he stared up at the splatter of stars against a pitch black sky. The scene grew blurry with each sweep of his lashes. He rubbed his eyes. His overly tired body demanded sleep, but his mind refused to give up the fight to stay awake. Sleep usually brought dreams. For Ryan, those dreams always involved her.

"Ryan? You awake?" Jordan whispered from the sleeping bag not more than a foot away from his.

"What is it?" Ryan whispered back.

"You alright?"

"Yeah, why?"

A minute or so of silence before Jordan answered, "Sorry about this morning. We all just wanted you to feel better and have a good time, if that's possible."

Ryan said nothing.

"I hate that you lost your company like that. It really sucks how it happened. I know you worked hard building it up."

"Jordan—"

"Barb did you wrong, you know. How she got the house-"

"And her cheating on you with the man who stole your company," Gabby piped in.

"Guys, stop," Ryan said.

"Oh, Ryan, I'm sorry. I'm sure it still hurts and all…" Gabby said.

"I'm tired. I want to go to sleep." Ryan's voice sounded gruff to his own ears. He waited a beat before he added, "It's been a long day. I'm not use to the hiking all over God's creation thing like you guys are."

When neither Jordan nor Gabby said a word, Ryan closed his eyes and sighed in defeat. "Just give me a little time to myself, okay?"

"We understand," Gabby whispered then paused before she added, "Love you."

Ryan cringed. He didn't have anything against Gabby, other than her ability to talk a man's ears off, but the last two words she said Ryan hoped to never hear from anyone ever again.

Several hours into a new day's journey the group stopped for a break. As usual, Ryan lagged a good distance behind everyone else. When he reached the rest area, Ryan noticed a few of the members conversed beside a lone female hiker. Coppery-red curls touched her pale ivory face like tiny flames. A loose ponytail barely contained the massive curls of her hair which hung half way down her back. Her slight shift in stance revealed all. Ryan's breath caught in his throat at the sight of her. She was beautiful and now headed his way while he choked and coughed. He quickly rubbed his watery eyes as he cleared his throat several times.

"May I join you?" His mouth opened, but nothing came out. She extended her hand. "I am Myra."

Still not a single word as Ryan continued to stand and stare at her.

"You okay, Ryan?" Jordan stepped up behind Ryan then patted him hard on the back.

"What is wrong with you?" Jordan whispered in Ryan's ear.

Ryan thrust his hand forward. "I'm Ryan." He grimaced as his introduction came out louder than intended.

Jordan laughed. "Yeah. I think we've already established that," he said moving to join Gabby. Ryan glared at Jordan's retreating form.

"It's nice to meet you, Ryan." His eyes shifted from boring holes in Jordan's back to the woman's hand locked with his in a handshake greeting. Ryan's gaze moved upward to her face and to the ruby red lips curved into a smile.

"Mind if I join you?"

Ryan glanced toward the other hikers on the trail.

"They are okay with me hiking with the group. Are you?"

Ryan shrugged. "Hey, if they're okay with it, then sure, why not. Besides, it's their hiking group, not mine. I'm just along for the ride, so to speak."

"I'm asking if you mind if I join *you* on your journey through the mountains."

"I don't have a problem with it if that's what you want."

"That's what I want," her gaze traveled the length of his body. "—for now."

"Yo, Ryan! What're you doing back there?"

Ryan's head snapped up at the sound of Jordan's voice. "Damn it," he said, surprised at how far Jordan and the others had traveled without him. He turned to Myra. "Um, we need to get going."

She smiled up at him as she placed her hand in his. Together they re-joined the group.

"Do you like the mountains?" Myra asked after they had traveled a while in silence.

"What?" Ryan's voice cracked. He cleared his throat. "Oh. Do I like the mountains? Uh...sure."

Jordan glanced back at Ryan. "Talking to yourself?"

"Rude," Ryan replied glaring at Jordan until he turned back around. He stole a glimpse at Myra and found her eyes upon him.

"There is such history in these mountains. A resting place for both the living and the dead," Myra said as her eyes moved from Ryan to the trees along the path.

He frowned as he followed her gaze; her comments on the dead left him a bit creeped out.

Hours passed with only the casual conversation of the other group members to break the silence. Fatigue slowed his steps until once again he drug several feet behind the others. Thankfully Myra stayed with him. Gabby turned several times to inquire of his condition, but never asked the same of Myra. To Ryan, it seemed Jordan's rudeness had rubbed off on Gabby.

The group finally decided to make camp for the night with Ryan ready to close his eyes and sink into oblivion. He dropped to the ground, exhausted to the core. His chances to hold out for the rest of the journey without body parts shriveling up and falling off seemed doubtful. The realization weighed heavy on Ryan's mind.

"So how's it going?" Jordan slapped Ryan on the back then sat down on the ground beside him. Ryan sucked in his breath as pain shot through his shoulder blades from the contact.

"Man, you okay?" Jordan raised a hand to Ryan's shoulders.

"Hands off," Ryan said dodging Jordan's hand. "Personal space, bubble thingy – whatever." He put his hands up as if to ward off Jordan. "Just lay off the hitting me routine."

Jordan's brows drew together in concern. "What is the matter with you?"

"What's not the matter with me? I got..." Ryan began until he noticed Myra watched the exchange. "Nothing. I'll be fine."

Jordan stared at Ryan for a moment before he cocked an eyebrow then said, "Aw ... so who's caught your eye?"

"Uh? What?" Ryan tore his attention from Myra to feign an innocent appearance.

Jordan motioned at the campfire with his head. "Who are you looking at?'

Ryan shook his head as he pursed his lips. "Don't know what you're talking about."

"Yeah. Right. So you're not eyeballing someone in that group of women across the campsite."

Ryan's eyes narrowed. His mouth opened to spout a denial, but gave up the charade and grinned. "It's that new chick."

"Who?"

"You know, that new chick." Ryan sighed when the blank expression remained on Jordan's face. "Myra."

"Myra?"

"Thought she told you guys her name?"

"Have you been drinking?" Jordan leaned closer to Ryan, took a sniff.

"What the fu – get off me!" Ryan gave Jordan a shove.

They glared at each other until Ryan muttered, "Whatever man." He returned his attention to Myra.

On the other side of the campfire, Gabby stood in silence beside Myra. Usually Gabby talked the head off anyone, stranger or not. However, not once had Ryan seen Gabby so much as look at Myra, much less speak to her. Gabby's snub of Myra when Jordan's wife had never ignored anyone else before added irritation to Ryan's previous anger. The day officially sucked.

"Hey, man. I'm sorry."

Ryan frowned then his gaze lowered to the ground.

"Guess I better get on over to Gabby before it gets much later." Jordan rose from his seat beside Ryan.

"Friends?" Jordan asked.

"Yeah. Whatever." Ryan said, before adding, "Everybody needs at least one asshole for a friend."

Jordan leaned down, hooked Ryan around the neck, and ran his knuckles over Ryan's head. "You little jerk. Should lose you somewhere in these mountains for being such a smartass."

Ryan laughed despite his sour mood, half-heartedly struggled to get free. Jordan released his hold then gave Ryan's forehead a little shove back. "Later, asshole."

Jordan turned to leave when Ryan taunted, "That's right. Copy me like you always do. We both know I'm the man that makes..." The words died on his tongue. The sorrowful expression on Jordan's face made Ryan wish like hell he'd kept his own big mouth shut. Damn. He hated pity- doubly so from his friends. They both knew the end of the phrase - 'makes things happen.' Just like they both knew the words no longer applied to Ryan.

Ryan bowed his head then waved Jordan off when his friend made a step toward him. He knew Jordan wanted to talk about what happened, but Ryan was in no mood to do so. He picked up a stick and drew random circles in the dirt of the bare ground while the other campers prepared for bed. Soon their low chattering gave way to silence, but Ryan remained seated on the end of his sleeping bag. Like so many nights past, sleep eluded him.

"Lay with me in the mountains," she whispered. The stick snapped in two. Ryan's eyebrows shot up, his mouth fell open. All sorts of mental pictures collided into each other as they entered his mind competing to play out his sex deprived fantasies.

Ryan glanced around the campsite for any apparent observers before he responded. "Are you serious? Because if you are we can go somewhere more private and—"

Myra laughed dropping her sleeping bag on the ground. She unrolled the bed then scooted it up to touch his. "I don't feel comfortable sleeping all by myself. If you were to sleep next to me..."

the words trailed off as, on hands and knees in the middle of her sleeping bag, she leaned in close to him. Her lips pursed as she studied him then slowly curved into a seductive smile.

Ryan lifted a hand to touch her, but Myra drew back and sat down. A mass of coppery curls brushed his hand tickling his fingers. She dug into the pack beside her bed. The smell of lavender filled the air. Ryan had a sudden vision of them running naked through flowers in a meadow. He blinked and snorted at the absurdity.

"What's so funny?"

Ryan shook his head at her question. Hell would freeze over first before he said a word.

Myra cocked her head to one side, grinned. "Keeping secrets?" Back on hands and knees, she placed a quick kiss upon his lips. A soft hand caressed his cheek before she swiftly moved away. Ryan sat in stunned disbelief as Myra opened her sleeping bag then dove inside. The sound of the bag's zipper ripped through the awkward silence. The colorful fabric enclosed her body until only her head peeped out from the top. She lay on her side with those amazing evergreen eyes focused on him.

"Perhaps one day..." Myra's eyelids grew heavy as she spoke, "I'll let you see my secret."

Ryan stretched out flat on his sleeping bag, but turned his head toward her. A long time passed before he joined her in sleep.

Another day on the mountain trail every muscle in Ryan's body cried out in pain. Ryan toyed with the idea of telling Jordan and Gabby he gave up. Even with Myra's presence in the group, he still had some serious doubts in his ability to complete the remainder of the hike. Once he had reached the conclusion he'd had enough, Ryan raised a hand to tap Jordan on the shoulder, but Myra seized his hand.

"Tell me your secret wishes and desires." She pierced his soul with sharp evergreen eyes. All his prior thoughts to leave the mountains disappeared.

"Climb with me higher and higher. Join me until we reach the peak." Ryan's eyebrows rose from the image her words created. He came to a halt which surprised Myra causing her to stumble back against him. The sudden contact of their bodies fueled his hard desire for her. A fine mist of perspiration covered his body as he fought to control his heated emotions.

"Ryan?" Jordan's voice echoed off the trees as he called out through cupped hands.

Ryan's heart raced like he'd ran a marathon. On wobbly legs he backed away from Myra. She turned to face him. Dark green eyes grew lighter until they resembled the shade of a new leaf bud on the stem of a spring flower. A timid smile touched her rosy pink lips. The meek expression created a calming effect. His eyes grew heavy as she stepped toward him.

"Ryan! What are you doing?"

Ryan flinched and whirled around to find an angry Jordan.

"We've been looking all over the place for you! Why didn't you answer us when we called? And why the hell did you leave the trail without telling someone?"

"I...I..." Ryan stuttered as words failed him.

Jordan held up a hand. "Just...just come on. Everybody's pissed off enough as it is that we had to stop and search for your ass."

"I'm not some little kid that needs a damn babysitter, you know."

"Could have fooled me."

"Screw you! If I'm such a burden to you and your precious friends, how about I..." a sharp tug on Ryan's arm stopped his rant. He glanced down then saw Myra press a finger to her closed lips.

Jordan spun around to face Ryan. "How about you what?" They glared at each other until Ryan broke eye contact.

Jordan ran a hand through his hair sighed. "Look. We don't have much further to go. Do you think you can hold it together for a little while longer?"

Ryan nodded as he continued to stare at the ground between the two of them. Although only a short distance, to Ryan it was like a huge gap growing wider. He had never felt more alone.

"No more going off on your own." Jordan wagged a finger at Ryan.

Ryan frowned in confusion. "But I wasn't-" he began motioning toward Myra.

"Shh," Myra captured his hand in hers then held it to her mouth to place a kiss upon his palm. In silence they walked behind Jordan to re-join the group.

"Sometimes, if you are real quiet and still, you can see the spirits of those gone long ago dance in the shadows cast by the fire's light," Myra said as she stared into the camp fire. Her gaze drifted to the trees behind them. "But the demons lurk just beyond the shadows, always waiting."

A chill shot up his spine. Ryan shuddered. Eyes darted to either side as Ryan checked if anyone else had heard Myra. Both Jordan and Gabby stared in his direction, but quickly glanced away.

"That's kind of a weird thing to say, you know."

Myra moved her head from side to side. Her eyes bore an alluring shade of deep green. Her movements reminded him of evergreen trees swaying in the wind.

"Why do you think it's weird?"

"Uh…seeing spirits…and…demons…and…Wait. You don't think that sounds a bit messed up?"

"Messed up?"

"Yeah. Creepy. Not normal. Messed up."

"Do you always look at the world through such a narrow view?"

Ryan's lips flattened. No matter how pretty, the woman sounded mental. He had enough problems of his own. Myra unzipped her sleeping bag, crawled in, and zipped it back up again. Good. He was through with her too. The sooner this hike ended the better. Ryan scanned the area, but avoided the campfire. If spirits and demons hung around the fire, he had no desire to see them.

Ryan fell back on his sleeping bag then stared at the dark sky. The only other person who bothered to talk to him turned out to be unhinged. Probably was the reason why no one ever spoke to her. He had teased Gabby about her willingness to talk to anyone or anything, even a fence post. Yet, she had not said two words to Myra that he knew of. Everyone else's rudeness he could accept. He reluctantly even accepted Jordan's, but Gabby was a tough one.

He drifted off into a troubled sleep, but awoke with a start bolting upright at the outline of a head above his face. The image retreated. He blinked several times before rubbing his eyes.

"Darkness is fading. Will you come with me?"

"Myra?"

In a panic, Ryan jumped to his feet as Myra disappeared into a thick gray mist. He squinted waving a hand back and forth, but couldn't make out a single thing past his own hand.

Myra grabbed his hand looping her fingers between his. "Come walk with me." She tried to use their joined hands to pull him along with her, but he held back.

"Ryan…I need you…come…be with me."

Still he hesitated.

"Don't you want to be with me?" The sound of her lost and forlorn compelled Ryan to comfort her.

"You know I do."

She tugged at his arm again. He finally followed. They traveled into the depths of the forest with the gray fog drawn around them like a curtain. Ryan grew anxious as time passed.

"Myra. Hold up a minute."

When she stopped and turned, the details of her body came into view as the fog lifted until only a slight fuzziness remained. Her coppery hair contained droplets of crystal shaped water that hung like ornamental jewels in the tightly sprung curls. Her skin glistened with dewy moisture. Her eyes blazed the darkest evergreen, almost a black with a green overlay.

"A few more steps and we'll be there." Myra took his hand in both of hers as she walked backwards.

"We'll be where?"

"Close your eyes." She said then paused.

His brows drew together. "Why?"

"I want to surprise you." When Ryan kept his eyes open, Myra bowed her head, whispering in a small voice, "Don't you trust me?"

"It's not that I don't trust...I don't see why you want me to...it's just that..." She sniffled as if on the verge of tears. He gave up. "Fine. Whatever."

Ryan fought the urge to take a peek from time to time as they traveled longer than he had expected, yet they moved through the forest at an amazing speed. Finally Myra placed a hand on his chest to stop any further movement. His eyes opened. She cupped his face pulling him closer so only she filled his vision.

"Kiss me."

Before he could respond, Myra rose on her tiptoes. She closed the gap between them pressing her lips to his. The contact was gentle, innocent in nature as her mouth blended with his. When he moved to take the kiss deeper, she broke away stepping to the side.

The view she stepped away to present baffled Ryan's mind. He glanced at Myra surprised to find her face beamed with pride and pleasure.

"Do you like it?"

Ryan nodded grinning as she took his hand once more and led him into a meadow garnished with colorful wildflowers. The rich green grass felt plush with each step he took into the little sanctuary hidden within the forest.

Myra twirled around with her arms spread out wide. The gaiety in her movement made Ryan laugh with her until she stopped then peered shyly up at him.

"Do you like it here?"

"Of course. What's not to like?" Ryan said.

"Do you want to stay?"

He shrugged. "Sure. Why not? For a little while, anyways." He glanced behind them frowning in concern by how far they had traveled into the meadow away from the trees. "But soon we'll need to get back to the group."

"Why?" She tilted her head sideways and asked, "Why do you want to go back?"

Ryan snorted. "Well, I sure as hell don't want to be left out here on my own."

"But you're not on your own."

"More reason to go back. I doubt I can even take care of myself out here, much less take care of you, too."

Myra smiled as she took a step closer to him. "What if I told you that I'm very familiar with these mountains?"

"Guess that would help," he said absently then glanced at his watch. His eyes widened. "Man, we gotta go."

"Go where?" She touched his face closing the gap between them. "What do you have to go back to?"

He was taken aback by her question, "What?"

Myra brushed her fingertips across his cheek. "What do you have to go back to?"

She moved her fingers to trace the pattern of his lips. "Is there a girl? A job? A home you have left behind?" She shook her head. "I think not."

Ryan scowled brushing her hand aside. He took a step back. "What the hell?"

"Maybe you just wanted to experience the mountains alone. Get a feel for nature and all it has to offer." She moved close to him gazing into his eyes. "Do you want to become one with nature?"

Something in Myra's tone made Ryan nervous. He took another step back. "Never have been much for nature and all that feel good get in touch with Mother Earth stuff. Besides, we need to get going."

A hurtful expression crossed her face. "I thought you said you liked it here?"

He shrugged. "It's okay. A place tree huggers would love to visit."

Myra moved forward to stand in front of him. A gentle scent of fresh lavender filled the air around them. She touched his face with both hands.

"Stay here with me. We can be together. Forever."

At first he laughed, but the laughter faded as Ryan gazed into eyes no longer green. Round pools of blue cast his reflection like twin bodies of deep water. He shivered.

"Kiss me," she whispered through shiny apple red lips plump and poised. Myra pressed against him. A sudden desire for her gripped his loins. She consumed his vision, his thoughts, and his senses.

"Join me," she said as she placed her hand to the back of his head bringing his mouth down to hers. He moaned as the sweetest of honey taunted his taste buds giving him an unquenchable desire to have more. His tongue delved deeper into her mouth while his body heated with long starved passion.

"Ryan." The faint sound of his name registered deep inside ringing like a bell of warning. Jordan?

"Ryan."

So intoxicated by her presence, he ignored what he thought to be Jordan calling his name. Instead he imagined the voice belonged to Myra begging him to give her more. His arms wrapped around her holding her body firm and hard against his. Ryan made love to her mouth with each thrust of his tongue. His pelvis ground against hers. The rhythm they created worked to drive him into a fevered madness.

"Join with me." Myra said lightly stroking him.

Ryan trembled at her touch.

A gust of wind whipped at their bodies bringing about a strong earthy smell as if someone had freshly raked rotted leaves to expose the dark moist dirt below. The air alternated between searing heat and frigid cold, a swirl of temperatures that burned flesh and froze bones. He winced shaking uncontrollably as his skin prickled with small blisters.

Fear tore at his soul, but lust burned in his loins as if consumed by fire from the inside out. His hands rose to touch her face. He gasped to find tiny splinters protruded through the popped blisters on his skin. He fell back a step in shock. She wrapped her arms around his waist drawing him back to her.

"Ryan!"

Jordan?

Wind ripped up the grass tearing small leaved-covered branches from the trees. A mixture of dirt, grass, and branches whirled around them. Ryan's eyes widened, his pulse raced. He fought to pull away from Myra as particles from the debris pelted him until every limb on his body went numb.

Barely able to stand, Ryan leaned against Myra peering into eyes that burned an evergreen fire. Warm hands soothed battered flesh as she gently cupped his face. "Kiss me with your spirit."

Myra pulled his head down as her lips rose to meet his.

"Fill me with your soul." Searing pain replaced pleasure as she drew his tongue into her mouth and sucked.

He couldn't breathe!

"Ryan!"

Jordan! Help me!

"Stay with me in the mountains." The words echoed in his head as his body jerked and twitched. He crumpled and Myra covered him with her body. Deeper he sank into the ground as the marshy grass crawled along his skin penetrating his pores. Half-glazed eyes watched as the grass consumed Myra's smiling face. Ryan's lips parted to scream. A muddy substance filled his mouth and continued down his throat. Day gave way to night as grass covered his face.

"Join me, be me, be the mountains."

"Ryan!" Jordan's voice grew fainter until silence reigned.

Angela Trumbo is a resident of Nashville, Tennessee and enjoys writing in the paranormal, horror, and thriller genres. She has one short story published, "Folly of Youth", in the anthology *Soundtrack Not Included*. Another short story, "What Happened to the Girl?", is scheduled to be published in the anthology *Nashville Noir* in September 2012. Check her website, angelatrumbo.com, for more information about the author and a link to her blog: Angela's Visions.

Iron Will, Broken Fingers

By Nathan Elberg

How many people would Simon Sheta kill—allow to die today? Half? Three quarters? More likely: all of them. If he authorized one appeal out of fifty, it was unusual. Two was exceptional; three, unheard of.

"Next is the case of a mother who shot an intruder, claiming it was to protect her baby. The victim was—"

"Did she have a lawyer?" Simon's questions were always the same. Other issues were irrelevant for him.

Alex, as the Justice Minister's assistant, had the job of winnowing through all the applications to appeal a criminal verdict. Once a week, after lunch, he would present the fifty petitions most likely to be approved, and Simon would quickly make his determinations. The hundreds, sometimes thousands of others were refused. Alex wiped the perspiration from his forehead and leafed through some papers. "Um... yes."

"Was the judge competent?"

Alex turned another page and scratched his head. "Stan... yes, Standard profile qualifications."

"Did anything prevent her from defending herself?"

"No." Alex rummaged through the file. "The question is, um... well, whether—"

"The question was for the presiding judge to deal with. Leave to appeal refused."

People wanted to appeal, especially when convicted of one of the many capital crimes such as murder, armed robbery, reckless endangerment... The week or so it took their application to be refused meant another week of life. Before Simon, the process used to last for decades.

That in itself was a denial of justice. A person who was supposed to be executed was not entitled to an extended existence. The gallows was constantly swinging, marking the rhythm of the relentless drive of the law. That satisfied the requirements of Justice.

What bothered him was Alex. Usually calm and efficient, today he was on edge, rubbing his thin nose, stammering, looking in files for answers he should know, scratching his brown, wavy hair. A sheen on his forehead reflected the light from the ornate office chandelier.

As Justice Minister, Simon Sheta's written word, signed and sealed, was law. Whatever whim, whatever fancy, it was binding. Of course he didn't rise to the Inner Cabinet by indulging those whims. That was by virtue of his discipline, his moral character, his zealousness to do what's right. He had been forced to leave the Education Ministry because of the outcry against his plan for universal education. The Prime Minister had then given him the task of cleaning up the Justice system, along with the authority to carry out the job. Simon had asked for the Ministry of Culture, or perhaps Sports and Recreation. He would have awarded literary prizes instead of death sentences; encouraged healthy living rather than enable quick executions.

The Prime Minister said Simon's iron will was needed at Justice. He didn't know that what looked like iron was actually a tremulous shadow, cast by Simon's servitude to responsibility.

Alex was his third assistant in as many months. The first had argued with him about all the appeals Simon had rejected. The second felt personally responsible for erasing the last hope of all the appellants, and tried to commit suicide. It was the assistant after all, who entered the rejections into the system. Alex was too soft, too effeminate for Simon's taste. Was he now showing signs of cracking?

"Next, um, is the case of a man who tried to burn down his neighbor's house, claiming she was part of a coven of witches. The neighbor is appealing the judge's ruling that she actually is a witch."

"What?" Simon put his hands on his desk, and leaned forward.

"Yes… Standard profile qualifications."

Simon waited for Alex to realize that he hadn't asked the regular questions.

"What did you say the man claimed? What's the appeal?"

"Um, that—"

Simon rose. "There's no such thing as witches." Was this file why Alex was on edge, or was it something else?

"Sir, the arsonist presented supporting evidence which the trial judge ruled valid."

Simon's nostrils flared. "The judge ruled…"

"That the neighbor is a witch."

He extended his arm. "Let me see that."

Simon quickly scanned the judgment summary, looking for some reason to dismiss the whole case as someone's ridiculous error. He couldn't find one, and it wasn't his role to do an in-depth review. He handed the parchment back to Alex, and ran his fingers across his thin, graying hair.

"What was the final disposition on the arson charge?"

"There was none. The judge resigned from the bench before rendering his judgment on the actual case at hand."

The Minister arched his eyebrows. "He can't do that." Sal wouldn't do that. The judge was a friend of his; he and Sal had been called to the Bar together. They had played together in a jazz band, stopping only because of Simon's ruined fingers.

"Well, the judge sentenced the neighbor—"

Simon frowned. "You mean he sentenced the witch?"

"Sir?"

"When a judge makes a ruling about something, it becomes part of the body of law. There's a legal judgment that witches exist. As crazy as it seems, it means there are witches, and the neighbor is one of them. I can't dismiss the ruling just like that."

"As you say, sir."

"You're not a witch, are you Alex?"

"Um, I…"

"I'm joking. You have to have a sense of humor when things are difficult. Anyway, continue."

"Judge Salvatore sentenced the neighbor… the witch to death and issued an arrest warrant for the other women supposedly in the coven. He read the sentence out loud for the court record but then quit before dealing with the alleged arsonist." Alex handed him the file then whispered, "The Court Clerk says that as the judge read the sentence, he looked terrified. He was pale and shivering."

Simon took a can of ginger ale from the small fridge next to his desk and leaned back in his high leather chair. "This is crazy. The existence of witches is now established by law in a modern, civilized society." He took a long swallow, shook his head.

Simon flipped through the file quickly then picked up a legal parchment and a pen. "Have Judge Salvatore jailed for dereliction of duty and contempt of court. No, make that for contempt of our entire legal system. That's a capital offense for a judge. Drop all charges against the arsonist if he cooperates, and is able to identify the rest of the coven. Arrest them all. If they're really witches, we'll hang them. If not, they may want to press charges against the arsonist." He took another sip of his drink. "If they live, they'll probably sue the life out of him."

Alex gaped. "You're not taking the witchcraft accusation seriously, are you?"

"There are lots of people who believe in them. Fear of witches can wreak havoc. I take that seriously. Am I wrong?" Simon glared at his assistant. He couldn't let Alex know that he agreed with him; the whole thing was ridiculous. But the judge had made a ruling, probably a stupid ruling. It was the law until overturned.

The Justice Minister scribbled a few lines on the parchment and grimaced. He signed it, grabbed his embossing machine, and legally sealed the end of his friend's freedom. "I want him behind bars by the end of the day."

"Sir, the arsonist said that there are eighty witches in the coven."

He sneered. "Eighty? I don't believe there's even one. It's probably a mahjong club or something like that. Not a coven."

"So then you grant the appellant leave to appeal being declared a witch?"

Simon put a hand over his eyes, then squeezed his temples, remembering some of the things he'd heard from Jason, his son. It made him tremble. "The whole case is insane. But I can't just let her go. Salvatore isn't a fool. He wouldn't have declared the woman a witch without having a good reason." He eyed the bottle of whiskey on the table. "I'll give it a few days before I decide." Simon put the file on top of a cabinet.

"No; I can't give it a few days." He frowned. "The rules I implemented." He picked up the folder again. "What if she really is a witch? I can't take a chance on her bewitching anyone during the appeal." He turned to the appropriate page and stared at it, pen in hand.

Alex shuffled his feet, scratched his head, and coughed. He stuck his hands in his pocket and pulled them out.

It was time to decide. She definitely wasn't a witch. The ruling was absurd. But what if she was already doing things to people? What if she was preventing Simon from seeing the truth, which was right in front of him? Jason, who was way smarter than him, took this stuff seriously. A wave of dizziness swept over him, which he washed away with ginger ale. Be a man; make the difficult call.

"Refused," he scrawled. Be a man who sacrificed an innocent—probably innocent—person in order to preserve the justice system, society, something... His reputation?

He handed Alex the order for the arrest of Judge, and for the arrest and hanging of the witches, if that's indeed what they were.

"Sir, this will take a little while to put in motion." Alex's eyes shifted to the stack of appeal files.

"I'll continue without you. Go ahead."

The Minister took the next file, scanned it quickly, and scrawled "refused." He did the same for the second, the third... He scanned the fourth file, then the dizziness roared back. So soon? He wasn't ready for it; he could never be ready for it. He placed Jason's file at the bottom of the pile. It was what had actually put Alex on edge. The Justice Minister poured himself a tall glass of whiskey, wiped the sweat from his brow, before taking a deep swallow.

Down the wrong pipe. Simon coughed and gagged as he spit his drink all over his hand, over his desk, over the last hope for life of desperate people. He grabbed some tissues, blotted, and surveyed the damage.

Not too bad. The files stank, but that would evaporate soon enough. He went back to work, going through them one by one, checking for the answers to his standard questions. He flipped through forms and documents, all the while wondering about the witches, all the while fearful of the application he had placed at the bottom. One by one, he scrawled "refused" on each then put it to the side.

He didn't like doing this alone. He was happier not knowing anything about the people whose lives he was ending. He preferred dealing with cases; with simple answers like yes or no. He hoped Alex would be back before he got close to the bottom of the pile.

He refilled the glass of whiskey and opened another file. He swirled his drink in his glass as he pictured the schoolyard brawl clinically described in the trial documentation. The appellant was the only one with a baseball bat; the only one with any kind of weapon, so everybody blamed him for the deaths. Nobody had run any forensics on the bat. It was the obvious cause of death, but that didn't mean that it actually was the instrument that had bashed in two skulls. Simon put the empty glass to the side, flexed his fingers, and carefully wrote "granted" across the page.

It was late afternoon when Alex returned. His hair was disheveled; there was mud on his shoes, dirt on his face.

"What the hell happened?" The whiskey had modified Simon's usual formality.

"The Police insisted I go with them to witness the arrest. Judge Salvatore resisted."

Simon arched his eyebrows.

"The Judge spat at me then slammed the door in my face. He must have escaped out the back."

Alex sat down in the guest chair. Simon decided to ignore the breach of protocol for the moment.

"I need a drink."

Did Alex think his boss was a bartender? "You want me to pour a drink for you?"

He nodded.

Maybe it was time for a new assistant. Maybe it was time for a new Justice Minister. Simon poured a small amount, and handed him the glass.

Alex downed it in one shot, and snorted. "Haa." He shook his head, as if shaking off a bad dream. He looked at the armrests on the chair as if suddenly realizing where he was. He rose a couple of centimeters, paused, then sat back down. He held out his glass.

The Justice Minister was not a bartender. He took the glass from Alex, set it on a table.

"When the Police finally broke into the house and couldn't find him, we tried to follow his trail. But he lives at the edge of the green zone. There are woods and streams; too many places to hide in. They lost him."

"And? Now what?"

"Fifty men were assigned to continue the search. Half of them refused."

"Refused? Why?"

"They're afraid of witches."

"This is what I was talking about before: the havoc that fear of witches can lead to. Let me make it easier for the Police. They're breaking the law by refusing. That makes them also subject to arrest for dereliction of duty. But who's going to arrest them? Other police?"

"What if they're also afraid, and refuse?"

"That's exactly the problem. I've got to get past that fear. Any suggestions?"

Alex shook his head, looking at the floor.

The Justice Minister walked to his desk, scribbled a few lines on a parchment, took a deep breath, then signed and sealed it. "The Police have more leeway to protect themselves when in hot pursuit, without fear of disciplinary action. Arresting Sal and the coven of mahjong players, or whatever they are, is now officially a hot pursuit. If the police are afraid, they can do whatever is necessary."

Alex's hands were trembling as he took the document. "Are you sure you want to do this? Maybe you should consult—"

He sighed. "I'm sure I don't want to do it, but I won't consult anyone. It's my responsibility; no one else's."

Simon's heart trembled. There were four files left.

Alex gave his summaries.

"Refused."

"Refused."

"Refused."

Alex picked up the last file, leafed through it quickly, and started to sweat.

The Justice Minister leaned back in his chair, whiskey in hand. "Well?"

"Next is the case of a man convicted of murder, who claims he was framed in order to get back at his father, the Justice Minister. The witnesses—"

"Refused."

Alex stared at his muddy shoes. "Sir, it's Jason, your—"

"I know who it is. Did he have a lawyer?"

Alex flipped through the folder.

"Of course he had a lawyer," Simon answered his own question. "I made sure he had a damned good one."

So why was Jason convicted? Was his lawyer as good as his reputation? Or was he part of the frame-up?

"Was the judge competent?" Simon asked.

"He had, uh, the usual; I mean the standard profile qualifications."

"Did anything prevent my son from defending himself?"

Alex closed his eyes and shivered. "No."

"Then why are you arguing with me?"

Alex swayed on his feet. "Don't you want to investigate, to—"

Yes, please, his heart cried out. Simon walked over to his assistant, grabbed his arm, and stared into his eyes. "Don't you think I want to do everything to save my son? But I'm the Justice Minister, not the Jason Minister. I can't treat him differently than anyone else."

"It's his life!"

"Don't you think I know that?" he shouted. Simon felt like beating Alex with a baseball bat. "I've had enough of you. Get me a hotel room for tonight, then get out of here."

"Yes sir, I'm going. Don't you want to be with you wife?"

Simon let go of Alex, and wiped his eyes. "She won't want to be with me."

***

Part of Simon's office furnishings included an overnight suitcase, equipped with everything he would need if he couldn't make it home on a given night. As Justice Minister, he had to be ready for many kinds of emergencies. Best not to be distracted in such situations by a lack of fresh underwear.

Simon opened his bag on top of the counter then stared at the contents. As expected, everything was there, neatly folded and arranged. He had a sour taste in his mouth from supper, though there had been nothing wrong with the food. The hotel restaurant was too good to allow that. But the leek soup, the braised veal, even the salad, all tasted rancid. He went to the washroom and swirled mouthwash for a full minute. It too, had a rancid taste. He returned to his suitcase and resumed staring at it.

The Justice Minister's meditation on his luggage was interrupted by the phone; Alex. He hastily pulled it out of his shirt pocket, and stared at the picture on the screen. He slid open the back cover, removed the battery, and put the whole thing on the night table.

It was foolish to have left it on till now. The Ministry would never disclose his location, but the GPS on his phone would pinpoint precisely where he was. Hopefully, his wife wouldn't think to check. He didn't want to have to answer to her. Hopefully Alex would leave him alone now.

He turned on the television. Football. Jason had been the ninth pro draft choice this year; his long-distance accuracy kicking field goals was uncanny. His talent was going to change the perennial loser that chose him into the team to beat.

Would have changed. His son wasn't going to kick any field goals after his hanging. Simon turned off the television as he remembered the party they threw after the draft. Jason, the reluctant hero, was more interested in talking to people about the history of some arcane central Asian mysticism than football. It sounded like witchcraft: riding a wind-horse, absorbing spirits of the dead... Sounded weird, mostly. Jason was more concerned about his graduate research than the millions of dollars a year he would earn splitting the uprights.

It hadn't been easy for Jason to become such a good kicker. More than once, he had broken his father's fingers when he missed the ball. Simon never let on, and never refused to hold the ball for him. The hand of Justice was powerful, but it was also crippled. Writing more than a word at a time made his fingers cramp up.

He flipped through the television channels; every station annoyed him or reminded him somehow of Jason. He threw the remote on the bed.

He shouldn't let himself mope. This was a full service hotel. He opened a little bottle of rye from the hotel mini-bar.

The Justice Minister picked up the TV remote again then went to the hotel menu page. Room service... business services... personal services... massage... No, he didn't want a massage. Intimate services... female... standard... He usually chose standard when traveling. But even if they sent the most beautiful, buxom brunette, it wouldn't be enough to distract him tonight. Discussion... voyeur... endurance... punishment. Punishment sounded like an appropriate choice, considering his accomplishments today.

"Estimated time of arrival: twenty-five minutes. Please shower beforehand." He shut off the monitor, grabbed his Grecian Formula, undressed, and headed towards the bathroom.

Simon liked the hotel shower; the water came at you from all sides at once. Turn it to maximum and it was like a storm of needles, stinging, penetrating, cleansing…

But that wasn't for today. The girl would no doubt provide all the pain he needed.

The steam itself was like a meditation, cleansing his mind, replacing his misery with fog. He scrubbed himself aggressively. He wanted to be at his best for his scheduled affliction.

There was a razor and shaving cream in the suitcase. Simon dried himself roughly, threw the towel on the floor, before stepping out of the bathroom. A stick smashed down on his back, knocking him to the hard, wooden floor.

A red leather boot shoved him onto his back, and a woman dropped down to straddle his stomach. She grabbed him by the hair, pulling his face towards hers. With the other hand she pulled a little card out of her pocket.

"Simon Sheta, Minister of Justice, suite 4509: you need to be punished," she hissed.

Simon tried to wipe the tears pooling in his eyes. She grabbed his hands and pinned them to the floor with her knees.

"Hey! I ordered this for entertainment. To make me feel better, not to be abused."

"You find punishment entertaining, do you? It makes you feel good?" She slapped his face, raking his cheek with a jagged fingernail. "Getting excited, honey? Enjoying yourself?" She bent over to lick the blood gathering on his cheek.

He had ordered this. It was more intense than he anticipated, but sex with pain was new to him. He should try to enjoy it.

"Yes." He yanked his arms out from under her knees and clamped his hands onto her breasts. She put one arm behind her back, reached between his legs, and twisted hard. Simon gasped as he let go. She didn't.

"I know you get a kick out of punishing people, honey. How do you like being on the receiving end?" She twisted the other way.

The Justice Minister tried to scream but was in too much agony. He struggled to focus the pain onto arousal, to transform it into pleasure.

He couldn't. It wasn't the torture, though; his mind was filled with an image of Jason, proudly holding up the jersey of his new team.

Tears clouded his vision. He squeezed her breasts, trying again to distract himself. Simon berated himself; he should have clicked "info" before selecting "punishment."

She let go of him to push her hair out of her eyes. Simon took the opportunity to look at who he was with. Tall, she had a thin, small nose, high cheekbones and wavy brown hair, falling luxuriantly around her shoulders. She wore a tight, plain, button-down blouse open at the top, and a knee-length navy-blue pleated skirt. Except for the fire in her eyes, there was nothing about her that looked threatening.

"Do you make all your customers suffer like this?"

"Not customers; victims. You're the first, my dear Simon."

That could be bad; trying too hard to prove herself. "What's your name?" he asked.

"My name?"

Simon had never seen such a sinister looking smile. He put his hands on her thighs.

"Are you sure you want to know?"

He rode his hands higher, and nodded.

She pulled up her skirt then lightly caressed his arms. "It's long."

"It's a long night," he said, licking his lips.

"Margaret," she whispered.

"That's not a long—"

"Salvatore."

"What?"

"Ryan. Julia. Joseph. Steven. Sylvia—"

"What the hell are you saying?"

She slapped him once more, this time raking his skin with all her nails. She resumed her recitation.

"That's enough; stop it." He grabbed her breasts and twisted with all his might.

She gently took his hands, put them back on her thighs, and continued the names. They were annoyingly familiar; probably because they were so common. "I'm almost done telling you." She kissed her fingers then softly put them to his lips. He flinched.

"Don't be afraid. I'm here because you need pleasure. Move your hands higher."

The Justice Minister was confused, but obeyed.

"Lianne. Shaya. Anthony. Sylvester—"

"Please. Can't you simply tell me what to call you?"

She bent forward and pressed her lips to his. She forced her tongue between his teeth then sucked his into her mouth. She reached again between his legs, but this time without twisting.

He moaned in pleasure. This was what he wanted.

She yanked with her hand and bit hard at his tongue. She sat up on his stomach, smiling, as he screamed and spat blood onto the floor. He panted for breath, his chest rapidly rising and falling.

"How are you enjoying yourself so far?"

"I'm not," he said with a gasp. "Are all punishment women like you?"

"I've got the standard qualifications. Don't you enjoy punishment? You inflict it all the time. What were you expecting?"

He used his arm to wipe more blood from his mouth. "I don't know. Maybe a toy whip; handcuffs… Something playful. Something erotic."

"I can do that, Minister." She gently patted his bloody cheek then stood. "Lie down on the bed and stretch your arms over your head."

She walked over to a small duffle bag and pulled some things out. She sat down beside Simon, picking up his phone. "This will be useful."

"It doesn't work."

"I'll fix it later." She took a few plastic cable ties and fastened his wrists to the headboard. She attached his ankles to the footboard before turning off all the lights. "I think you'll like the next part. Have a drink first." She held a bottle of foul-tasting whiskey to his mouth. He couldn't avoid swallowing some; more of it dribbled onto his chest.

He heard her rummaging through her bag. "What do I call you," he asked.

The whip made a horrifying noise as it cracked through the darkness. "How about that?"

"What?"

She cracked the whip again, but closer. Simon could feel the air shiver in response. It didn't sound like a toy, or an instrument of pleasure. He braced himself for its cut.

Another crack and the bed trembled. His left hand was free.

Simon struggled not to wet himself. If the whip could cut through the dense plastic of his improvised handcuffs, what would it do to his flesh?

A tongue touched him instead.

It started at the top of his chest, and began working its way downward. In the utter blackness of the room, it was exquisite.

Simon felt her finally roll off him. He lay on his back, stroking her long, lush hair, listening to her soft breathing, smelling the radiant warmth of her bare skin. He tried to look at her face, but his eyes still hadn't gotten used to the dark. He looked at his watch; the blackness seemed to have swallowed the phosphorescence. He would have been annoyed that he still didn't know her name, but he was too overwhelmed by what she had done to him, by what they had done together. He touched his finger to the cheek she had raked. When they were making love her hands were all over him, not bringing pain; just ecstasy.

She kissed him on the cheek and rose from the bed. "How do you feel?"

"Your talents are truly wondrous."

"Thank you, Minister; it's good you enjoy punishment. I have a present for you."

"Simon. Turn on the light. I don't want you to fall or get hurt."

"Don't worry about me." She pressed something into his hand. It was metal. It was a gun.

He flinched. "What—"

"Shoot me."

"This feels real." Simon had ordered lots of people to fire guns, resulting in many deaths. He had never held one himself.

"You're in hot pursuit; you need it to defend yourself. You set my neighbor free: the one who's spent the last two years vandalizing my house, terrorizing my children. Capture or shoot me, and then there are only seventy-nine members of my mahjong club left for the police to worry about."

"Who are you?"

"I tried to tell you before, but you wouldn't let me finish. Should I start over?"

"No, no..." The Minister tried to break his other limbs free of the restraints. They dug deeper into his flesh.

"Tell me the names you remember."

Simon shuddered as something passed lightly over his exposed crotch. He shuddered as he realized it was the business end of the whip.

"I'll make it easy. Tell me my first two names, and then I'll tell you the last two." The lash passed gently over his chest.

Simon pointed the gun towards the voice, and fired. The unexpected recoil made him lose his grip.

"You like playing with guns, don't you? How do you like when it's your finger on the trigger, instead of one of your subordinates?"

He felt the lash trace its way gently from his forehead to his feet. "I have to go to the bathroom," he whimpered.

There was a clicking sound near his head, like something snapping into place.

"I bet your wife's furious at you. You fled to the hotel because you're afraid to face her. Well, Minister, it's time for you to get back to work. Be a man. That's important to you."

"How do you know—"

"I fixed your phone. Your wife is probably wondering where you are. I'll send her a photograph and leave the GPS on, so she can find you. Say "cheese.""

The lash teased his genitals, terrifying and arousing him.

Simon heard the simulated click of the shutter on his camera phone. It was pitch black in the room. How could she take a picture? He ran through the possibilities. He remembered the foul taste in the whiskey, and wet the bed.

"What did you do to me?"

"Do you remember my names? I'm losing patience. Two, at least? Otherwise it's one lash for each that you've forgotten." She ran the whip along his leg.

"Don't, please."

"You have a gun. I don't. You can't say I prevented you from defending yourself. Isn't that your benchmark? Come on. Give me the names. You've heard them all before."

Yes. They had sounded familiar. What were they? The Minister raked his nails through his mind, trying to remember. He knew the names. Sal, she mentioned. His friend. Salvatore, his friend who he'd ordered arrested, and probably executed. Who was first? The mother trying to protect her baby... Simon certainly hadn't protected his own child.

"Margaret, Salvatore..." All the names from the day's appeal files spewed like vomit from his mouth.

The lash caressed his face. "Very good, Minister. It seems you know who I am: your victims. Now I'll tell you the last two names. Jason..."

"Jason," Simon whispered.

"You know, the son you didn't care to protect. You were so unhappy when you had to spend your precious time playing football with him. Don't think he didn't notice your grimaces."

"I didn't want him to see—"

"Oh, he saw how much you hated holding the ball for him. He knows you think posts are for hanging people, not kicking balls through."

"No, that's not true!"

"Don't bother to deny it, Minister." She dragged the whip across his face, ending the argument. "You asked before what you should call me. Why not the usual name: Alex."

"Alex? You're Alex? You're no victim."

"I'm your witness, Minister."

Terror and trembling were washed away by a wave of fury over the deceit. "Untie me now! Turn on the lights." Simon paused, and took a deep breath. "You're going to pay for this. I'm giving you two weeks' notice. You're fired."

There was a soft click. "There. All the lights are on. The shades are open, and the sun is streaming in."

"Liar." He tried to roar, but it came out a hoarse groan. "It's pitch black in here."

"No, the world is a bright, sunny place, but every day you've been tugging at the shadows. They've enveloped you now. I was summoned by Jason as part of his research; I'm from what you would call fourteenth century western Mongolia. Unfortunately, your son is swinging from the end of a rope now, stranding me here. I'm going to watch you to the end, to make sure there'll be no light coming into your life."

Simon digested this silently for a few moments.

"Does that satisfy your sense of responsibility, Minister? Has justice been served?"

"No! I did what had to be done, to prevent lawlessness."

"What about mercy, Minister? What about serving kindness?"

"I punished the guilty. A person who is kind when it's time to be cruel will end up being cruel when it's time to be kind."

"Guilty like Jason? You know he was framed. Was it a time to be cruel, or for kindness, for mercy? For love?"

Simon took a deep breath as his free hand quietly reached for the gun. He put it to head, and pulled the trigger.

"Sorry Minister. You only deserved one chance, one bullet. It's more kindness than you showed your victims."

Simon started to laugh. "Thank you, Alex. You're the best assistant I've ever had."

"Thank you? What the hell do you mean by that?"

"You've given me what I really need. At least, what I deserve."

Nathan Elberg is a commercial real estate agent who has hunted and trapped with Eskimos and Indians. He's negotiated multimillion-dollar transactions, traveled the Trans-Canada Highway with hobos, and lived in a tipi at -40F. Four of his short stories have been accepted for publication. Three non-fiction essays have been published, in print and online. He is Chairman of the International Board of a Canadian research institute.

MASSACHUSETTS

BY MICHAEL SIDMAN

Lev parks the station wagon at the foot of the mountain then lets Pickle out the back. He got the car as a hand-me-down from his father on his twenty-first birthday. Five years later it remains his most adult possession. In his head he reexamines the list of supplies he was too lazy to write up: tent, wool sweater, parka, underwear and such, toilet paper, umbrella, hot dogs (buns, mustard, ketchup), sleeping bag, water, lucky Swiss army knife, flash light, pen, and notebook.

"Oh shit," he says running to the front of the car. "Where is it?" he says, twisting his arm under the passenger seat. Pickle sticks his wet nose into the seat of Lev's pants. With his free arm Lev tries to shoo the dog away.

"Pickle!" he shouts. The dog cowers slightly, bowing its head, as if waiting to be hit. Lev feels instant shame. He kneels down, Pickle approaches for an embrace. "What a good dog you are, it's OK, sweet puppy." Pickle is certainly stunning: a four-year-old gray and white Akita with eyes bluer than Paul Newman's, plus a coat and posture that would make the members of the American Kennel Club cream in their seersucker slacks.

As he reaffirms his love for his dog, Lev sees the doggie backpack that (he had forgotten) has been draped over Pickle since the beginning of their car ride from Brooklyn to the Catskills.

"Yes! Yes!" he shouts, throwing his arms into the air in triumph. He opens the two side pockets of Pickle's bag. In one is an unopened bottle of Maker's Mark; in the other is a big bag of weed, rolling papers, business cards to make filters, matches, lighters, and a glass pipe.

His brief crisis now averted, Lev stands facing the mountain that will be his and Pickle's home for the next two nights. It's a beautiful October afternoon. The dead leaves at his feet trail up the foot of the mountain where many of their brothers still burn a defiant array of reds, oranges, and yellows and the vastness of the crisp-cool sea of the autumn sky.

He reties his Merrells, straps on his oversized camping pack, then with a whistle and a smile trots past the tree line with Pickle following just behind. For the last two years, Lev has made this annual fall pilgrimage to the Catskills to purge the city and its artificial life from his system, and hopefully to write. His therapist applauds this ritual, citing first and foremost that an anxious basketcase like Lev can only benefit from nature's solitude. The city paralyzes him with fears of success and failure, of upward mobility and collapse. Talk of the retreat keeps his therapist from suggesting new pharmaceutical remedies for his debilitating anxiety; a subject he despises, though a steady dose of Lexapro has successfully turned Lev from a suicidal mess of self-deprecating anxieties into a surviving mess of self-deprecating anxieties.

After hiking a few hours, Pickle stops to scratch his ear then lick his ass. "Come on," Lev says. "Look at what you're carrying compared to what I am. You have no excuse."

However Lev has no desire to keep trekking up the mountain, so he surveys the area. Crunching through the millions of dead leaves, he takes a breath in feeling the chilled air shock his lungs.

Up ahead amid a boulder cluster, Lev sees small lichen communities dotting the rocks, pioneering the unforgiving terrain at the slow speed of life. Nomadic bands of moss creep up below the lichen patches then feed on them, spreading over the surfaces they have terraformed. Soon the grasses and small plants will arrive, followed by bushes and trees. Lev applauds himself for recognizing the process. Most people wouldn't notice.

When he arrives at the other side of the boulder cluster, Lev releases a sigh that dances in midair as a cloud of condensation. Through it he sees his perfect spot: a slightly protruding cliff containing two cat-sized rocks sheltered by three elm trees whose leaves are exploding in the ecstasy of a golden death. Far beneath the cliff, at the base of a long, steep slope, is a lake, crystal clear and still. Two small mountains share the borders of the lake with the cliff he is on, hiding and coveting the oasis, slowly depositing a year's worth of leaves against its shores.

"Jesus, the clarity!" he yells to Pickle, who seems unimpressed but nevertheless responds to the tone of Lev's voice with an enthusiastic tail wag. "This is the best spot we've ever found. Whadya say, buddy?" Lev tosses his bag then sits with his legs hanging over the side of the cliff, pondering the image and plausibility of living happily as a mountain man.

***

The sun begins to set behind the mountain across the lake. Lev removes the weed and whiskey from Pickle's bag. He'd spent the last few hours pitching his tent, collecting firewood, chastising himself for not writing, jacking off over the edge of the cliff, singing the finale from *Gypsy*, and playing fetch with Pickle. Now the dog gnaws at a rawhide bone with the dedication and commitment of a master sculptor.

The sky turns from blue to gold. The colors of autumn blend and fade. The transformation of the landscape in the sun's absence is most dramatic at this time of year. The moment a sun-lit spot is overtaken by shadow, it begins to freeze. The bold colors of the mountainsides become a blur of charcoal and ash. Soon even the branches in the trees directly above Lev's head retreat into the darkness. The chill fall air becomes cold. The vast space of the mountain and its valleys becomes a lurking monolith of darkness that creeps up to within an inch of Lev's face, threatening him.

"Pickle?" he calls. "You there? C'mere, buddy!" His eyes have mostly adjusted to the dark, but he panics as if stricken with blindness. He hears the dog's feet crinkling leaves and crunching sticks. He is comforted when he feels his companion's soft, strong body press against his own. "It's real dark, huh, buddy? You scared? Don't be scared, I'm here.

"Why don't we get the fire started? I'm freezing my titties off." He reaches behind himself for the crumpled newspaper and lighter. Ever year Lev fails to fully comprehend just how challenging a night alone in the mountains can be. In the city he rarely spends a night without company, finding that time alone turns his thoughts against himself.

The first year he came to the woods Lev had been absolutely terrified. He had spent the night in his tent holding his knife, crying quietly. Since then, part of the purpose of the retreat has been to confront the terrible fear that Lev creates from loneliness—darkness and silence being the ultimate environment for his self-made terror: an easel upon which he'd painted his most vividly imagined ghosts and demons since childhood.

Lev grew up on the North Shore of Massachusetts. He had reveled in the distinctly American-gothic landscape of pumpkins, Puritan architecture, and four-hundred-year-old gravestones etched with winged skulls. Some nights near Halloween he and his friends would walk through the old cemeteries with flashlights. Although he was petrified with fear, Lev would tag along, fearing most that someone would call him a faggot, and that his own dark secrets would be exhumed. He'd watch the beam of his flashlight pass over grass, stone, graves, and tombs. His heart would skip beats because Lev was sure that his light would fall on the figure of a rotting person. The person would have a bloated white face with blood and bile seeping from its eyes, ears, and mouth; then it would lurch and slouch toward him with the unease of a toddler in leg braces.

Every time it was the same nightmare. Lev never allowed himself the power to believe that his worst fears were simple impossibilities. Even if he temporarily accepted that zombies didn't exist, he would remind himself that undocumented serial killers lived in the darkness, some of which ate the flesh of their victims. This would ignite and feed a more rational fear. Soon the zombies would return, protesting the thought that anything could ever be considered impossible.

Lev lights the crumpled newspaper. He dreads illuminating the ghoulish company he might now have stalking his camp; but he knows he must. The light only reveals Pickle, calm and bored. Lev laughs a little then builds the fire.

"I'm such a fucking man-child," he confesses from the center of his camp, taking in what he can see in the firelight. Ahead of him the light reaches the cliff then surrenders. Behind him the light only ventures as far as the front of his tent. Above, the lowest branches of the elms dance casting shadow puppets on their wrinkled trunks. Over the crackle of the fire Lev can hear the ever-present drone of crickets as well as the occasional hoot of an owl waxing philosophical as it awaits its prey.

"No time like the present!" he says crushing a large bud of weed onto a rolling paper. He licks it closed, lights it, and breathes in the skunky smoke. Lev blows out the hit then coughs up excess saliva. Pickle stares with concern, putting his face between his paws, watching his owner get high.

After inhaling the next hit, Lev holds Pickle by the snout and slowly exhales the smoke in the dog's face. Pickle pulls and bucks, but Lev keeps him still, hoping that his dog will share his bad habits for the night, as a good compatriot does.

The rush is grand and sweet. Lev's concerns drop from his shoulders, with a heartbeat like a hummingbird's he can't help but smile and laugh. The darkness ceases to be alive. Lev imagines himself safe, somewhere familiar, in a small room with black walls.

"Y'hungry, boy? Want some food?" Pickle jumps to the sound of Lev opening the plastic hot dog container. He brought enough for both of them, because no dog should have to eat kibble in the mountains.

Lev cooks the hot dogs over the fire then is inspired to write new stories. He considers taking a crack at a gay vampire novel or a fictionalized account of the Salem Witch Trials. In the end he'll probably write some bullshit about a guy who broke his heart.

The hot dogs are taking too long, he thinks. Lev asks himself why the hell he's lame enough to be alone in the mountains. He hears leaves crunch, but has no room to process it in his already crowded mind.

"You think that if I dropped my joint the whole park would catch fire? What if there are so many dead leaves on the continent right now that one spark would destroy it all?" Pickle looks at him with an excited anticipation. "I'm not feeding you. I just wanted to ask a question! Jesus!"

Leaves crunch back near the boulders. Now Lev hears it. He freezes.

He looks to Pickle who has also heard the noise and is staring in the direction of the source. Lev watches his dog waiting for Pickle's reaction before he fashions his own.

Pickle lowers his head onto his paws and looks at Lev.

"Nothing, buddy?" Pickle walks over to him puts his head in Lev's lap. "Nah, just one of our many animal hosts tonight."

Pickle's head shoots up staring over Lev's shoulder. He can sense the dog's muscles tense. Lev begins to lose his breath. The dog burps a low growl, exposing his fangs. Lev refuses to turn but sees it all in his mind: a man with wiry hair and wild eyes clutching a dull butcher's knife, or a pack of crazed mountain folk looking for the night's man-wich.

Pickle shifts slightly, his growl growing louder. Lev gathers enough strength and self-control to reach for the knife in his pocket. He unfolds the blade without moving anything but his fingers.

Pickle bolts. Something in Lev's mind uncoils. He lets out a whimpering scream as he tosses his body away from the action, almost dumping himself headfirst into the fire. Lev grabs his flashlight. He holds his knife straight ahead, trying to follow the sound of his dog. Pickle has not gone far, but is frantically running, changing directions every so often in an energetic frenzy.

The fire in Lev's mind begins to dim when he hears the squeak of a chipmunk or vole or some other stupid animal like that. "Pickle!" he calls. "Come here! Come back here! Leave it alone!" His light finally rests on Pickle, who has cornered some kind of small rodent between two rocks. "Pickle, you stupidfuckingpieceofshit! Get over here now!" Lev screams with a force and volume the dog has only heard a handful of times.

Pickle retreats from the pursuit of his game then sits at his master's feet. Lev falls to his hands and knees, wheezing slightly. He looks at Pickle with resentment mixed with accusation. The dog is too startled to return the stare. He knows his master only has three gazes: one of love, one of indifference, and one of anger. Pickle arches his neck as he puts his head down, demurring to the side in submission. Seeing this, Lev feels like an abusive and irresponsible parent.

"You can't do that, big boy," he says while scratching Pickle's ears. "It's scary out here. You almost gave me a heart attack just now." Pickle tries to lick Lev's face, and as is warranted in such rare occasions, Lev allows it. "I need you here, protecting me.

"Jesus Christ, look at me. I'm old enough to have a baby and I can't even handle you." Pickle sneezes then licks his chops. Lev blows a grunted laugh through his nose and smiles.

"Or maybe I'm just a little too high." He reaches for the ground, picks up his bottle of Maker's Mark. With a *squeak* then a *thunk* the cork pops out of the glass neck. Soon the antiseptic smell of whiskey climbs into Lev's nostrils. He raises the bottle to his lips feeling the firewater rush from his tongue to his gullet. The alcohol brings him back to his body pulling him away from the ethereal madness of the weed. "Nothing like a little whiskey to take the edge off. Anyway, it's not like I'd be smoking up if I had a baby, or if I had a boyfriend. Then again babies don't run off in the dark to chase chipmunks."

Lev sits down as he tries to remember the moment before the hubbub. He was thinking something about the leaves, something about fire, wasn't it? A small slice of moon rises above the peak of the mountain to the left of the lake, providing only enough light to illuminate its place in the sky, yet cover the surface of the water with a silken shimmer at the same time. Lev's mouth is cottony. He drinks from his plastic water bottle, imagining that he can taste the glimmering water down below. He picks up the Maker's Mark again, takes a few sips, drapes his sleeping bag around his shoulders and takes a few sips more. The alcohol takes effect quickly since Lev hasn't eaten—the hot dogs now nothing more than crispy black sticks crackling in the fire.

"That's okay," he sighs. "We have plenty more where those came from." With new food cooking and a lovely anxiety-reducing buzz, Lev opens his small journal then begins to write:

Some people think that vampires don't exist. Especially Jews.

He looks over his opening line and slaps himself in the face with an open palm. He tears up the entire sheet of paper. "Stupid ass," he says to himself. He starts again:

The basement of Sarah Lerner's house in the colonial section of Salem, Massachusetts is made of old wood and stone. It is lit by one sixty-watt bulb that swings from a yellow cord. The basement terrifies her, especially a hole in the wall far off in the darkest corner. She believes it leads to another room where bodies are stashed and fed upon by a mutant race of humans that have been living in the basement for hundreds of years.

He puts down his pen as he sees the skins on the hot dogs beginning to bubble. "Good start," he declares slamming his notebook shut. "Time for dinner."

As Lev finishes eating he eyes his notebook with a complete lack of enthusiasm. He walks past it a few times, stopping to pet Pickle or to meditate on the view of the lake at night. He sits down on the ledge and jacks off again. It's slightly awkward this time as Pickle keeps trying to sniff Lev's dick, then is saddened when Lev pushes him away. Pickle sits back looking into Lev's eyes as though wondering: *Why the furious pumping? Why can't I sniff your dick?* Lev chooses to ignore him. Pickle's seen worse, much worse. It is best not to consider the impact of one's sexuality on one's dog.

The weed makes Lev prematurely sleepy. He ends up too tired to do more writing tonight. He regrets not bringing his laptop so that he could have watched a movie or cartoons. He left those things at home with the hope that the lack of distraction would help him write more. He picks up the joint where he dropped it earlier then takes Pickle for a walk down to the lake. The downward slope is gentle. Even Pickle doesn't mind braving it headfirst. They make a lot of noise on the way, clearing a path through the leaves with their feet. There is now enough moonlight that Lev doesn't need the flashlight. A silver-blue glow dusts the mountainside, giving light to objects, but remains unable to penetrate the darkness of the empty spaces.

Lev sits on a rock at the water's edge before lighting the joint. The water is still and beautiful. It calms him, as water always has. Back in Massachusetts he would sit on a floating platform at the edge of the pier late at night, get high, and let the waves rock him into a state of infantile comfort. Sometimes during the day he'd sit on the rocks, those incredible red rocks of northern Massachusetts beaches, contemplating the fears in his life that stood as obstacles. He'd lose himself in tide pools, watching snails and barnacles do nothing, or watching small hermit crabs abandon the shelter of water plants to brave a competitor in the open sand.

The lake is not as spectacular or as sublime, but it has mountains to boast. In the glare of the moon Lev can't see any life in the water, but he's sure it's there—some small, insignificant fish or a swarm of leeches. Pickle shits a few feet away. Lev admits his own fatigue. At home he'd keep himself awake with television and the panic of lonely thoughts that dance in his head. Now, however he thinks it's best to go to bed, to sleep through the long mountain night then wake up early in the morning rejuvenated for an entire day of serious writing.

The two friends hike back up the mountain, following the trail of displaced leaves—a journey much less fun on the way back up. Lev sleeps in the tent with the flap open, as Pickle sleeps just outside. Lev keeps him out there to feel safe and protected; he leaves the flap open so they can watch each other sleep.

***

Lev dreams of his late grandmother playing *Hernando's Hideaway* on an old wooden piano that is drifting away on a floating platform in the ocean. Her back is to him, she takes no notice of him. He tries calling to her, he misses her so much, yet he has no voice. He tries reaching for her, swimming for her, she always knew him best, but he has no legs or arms. In fact, he has no body as far as he can tell. The music is beautiful and peppy (she plays it well, with a skill he never bothered to learn from her), but still he feels distressed.

Finally, mercifully, she turns her head to him, and with a sweet smile, barks ferociously.

***

Lev's eyes open to the darkness of the tent. He hears another loud bark followed by a growl. He whips his head around to see Pickle framed in the tent opening. He's facing the boulders again, but this time the hairs on his back and tail are standing tall.

"Pickle, shut up!" Pickle whimpers, taking two frightened steps backward. Another noise pierces the silence. A slow, loud gurgle erupts from just a few feet behind the tent. It is the sound of air being forced through a tar pit, but there is tone behind it, an almost musical tone that differentiates human communication from that of other animals. It's a scream covered in mucus. It is dull and dumb: the scream of a Neanderthal responding to the thunder.

Pickle cries at the sound, cautiously stealing glances at Lev. Lev reaches for his knife then bursts through the tent flap, shining his flashlight in the direction of the noise.

Nothing. Lev can't hear the movement of the creature or the rustling of leaves. He realizes that a pervasive silence has covered the mountain. Even the crickets dare not make a sound.

A phlegmy exclamation rolls toward them from behind, just below the cliff. Pickle turns in a blur of teeth and tail then shoots down the side of the mountain in hot pursuit. "No! No!" Lev screams. "Pickle!" He runs, following the sound of the dog's strides, calling out to him all the while. His thoughts stop as his limbs function on their own.

The sounds of pursuit become the sounds of violent struggle. He hears Pickle's mouth close around an object, viciously pulling and thrashing at it. Lev runs even faster, hoping that Pickle has the upper hand. Just as Lev is getting near, a noise bursts into the air: a shriek, a yelp.

"Pickle!" He hears the dog squealing. Lev skids to a halt a few feet away from the water's edge. He shines the flashlight in every direction. He catches glimpses of steam rising from the lake's surface, of grasses bowing and bending at the shore, the quick-moving legs of a spider escaping the light under a muddy rock, and finally a thick red puddle of blood slowly snaking through the mud into the water.

Lev holds the light on the blood, examining it repeatedly. He hopes with each fresh glance that it isn't real. A wave of white fur enters the outer perimeter of the light beam. He turns, following the trail of blood and fur. The light falls on a paw, motionless and blood-soaked, flayed up the center of the muscle where the knee has been almost completely torn from the leg. It remains connected by a flimsy tendon as well as a single vein. The leg continues to the shoulder, which has been torn out completely, the ball-shaped bone is left exposed in a massive puddle of fresh blood with fragments of muscle.

"Oh Jesus, oh Jesus," Lev says. The blood trickles off the bone into the larger puddle, spreading ripples.

A gurgle breaks the silence just a few feet to the left. Lev shines the flashlight in its direction. At first the light falls directly on Pickle's white face looking back at him. For a moment Lev's spirits are lifted. But then a thick brown tongue washes over the dog's face smearing it with translucent slime. Rows of broken, jagged teeth appear above and below Pickle's head. It sinks deep into the black tunnel of a gaping throat while something cackles and grunts with satisfaction.

Lev's eyes now focus on the thing: its mouth is so large that it holds almost all of Pickle's body inside. The mouth hangs open. Lev can see multiple rows of sharp teeth held by black gums stained with blood. It laps up dribbles of blood with a tongue as large and flat as a toilet seat and the color and texture of a sick man's shit. With one more swallow, Pickle disappears completely into the darkness inside the creature.

Two holes above the mouth serve as a nose. Lev hears air struggling to get through when the creature breathes in. Mucus explodes outward when the breath is released. Snot spills onto the creature's face, catching in the protruding basin that is its bottom lip. The skin is green-brown, almost reptilian, but is covered in a slick matte of short brown hairs. The creature carries its bladder-shaped body unbalanced on two legs. Its posture suggests a quadruped, but the two hind legs are the only useful ones, excessively muscular next to the rest of the creature's dumpy body. Six sharp talons twitch on each foot.

The two forearms, long and skeletal, hang limp from the body.

The eyes are worse, sunken and yellow. One watches Lev with retarded comprehension. It stares into his eyes as he stares right back. The other eye wanders with manic energy scanning the surroundings.

Lev is silent and still. He hardly allows himself to blink in this standoff. The thing coughs then snorts. A pond of mucus builds in its throat. It gurgles violently.

Both the creature's eyes focus. Its body shakes under some internal strain. A crackling sound emerges from the creature's backside, releasing a terrible smell into the air. In one push the creature defecates. Lev watches in horror as Pickle's entire carcass rip out the back of the thing. Small explosions of undigested fur burst around the corpse as it emerges. The dog has been stripped almost completely to the bone. One eye remains lodged in its socket. A single foot is completely intact—muscle, fur, and all. The skeleton falls in a fecal pile on the ground, the creature's noises subside. It closes its mouth as it watches Lev.

Lev lifts one foot in the air taking a step back. Both of the creature's eyes focus on the foot. He raises the other foot, repeating his previous movement. The creature's talons tap the wet soil. Lev takes one more step back then turns to run, but the creature has already lunged. It swings its lanky forearms like hatchets, building momentum. A sudden pain in Lev's right buttock stops him in his tracks. A sharp claw digs into the muscle, clasping and tearing. Another arm lands on Lev's left hamstring, immobilizing the leg, bringing Lev crashing to the ground.

"No! Oh my God—no!" he screams. Lev looks down as the creature attempts to get its mouth around both his feet, using its arms to drag his body down deeper into its throat. Lev struggles. The shooting pain of the claws tearing at his flesh paralyzes him. An acid goop covers his feet, burning through his shoes then his flesh.

"No!" Lev digs his hands into the ground and pulls himself forward, setting the creature slightly off balance. He gives a kick with both of his legs into the back of the creature's throat kicking again several times as he screams at the top of his lungs. He pushes himself off the ground with inhuman strength, sending the creature, mouth still clamped tight around Lev's legs, into a backward roll that flips Lev over the creature dumping him into the lake. He runs deep into the water then turns. The cold water numbs his burning and aching wounds. The creature returns to its feet then stands calm. It watches him from the shore. Lev stares back.

The thing paces back and forth at the water's edge, but is anxious about getting wet. The creature stops. It looks at Lev, and lets out some kind of call, a brief alarm like one quick note from a trumpet. It lingers for a moment more before bursting into a fast run, disappearing into the trees.

***

Lev stays in the water for what feels like hours. He holds his hands to his mouth as he rocks back and forth, mumbling incoherent phrases, keeping watch for any movement nearby. The lake is quiet and peaceful; the mountains continue their slumber undisturbed. Gradually he returns to his body. He is freezing, his feet are burned, and his puncture wounds ache. His bladder is about to burst, so he crouches in the water then pisses through his pants.

You have to leave, he thinks. Do it, man. Run, get your keys, and just drive. Don't take anything except your keys.

But what if that monster is up at the camp?

Then you fight it again. You can't stay here. You have to get your shit together, get to your car, and get some help.

He takes some deep breaths struggling to focus his attention. "On three," he says. "One, two."

Lev splashes out of the water as he starts back up the mountain, grabbing a stick on the way. His eyes watch only the path. He doesn't lift his head or think. He just runs. The dead leaves pass under his feet in a blur.

The campsite seems darker. The elm trees are blocking the moon. Lev is on his hands and knees searching for his bag. He stumbles across his journal, tosses it to his left, where it hits something soft and falls to the ground. A quiet grunt stops him. Lev turns his head then notices the blurred edges of a shadow standing in the fire pit. He freezes, staring in shock.

The shadow scratches at the dirt and ash then leans down to sniff at it. Lev sees the plumes of gray dust forming under the creature's heavy breathing. It laps something up with its massive tongue. Lev remembers throwing the burnt hot dogs into the fire, like an idiot. He reaches into his pockets to find nothing. He can't remember dropping the knife. It must be somewhere down near the lake, probably sitting next to the flashlight, wherever that may be. Lev feels around for any semblance of a bag. His fingers brush canvas before falling on the cold metal of a zipper. The keys are in the front pocket, he remembers. He grips the zipper then begins to pull. The dull sound is muffled under the creature's lapping and snorting. Lev decides to act. With a swift yank opens the bag and grabs the keys.

The noise is louder than he expected. The creature shoots its attention in his direction. Lev can't see its face, however he doesn't need to. He recognizes the posture. The creature lunges toward him and he runs. He's not sure in what direction he's running, but he doesn't stop. He can hear the creature not far behind.

He climbs on top of a large rock then stops to listen. Unfortunately his breathing is too heavy to hear anything else. He tugs at his hair crying out. He doesn't remember the direction he came from. Even worse, the moon is hidden behind a cloud. He yells again. A gurgled call responds from somewhere ahead, mocking him. There is no adjusting to this darkness. It is a temporary blindness so palpable that Lev feels that his eyes have simply failed. He removes a small stone from the sole of his sneaker then throws it ahead. It lands with a soft paper sound in the leaves. Something rushes toward it with grunts and gurgles. Lev hears the small explosions of the creature's nostrils. It's near. Waiting. He sits cross-legged on his rock, listening.

Leaves crunch to the right, a whine echoes from behind. Soon there is nothing. Lev sits in the center of darkness and silence, a veritable void if not for the rock underneath. He comforts himself by adding imaginary color and sound to the terrible nothingness that surrounds him.

There is the ocean harbor of his childhood. Boston is in the distance surrounded by heavy gray clouds. A storm is coming. The ocean responds with violent glee. The waves are choppy like jagged teeth. They spray over the barriers onto the pedestrian walkways. Gulls hover above the water line, not bothering to challenge the roar of the sea with whining calls. The whipping wind holds the gulls mid-air, but they maintain their ominous invisible perches with wings outstretched.

In his childhood, Lev would watch the red rocks disappear under the rising tide. He would worry for the small creatures that depended on the rocks for shelter. He'd wonder if the water was calmer underneath the surface, but he knew that shallow waters were the most tumultuous. He knew the gulls were watching for the helpless creatures that had been blown from their shelters. They'd swoop them up, then that would be the end. Lev would pray that most would find shelter, riding out the storm under the cover of tall seaweed.

When the storm was over, the sea would be calm and gentle once again. Fishing boats would rock gently at their buoys. The waves would lap apologetically against the land. The gulls would call and the blackened water would settle, once again clearing to reveal the universe beneath.

Lev hears the creature call from far behind. He climbs down the rock then runs in the other direction. He trips on trees and rocks but doesn't stop. The pain in his feet and legs is unbearable. His lips stick to the front of his teeth, begging for water. He runs slower now, pausing occasionally. He can't seem to sense his surroundings. The ground could be the sky. He walks, slowly now, his hands on his hips.

It dawns on him, just as his pace couldn't grow any slower, that he's not scared anymore. Chalk it up to desperation or fatigue, Lev thinks, but then again it may just be the end of shock, that moment when you've gone over the rollercoaster's first drop and you finally have the guts to put your hands in the air. He doesn't want to die here, doesn't want to be another missing person. He can't put his family through that.

Let the thing come to him, he thinks. Let it all be done. Lev waits, trying to quiet his angry breathing so he can hear any sign of the creature's approach. However the more he waits, the quieter the night becomes, as if the power of the night were receding, the darkness itself growing thin and porous.

Sooner than Lev could have imagined, the night retreats. Darkness gives way to a soothing silver. The symphony of crickets is replaced by the gleeful chatter of the earliest of birds. It's over, Lev thinks, just when he was raring for more. But he can feel it in his bones: the creature is gone.

Accustomed to the pain now, Lev finds his way back to the camp, collects his things, and walks down the mountain to his car, the necessary steps so monotonous now without his companion. Lev sits in the car without turning it on. Should he go to the police? How could he? As if they would believe him. What would he tell his friends and family? He'd have to make up some story about Pickle's demise—he wouldn't have to feign his grief. From his bag he hears his notebook calling to him, its empty lines sore with atrophy. In the rearview mirror he sees the mountain in all its beauty.

Tonight he'll write.

Having grown up amid the reminders of the Salem Witch Trials, **Michael Sidman** was always most interested in those things dark and strange. Now living in Park Slope, Brooklyn, he has to create those things for himself.

MY GYM

By Gary Wosk

The restless, quite angry, and disheveled mob was growing. Their faces were pock marked made even more unattractive by deep scrapes and abrasions. I was not something to write home about either, yet compared to these weak looking characters, I was Adonis.

They pounded on the front door of My Gym, but it seemed unlikely the glass would break because the underfed collection of stick figures lacked the power to accomplish such mayhem.

It was a Monday morning. Apparently the troublemakers had too much to consume over the weekend and couldn't wait to start working it off. On further reflection I realized that couldn't be, because they appeared so lean.

It was a scene right out the Great Depression — the run on the banks — but this was only a fitness center that wasn't supposed to open for another ten minutes. The hours were clearly marked on the front door. Anyone with half a brain would know the gym was not going to open any sooner no matter how much everyone chanted in unison: "OPEN, OPEN, OPEN, um, um, um."

I noticed that the tops of some of their heads were caved in and shaven with a patch quilt pattern of uneven stitches. Perhaps they did have half a brain after all.

It was nice to think that they were apparently devoted exercise enthusiasts, but this was ridiculous. It bordered on anarchy. I hoped the staff inside the gym had called the nearby police station. My hope was that these hooligans would soon be arrested and prosecuted to the full letter of the law. I was no elitist however we could not allow our societies to fall into the hands of thugs.

I first noticed the ruckus as I pulled into a parking space that was only fifty yards away from the near brouhaha. I called over to my workout friend in the parking space next to me.

"What's going on over there? Someone is going to get hurt."

Billy Williams, an ex-cop who worked out nearly everyday, appeared years younger than seventy-two years old. He had the sinewy frame of a man half his age. He was not someone to mess with.

Many of our conversations centered on what we perceived as the decline of Western civilization. The scene before us seemed to prove his theory that modern day technology, the Internet and social networking primarily, had contributed to boorish behavior on the part of humanity. One punch to the chin of one of these moribund humanoids and they would quickly dissolve into dust, I feared. Billy would be charged with murder and I would be called as a witness. Oh, what fun that would be.

He shook his head in disbelief.

"Well, Lewis, I'm just guessing, but I believe those are the new members," he said. "This gym is going to the dogs. I wish I had a stun gun. Even a little mace would be fun." He laughed, but I could tell he was serious.

"New members?"

"Yeah, I heard My Gym just purchased this little known fitness chain. I think it's called Dawn…Dawn of the something. As you can see, they're a different breed of people. They only pay about fifty dollars a year, which is not fair, compared to what we're shelling out."

He kept shaking his head. It's the end, I tell you, the end of the world. Look at those lost souls. They're pathetic."

I became a little uneasy after hearing his remarks. Like I said, I was not an elitist.

My parents taught me to treat everyone equally and not be judgmental.

We slowly made our way to the entrance staying as far away from the rabble rousers as possible. Billy gave them a dirty look. I was prepared to restrain him in case he tried to intervene and break up the crowd. He was not one to put up with any nonsense. I didn't want to see him get hurt; even though it seemed likely it would be the other way around, because the opposition looked very slow and emaciated.

"They're kind of grungy looking," I whispered to Billy. "You would have to put them under a microscope to spot any muscle tone. They really do need to get in shape. I would be shocked if they could pick up a twenty pound weight. What a measly bunch." I tried to resist laughing, but they wouldn't have noticed anyway because they seemed singularly focused on something else.

"They also reek to high heaven," he said. "Hold your nose, man. And the skin on those suckers, yuck. They look like worms living under a rock."

"Obviously their last gym didn't have a tanning booth."

It was 8 a.m. when a pale, slender employee with jet black spiked hair and long, narrow side burns with pointy ends, opened the front door. His name tag read: Ray Zucco.

The people in the mob nearly stumbled over each other as they dragged themselves inside. We followed behind but not too close. The rowdy crowd quickly formed a line behind a table manned by Zucco, the recently hired training director, who also doubled as a trainer. He recognized me then gave a forced half smile. The introvert never made direct eye contact with anyone. What a snob, I thought.

Zucco, very pale, I believed, for someone who encouraged other people to get in the best shape possible, greeted the members with a barely audible, slow "Halloo" and nothing else. He checked their names off a list then handed them what appeared to be a manual. They grunted back something. There were no smiles. Just a look of determination or hollow eyes.

The new members looked grim. Many of them wore torn workout clothes. Their hair was matted. We were living in tough economic times, I realized, and should be more sensitive to their plight.

I was not happy, neither were my other workout friends, including Joe Bongolooza, a former boxer whose pugilistic nose and cauliflower ears gave him away. The new members brought out the worst in everyone. The new members, I knew, would not like the tough Bongolooza.

"They ought to line those poor bastards against the wall and shoot them," he said. "Hell, I'll do it. Line 'em up, pow, pow, pow."

It was bad enough that the equipment was falling apart, which the new members haphazardly knocked into, but now the surge in membership would mean longer waits for everything including the machines, lukewarm showers, overcrowded sauna room and pool. I dared not venture into the pool anymore for fear of catching something from the new members. I did not want to wade in flaky skin that had fallen off their gaunt bodies.

The weeks passed. The gym grew mustier and mustier. The complaints I lodged with staff fell on deaf ears. "It will get better, it will get better," was the typical response I was offered.

There were fewer and fewer familiar faces. I tried to strike up a conversation with the new members from time to time. I joined the gym not only to get in shape but also to make friends.

It may have been a coincidence, but it seemed like each time Zucco weighed the people I had known for years to chart their progress, I never saw them again.

I overheard a few of the conversations at the weigh in when I worked out nearby.

"Excellent, excellent," Zucco told the chunky Fred Anderson. "You are a seasoned athlete and are more than ready for the next stage in your workout regimen."

He was not as complimentary to the frail Ted Krague, the juicy gossiper of the gym.

"You need to stop eating like a bird or you will not be ready for the exercises I have in mind for you," Zucco told him. "I'll fix that. Let's visit the snack bar together."

When I asked Zucco if my friends had quit the gym, he said, "Oh, no, they are still with us. They have put their memberships on hold. Apparently, they've gone on vacation or something. They will be back. I assure you. You will see them again."

I was very surprised when I heard Zucco take a harsh tone with a new member. I didn't quite make everything out or understand what it meant, but it went something like this: "We've gone over this before, Hector. We want to change the perception. Your legs are still as thin as toothpicks. Do you want to make the final cut?"

I never thought of myself as paranoid, but the new members seemed to be staring at me. Could it be that I was staring at them? Whatever the case, I told myself, I can do this. Someone has to break the ice. Don't be so prejudiced.

I approached the man with the grayish, blistered face with bags under his eyes. I introduced myself and tried not to stare at his ghastly facial features. Upon closer view, there were missing chunks of flesh that formed craters exposing bone. Poor man, I thought. I also realized I needed to order a new pair of glasses if it took me this long to notice such a hideous sight.

"My name is Vladimir. I work out. I go," he answered in a staccato tone, also unable to make direct eye contact.

I could not resist asking him what had happened to his face.

No reply. He walked away with a slight limp in his step, which reminded me of my last bout with gout and Boris Karloff as *The Mummy*.

And that was how it usually went with the new members. They were so cliquish, I thought. Billy was right — a different breed. I had not seen Bill in quite some time. He was probably as fed up as I and was staying away. Perhaps he, too, went on vacation.

Having no one to talk to anymore was bad enough, then an announcement was made that the facility would only be open from 7 p.m. until 2 a.m. because of daytime remodeling for a special new facility. And that was it. No details.

There was, however, some good news. A new marketing campaign was launched. Throughout the gym, banners and signs proclaimed, *You're Only as Healthy as You Eat,* and that free energy bars, power drinks, as well as other healthy goodies, would be given out at the snack bar. Zucco and his staff of trainers set their sights on longtime members such as me to take advantage of the promotion.

"It is our way of saying thank you for your many years of loyalty to the club," he said. "The snacks will help add some bulk to your frame, which will accelerate muscle growth," Zucco said to me in his usual low decibel, monotone voice.

The place was eerily feeling like a mausoleum. I had enough. Zucco handed me a special telephone number to call to make my complaints known. He gave me a menacing, red eyeballs glare.

I called as soon as I arrived home.

"Hello, my name is Lewis Resnick," I said. "Your guy, Zucco, at the Valley referred me to you. I don't like how things are being run out there. The new members are really creepy. And the construction? What's going on?"

"Yes, Mister Resnick. I have been expecting your call," said the man who identified himself as Gruco Drugic. "Here's what's happening. We are adding another room in the back of the facility. We are...expanding Mr. Resnick to...accommodate the growth in membership.

"When the renovation is completed you are going to love the new room. Give us a chance. Things will get better. And please, be open-minded about the new members. They're just as unsure of you as you are of them. People are people. Embrace them. Their last gym was not so great. That's why they look...fragile."

"Will there be more machines? More lockers?"

"I cannot say more, but before it opens you will be invited to take an exclusive tour. Be patient, Mister Resnick."

Two months later, the expressionless Zucco asked me to accompany him on the exclusive tour.

We cut across the gym, walked down the long hallway to a small, dark corridor that reminded me of the catacombs. He took out a key, opened a door and invited me in. It was pitch black. I heard the sound of a dead bolt closing.

The lights suddenly came on. My pupils were dilated as I began to refocus. It was a cavernous room.

I felt a panic attack coming on as my eyesight was restored.

"This used to be Albertsons Supermarket," he said. "It is now the home of our new members" — and all about me they stood the undead.

Several of them who wore *You're Only as Healthy as the Things You Eat* t-shirts converged on me in a slow gait grunting in unison. Among them were Vladimir, Billy, Fred Anderson, and Ted Krague. And the man Zucco referred to as Hector was present. He held a manual entitled: "Zombie Boot Camp," then dropped it to the floor.

"You see, Lewis, Our new members want to be friends with you too. They want to...shake your hand. They want to be the most fit zombies possible, not the types depicted in low budget motion pictures and on TV. There will be no getting away from them. Now, please Lewis, extend your hand to them, so we can get this over with as soon as possible."

I tried to break away but they pounced on me from all directions. If only I would have worked out harder, I lamented.

The feeding frenzy began as they tore into my stomach removing intestines and other various innards by the handfuls, stuffing the gummy delights into their drooling mouths.

I was still alive as they then went for my jugular, washing down bits of bone caught in their throats with my blood.

Their ravenous appetites were not satiated. They behaved as if they had not eaten in months. It was now time for dessert as they dug their yellowing teeth into my skull, busting through my cranium, and extending their coarse tongues into my brain, sucking out the membranes.

When I awoke, I had become one of them. Surprisingly, I was not in pain.

"You are in great shape, Lewis. The snacks helped. Welcome. Say hello to your new friends. You can never have enough friends."

A resident of North Hills, Calif., **Gary Wosk** writes in the horror and fantasy genres. He has an extensive background in communications as a newspaper reporter, public relations specialist and media relations manager. When he worked for Metro in Los Angeles, he was a senior communications officer and spokesperson.

PANGS

By Lizz-Ayn Shaarawi

Silas trudged up the stone steps of St. Ignatius, pulling his coat closed against his slender frame. He glanced up at the gothic architecture then gave an involuntary shiver. He always hated churches that seem to loom over you like they were monsters just waiting to swallow you up. God and the Devil didn't battle over your soul as far as he was concerned. People made their own beds and had to lie in them. It didn't make things easier; it's just how it was.

His thoughts were interrupted by a large gust of wind that sent various pieces of litter swirling around him. A large piece of paper whipped against his leg. He pulled it off then looked at it. A rotund woman's face stared back; another missing persons flier. He crumpled it up then tossed it in the trash bin by the church's front door.

As he reached for the door handle, he caught sight of his reflection in the large glass door. He winced at the narrow face, the hollow cheekbones, and sunken eyes. He yanked the door open before rushing inside.

A few people milled around the church's foyer. No one met anyone's eyes. Guilt and shame hung heavy in the air. Silas made his way to a large bulletin board. His gaze darted over more missing persons' fliers, free kitten announcements, and a sign-up sheet for the post-mass potluck lunch. His focus snapped onto a neatly typed list.

He scanned down until he saw his group. His finger slid across the crisp paper to the room number.

Silas pulled his coat even closer as he navigated the maze-like basement. He stopped in front of room B-5. "Why are basements always colder than it is outside?" he thought as he opened the door then stepped inside.

A group of morbidly obese women sat in a circle. They looked him over- some with bemused faces, some with disgust. One woman, name tag Lacey, smirked at her companion and mouthed *manorexic*. Her companion, name tag Shauna, snickered. The counselor, a slender balding man, ushered Silas from the room.

"This is Overeaters Anonymous. I think you're looking for the group next door," he said as he hustled Silas out. "B-4."

Silas peeked cautiously into the next room. A group of skeletal women and girls sat in gray metal folding chairs. Unlike the other groups, this one did not have the usual plates of cookies and doughnuts on a table shoved to one side. Instead, a large cooler of water and Dixie cups sat in their place. Silas poured a cup of water then hovered to one side.

"Take a seat if you're staying."

Silas jumped at the voice. A pleasant looking woman stood behind him. "The meeting is about to begin." She smiled at him. Silas quickly looked away. He nodded then headed to an empty chair in the circle.

He spent the next hour staring at his Dixie cup. He was, as usual, the only man that came to the meetings. He had heard all the stories before. There were women who didn't eat just to have some type of control over their lives. There were girls who looked in the mirror at their eighty pound frames and saw a leviathan. The binging, the purging, the stories went on and on but were always the same. How they'd guzzle water before doctor's appointments to make it look like they'd gained weight. How they'd hide rolls of pennies in their underwear. He knew all the tricks though he never used them.

Finally the group turned to him. The pleasant-looking woman glanced at his name tag. "Silas, would you like to speak tonight?"

Silas nodded. He drained his Dixie cup and crushed it in his hand. He stood then cleared his throat before beginning his story. "I'm Silas and I have an eating disorder."

"Hi, Silas," the group intoned.

"My main problem is portion control. I used to be able to eat small meals here and there. But lately I only want to eat huge meals. I eat until I'm sick. I feel huge and disgusting."

Some of the women nodded sympathetically.

"I won't eat for weeks afterward. I swear I'll never do it again. Then the hunger comes. I can hold it off for a while but it always gets the best of me." Silas' voice broke, "I always give in. Then it starts all over again." He choked on a sob. "I'm so hungry."

***

Lacey carried the green and white box out of Stan's Donuts while a uniformed teen locked the door behind her. She held the box close to her as if it was a precious treasure that might be stolen at any moment. The store's lights went out as she rounded the corner into the parking lot. She glanced around. It was darker than she remembered. Her feet crunched on plastic from the security light.

"Everything okay?"

Lacey jumped. She twisted around to see Silas step from the shadows. She relaxed when she saw him, remembering him from the church. "I'm fine." She waddled toward her car.

"Those smell good."

Lacey stopped. She looked down at the dozen doughnuts in her hands. With a snarl, she turned to Silas. "You caught me. Satisfied? Feel like a big man now?"

Silas stepped closer. "No."

Confused, Lacey narrowed her eyes at him. "What do you want?"

"Nothing." His stomach gurgled.

"Then take your skinny ass home."

Silas stood in her way. "I know why you eat. I know you're unhappy."

"Piss off."

"That's why you're so mean. You're just shielding yourself. It's okay."

"Shut up."

"That's why you'll take those dozen doughnuts home, sit in front of your TV, and eat them. You'll eat every single one."

"Shut your mouth. I mean it."

"You'll gorge yourself. And you'll feel better, for a while. Then the hate will seep in."

Lacey sniffed wiping away the tears that wouldn't stop falling. "You'll swear it's the last time- and it is- until the next time." Lacey bawled.

Silas held his arms out to her. "It's okay. I understand."

She stumbled into his arms. He held her close. "It's okay."

"I can't help myself. I try and try, but I can't."

"I know." His arms wrapped tighter around her. "I know. I can't help myself either."

Lacey squirmed against him, uncomfortable. "Stop. You're squeezing too hard." Silas held her tighter. "Stop," she cried, "You're hurting me!" Lacey opened her mouth to scream, but only gasped for air. She tried again but every time she took a breath, Silas tightened his grip. Her eyes bulged. Cracks and snaps filled the air as her bones broke. The box of doughnuts fell from her hand.

Silas open his mouth. His jaw unhinged as he forced his mouth over Lacey's head. The muscles of his throat flexed and released, expanding to accept the large meal. He pulled himself back into the shadows as his body distended.

Under the cover of night, Silas pulled his bloated body across the parking lot to his SUV. He heaved himself up into the driver's seat. Adjusting the mirror, he caught sight of his round, fleshy face. Self-loathing washed over him as he turned the key in the ignition and slammed the car into reverse.

The SUV's tail lights faded into the night as the back door of the doughnut shop opened. The pimpled employee, cigarette dangling from his lip, hauled the night's trash out to the dumpster. He spotted the box of doughnuts lying open on the pavement, the contents scattered. Cursing under his breath, he picked them up.

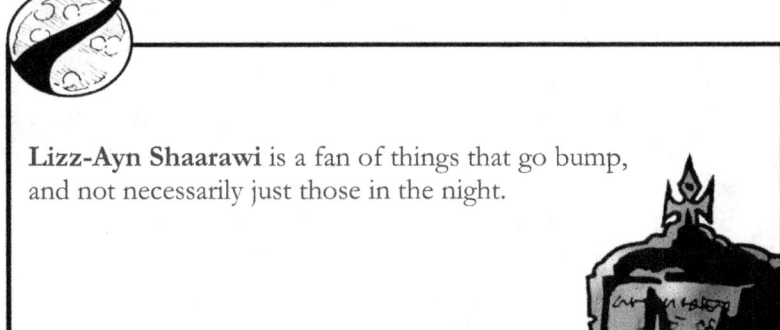

Lizz-Ayn Shaarawi is a fan of things that go bump, and not necessarily just those in the night.

PRODUCTS-193

BY W. B. STICKEL

Dead leaves tumbled lazily across the driveway as Evan pulled in.

"Jeez," he said, scanning the front lawn, which obviously hadn't been tended to in some time. The grass was overgrown and covered in sticks and leaves. "Looks like Dad's been slacking on the yard work. He's usually on top of that crap. I bet he threw out his back again."

Katrina, his fiancée, surveyed the yard then glanced at the neighboring houses. All of their yards seemed equally unkempt. "At least he's not alone in the slackage."

Evan looked around and saw what she meant. "Guess not."

They got out of the rented Malibu then headed to the house's front stoop. Like the yard, it was caked with the droppings of autumn. "Yeah," Evan said, clearing off the foliage with his boot. "He must have hurt his back. I'll have to ask him about it when he gets home from work." He looked at his watch. "Which shouldn't be for another two hours yet."

"He'd still go to work with a bad back?" Katrina queried.

"Dad's old school like that. He's like Charles Bronson, John Wayne, and Clint Eastwood all rolled up into one. You'll see."

"You're sure he—they—won't mind that we've shown up out of the blue?"

Evan sighed. They'd flown from Palo Alto to Wichita as a surprise to his parents and to introduce Katrina to them. He'd already met her folks and she was eager to meets his, so he'd suggested using the Thanksgiving break to drop in on them. He'd assured her a dozen times that they'd be ecstatic about the surprise visit, but his assurances didn't seem to carry much weight with her. "For the eightieth time, they won't mind," he told her. "So please quit asking."

A cold gust swirled around them then. Katrina huddled close to Evan shivering.

Evan smiled nodding at her faux schoolgirl sweater-and-skirt ensemble. "Told you Thanksgivings in Kansas are a bit different than those in California." He put his arms out, indicating the tan corduroys, black Stanford hoodie, red beanie, and plain black jacket he had on. "Next time, take a cue from your man."

Katrina jabbed him in the ribs. "Whatever. Just open the door."

"All right, all right," Evan said finally opening it.

Warm air enveloped them as they hurried inside.

"Oh yes," Katrina practically moaned. "Much better."

Evan shut the door then switched on the foyer's hanging light. Next to the light switch sat an old school dial thermostat. Evan leaned over and saw that it was set to seventy-five. "Lots of changes around here," he said. "Dad never used to let us put it above sixty-five." He took off his beanie, pulled back his black mop of hair, and rubberbanded it into a ponytail.

Katrina ran a hand through her own tawny mane, tossing the excess locks over her shoulders. "You haven't been home for over a year," she said. "I remember when I visited my parents after my first full semester away, I came back to find my mom had cut her hair lesbian-short and my dad had bought a freaking Segway. Who knows? Maybe your dad's just growing."

"Growing," Evan echoed dubiously. His father wasn't exactly the growing type. The man still used Old Spice and refused to quit smoking despite a recent run-in with the Big C. "Weird. Anyway, let me give you the tour."

The house was a split-level ranch built in the early eighties. It had four bedrooms and two bathrooms upstairs plus another bedroom and bath downstairs. As ever, it was cluttered with the myriad trinkets and knick-knacks his mother had accrued over the years—a vice of hers that drove Evan's father nuts and had caused many of their arguments.

They concluded the tour in the downstairs bedroom, which Evan had inhabited during his high school days after his older brother Dave had left to join the Navy. When he opened the door he was surprised to see that it had been overtaken by storage containers as well as a host of generic cardboard boxes. It hadn't been that way the last time he visited.

"What's all this?" Katrina wondered.

Evan approached one of the boxes sitting on his old bed. It, along with three others, bore the cryptic label "Product S-193." "Looks like Dad turned this into a catch-all for all his junk." He opened the box's lid. Inside sat a dozen red spray canisters with yellow caps and S-193 stenciled across the side. "Oh," he said, remembering. "Right. Dad had said something about this stuff the last time I called." He shook his head. "Dad and his special deals."

"What is it?"

Evan removed one of the canisters. It was light, empty. It had no lettering printed on it other than its name. "Kansas isn't the most glamorous state, however it is known for a few things. The Wizard of Oz. Dodge City. Sunflowers. And Fiddlebacks."

"Don't forget the band Kansas," Katrina teased.

Evan turned and grinned at his fiancée. "What's that you ask? What are Fiddlebacks? Oh, well, they're what some people call brown recluses."

Katrina's face paled. "You mean, like, spiders?" She was deathly afraid of insects.

"Oh, don't worry. They get a bad rap, but it's mostly undeserved."

"Mostly? Why would they get a bad rap?"

Evan shrugged. "Their venom, I guess. It won't kill, but it can sometimes rot the skin. I think because of this, people think they're inherently aggressive creatures and want to bite you. But it's not true. They won't bite if they can avoid it."

Katrina frowned. Her eyes drifted to boxes of S-193. "So what is that stuff?"

Evan glanced at the can he was holding. "Supposedly we had a bad infestation this spring. There's a big woodpile out back, which is kind of a breeding ground for them. Dad said they were crawling all over it. Got bit once too. Had the skin-rot and everything. To get rid of them he tried a bunch of different bug killers but nothing worked. They kept coming back. Even worse, he started finding them in the house. In the hampers, under the sheets. Behind towels."

"Eeeewww."

"I know," Evan said. "Then Dad being Dad got fed up and started looking around on the internet for something. Apparently he ended up finding some fly-by-night website that sold a product specifically designed for brown recluses. Product S-193. The site guaranteed results or your money back. Dad said he bought a bunch, supposedly it did the trick. Within a few days, they were all gone."

"Good," Katrina muttered. "I hate spiders."

Evan came over then pressed himself against her. "I know." He kissed her on the lips and gave her a playful smack on the butt. "Listen, let me go get our suitcases and stuff so you can get settled in and take a shower. While you do, I'm going to try and track down my old comic books."

Katrina smiled then returned the kiss. "My little geek."

"My little fraidy-cat," he returned. He gave her breasts a quick squeeze, then, fearing reprisal darted out of the room and up the stairs.

Katrina called after him to be prepared to finish what he started. Evan promised that he would. Money back guaranteed.

***

Evan experienced a flush of euphoria as he unloaded their luggage from the car. He'd done well to find Katrina. She made him insanely happy, and he believed he did the same for her. He hated corny terms like soul mates, but that's what she felt like to him. A soul mate.

They'd met at the start of their sophomore year at Stanford, playing darts at a bar in downtown Palo Alto. They recognized each other from the Intermediate Fiction Writing class they both attended and made an immediate connection. The first date went well, as did the sundry that followed. Before Evan knew it he was at Arnoldi's buying her a ring. To his great relief she accepted his proposal and that weekend she introduced him to her parents in Del Mar. He'd made a good impression. Afterwards she'd begged to know when they could meet his folks. That was when he'd suggested surprising them during Thanksgiving break.

Evan shut the trunk then gazed down the street. About six houses up he spotted a man milling about his front lawn. The man, whose features were too vague to make out at this distance, raised a hand and waved at Evan. Evan waved back then noticed that he and the man were the only two presently out and about. The man lowered his hand but remained in the yard, facing him. Evan gave him a nod, then grabbed the luggage and headed back inside.

He found Katrina in the downstairs bathroom, staring at herself in the mirror.

Evan put their suitcases down and joined her in the bathroom. "All right, baby," he said, wrapping his arms around her. "I'll be up in the attic, looking for those comics."

Katrina looked at his reflection in the mirror. "Evan, you're sure they're going to like me?"

Evan groaned biting back his frustration. "They're going to love you, baby. *I promise.* Just remember not to say anything bad about the Chiefs and you'll be fine."

"That's baseball, right?"

Evan pecked her on the cheek. "Funny." He pulled away then started towards the stairs leading to the first level. "Oh," he said, looking back. "In case you get finished before I do, the attic is above the garage, which you get to through the kitchen. You'll see the pull-down ladder."

Katrina gave him the thumbs-up. "Okay, there 'Sheldon'."

Evan pursed his lips at her *Big Bang Theory* reference and continued up the stairs. "I'm more of a Leonard," he said. "Besides, everyone's geeky about something. Remember I've seen your Fleetwood Mac CDs."

Katrina affected a hurt expression as she flipped him the bird. "Stevie Nicks is awesome," she declared then promptly shut the bathroom door.

Evan smiled. There were a million reasons he loved Katrina. Her obsession with Stevie Nicks was but one of them. "You're a lucky guy," he said as he reached the top of the stairs. "Don't screw it up."

***

After her shower, Katrina dressed in a more conventional blouse and jeans, then wandered the house in order to familiarize herself with its layout. It was a much different house than the one she'd grown up in. Smaller, more rustic—but in a cozy kind of way. She liked it. It was a place where a kid didn't have to walk around on eggshells all the time, worrying about ruining something expensive. She imagined Evan had had a pretty happy childhood here. For that she was a little jealous.

About the only thing she didn't like about it was its lack of cleanliness. She was by no means a neat-freak, but it appeared as if the place hadn't been cleaned in weeks. There was grime on the windows and dust everywhere. Wondering if she should broach the subject with Evan, she found her way out to the garage.

The pull-down staircase was where Evan had said it would be, near the back, extended down to the garage's gray cement floor. As she drew upon it, a string of goofy snickers tumbled down out of the space above.

"Hey, babe!" she called up. "Still looking at comics?"

There was a shuffling from above then Evan's head appeared at the top of the staircase. "Hi there. Come on up. You gotta see all this stuff."

"But I just showered."

"Don't be a wuss," Evan replied, retreating out of sight. "Besides, it's actually pretty clean up here."

Katrina huffed as she rolled her eyes but climbed the staircase all the same.

At the top she paused to have a look around. The attic wasn't at all what she expected. Tidy and spacious with sheetrock walls, nice hardwood flooring and plenty of space, it was more like a loft apartment than a place to store things. All it needed was a better means of access.

Contents-wise, it was filled with standard attic fare: boxes, old lamps and stacks of unused picture frames. What caught her eye, however, was the pair of old steamer trunks nestled against the far wall, one green, the other a faded brown.

Evan's voice brought her attention to the middle of the hardwood floor, where he was sitting Indian-style, his box of comic books stationed next to him.

"I'd nearly forgotten about these," he said, gazing at the comic in his lap, an older issue of *Punisher.*

Katrina went over and crouched beside him. "Forgotten? You only left home two years ago."

Evan put the comic back into its clear plastic protector, then removed another from the box, this one an *Uncanny X-Men* with Captain America, Wolverine, and Black Widow on the cover. "I only collected comics for a few years, back in Elementary. I guess I got bored with it though and stopped collecting. Put them in a box then the box ended up here. Wasn't until we got inside the house today that I even remembered I had them."

Katrina tousled his hair as if he'd just said something adorable then panned about the attic again. Her eyes drifted back to the two steamer trunks. "You know," she said, motioning to them, "I've always had a thing for those kinds of trunks. Kind of wouldn't mind having one as like a coffee table or something when we get our own place."

"They belonged to my grandparents," Evan told her. "I doubt Mom or Dad would care if we took one, though. They've been up here since we moved in. I'll ask, if you want."

"I want," Katrina replied. She wandered towards the trunks for closer inspection. "Is there anything inside them?"

Evan shrugged. "Don't know. Take a peek and see."

Katrina hesitated for a moment then continued toward the old travel cases. As she crossed the hardwoods, she noticed several more of the "Product S-193" boxes stacked to her right. Seeing them brought to mind the spider conversation they'd had, and she began scanning the place for webs. She looked high and low but didn't see a single gossamer strand anywhere. Guessing the pesticide really had worked, she paused in front of the trunks.

They were big, she saw. The size of beer barrels, each sporting an array of stamps indicating the various destinations they'd visited. Katrina beamed at this—she loved vintage stuff—and opened the leftmost steamer. Once she had its lid all the way up, she looked down at its contents. And looked. And looked.

"Um, Evan," she finally said.

"Yes, sweetums?"

"Weird question, but did your parents own mannequins?"

Evan's head cocked to the side. "Mannequins? Not to my knowledge. Why?"

Katrina closed the left trunk then lifted up the right one's lid. "There's another in here. They're both like covered in, I don't know, some silky material or something."

Evan put his *X-Men* back into its protective cover then came over to the trunks. He peered into the one she had open, knelt down, and swiped his hand across the silky material. The motion cut a rift in the stuff, which felt like cotton candy. Within the rift he could see one of the mannequin's arms. The appendage did not look like it belonged to a mannequin, though. It was grayish, decayed, and bore the smell of rotten meat.

Evan stepped back pinching his nose. As he did, his eyes caught sight of a metallic glimmer originating from the arm's wrist.

Katrina saw it too. "What is that?" she said, choking back a gag.

Evan leaned forward, held his breath, and had another look. The glimmer, he observed, was from one of those stainless steel medic alert bracelets. He edged even closer and read the inscription: *Penicillin Allergy, Diabetic.* For a long moment his mind refused to process what the words meant then a gasp escaped him. He stumbled backwards. "No ..." he murmured. "Can't be."

Katrina took hold of his arm to prevent him from falling down. "Baby, what's wrong? What did you see?"

"Dad," he said, brow furrowed. "He has a bracelet just like the one in there."

Katrina gazed at the open trunk. "Evan ...you're not... I mean..."

"I think so." The full weight of this struck Evan hard then brought him to his knees. Someone had put his father in there, and left him to rot. "Jesus," he said, as a torrent of how's and why's stormed his thoughts—all of which invariably led to grim conclusions. He started to examine them when his attention suddenly deflected to the other trunk.

"Mom?" he mewled.

Katrina stared at him, her face draining of color.

Evan mumbled something, forced himself to stand. He was about to tell Katrina that they needed to be certain it was his parents and not just presume when a loud clicking erupted beneath them as the floor began to vibrate. Evan and Katrina exchanged bewildered looks then Evan understood what was happening.

The garage's automatic door was opening.

***

The torrent assaulting Evan's brain doubled in intensity. Through it a stark and logical realization rose to the surface, compelling him to move. He scrambled to the staircase's opening looking around frantically. Sticking out of one of the cardboard boxes was an old aluminum bat. He snatched it and glared at Katrina, who hadn't yet budged.

"Kat!" he bellowed at her. "Kat!"

Katrina looked at him but said nothing.

"Someone's pulling in!" he said, eyes conveying a million things at once. "We've got to get down from here! Now!"

Katrina blinked, snapping out of her spell, then rushed over to him.

"It's okay," he whispered. "It'll be okay."

They quickly descended the staircase. Down in the garage they found an older model Bonneville with tinted windows parked in the rightmost spot. Evan knew the car well. It was his father's. Whoever had driven it into the garage was nowhere in sight. Fuming, wanting answers and revenge, Evan gripped the bat tight and held it ready.

"Where are you!" he shouted. "What did you do to my parents?"

Behind them stood a particleboard workbench strewn with various tools. Katrina snatched a hammer off one of its shelves then turned to Evan. "Baby!" she said, pointing at the Malibu, which sat thirty short feet away in the driveway. "The car's right there! Let's go get the police!"

Evan flitted a glance at the car. He knew what she was saying was the smart thing to do, but he wanted answers. Further, his primal side needed to use the bat on the person responsible for what had happened to his parents.

"Evan!" Katrina urged.

A moment later, the driver's side door of the Bonneville popped open and the garage door began to descend. The simultaneous occurrences made Evan and Katrina jump back. Before they could think to make a run for it, the door was all the way down, leaving them trapped inside the garage with the person getting out of the Bonneville.

"Greetings," the person said, a tall man dressed in a nice gray suit, black leather gloves, and a black fedora. Evan studied the man's face. He thought the man looked a lot like his father—if his father had recently undergone a facelift or botox treatment. The skin was just too smooth, wrinkle-free, and it bore no scars. Evan's father had a prominent one along his left cheek, a souvenir from a bar fight from his youth.

The lookalike shut the car door then halved the distance between them. He paused about eight feet away and stood gazing at Evan and Katrina. After a few seconds, he grinned without showing any teeth. The grin didn't look quite right; the symmetry was all wrong. "You are the son," the lookalike said in a voice that sounded like Evan's dad, only much hoarser. "A killer also?"

Evan's face twisted with confusion. "What?"

Disjointed laughter bubbled from the lookalike's mouth. "No relevance," he said. "The stimulant is everywhere now." A strange moment passed, wherein they just stood there staring at each other, then the lookalike's features abruptly disintegrated into legions of small independent specks, an effect that made it seem as though he had begun to melt. Before long the specks were pouring out of his pant legs spilling out across the garage floor. As they did, the suit and fedora collapsed to the ground in a shapeless heap.

Katrina saw that the specks were moving about each other. "Are those ... spiders?" she cried, dropping the hammer.

"Fiddlebacks," Evan said, flinging his bat at the mass of crawling things. Several got close to his foot, so he stepped down hard on them. There was no crunch, as he expected and when he pulled his boot back, he saw that they were still coming. Aghast, he grabbed Katrina's hand pulling her towards the garage's back door, which led to the house's the fenced-in backyard. He ripped the door open and they fled out onto the yard's covered back porch. Eyes bouncing back and forth, Evan scanned the yard closely for signs of other spiders. He was instantly struck by the fact that a brown wasteland of sticks, branches and old logs now existed where the lush green yard had once been.

"It's one big woodpile," he said, leading Katrina around the side of the house, where the fence's gate stood. The gate opened without resistance. Evan ushered his fiancée along the side yard out to the driveway. As they went, Katrina made a low, keening sound and started repeating, *It's not real, it's not real* over and over.

Evan dug into his pocket retrieving the key. "Thank Christ," he said, half expecting it not to be there, then they clambered into the Malibu. Heart pounding, head reeling, Evan threw the gearshift in reverse and peeled out of the driveway.

"Evan, look!" Katrina cried. Evan followed where she was pointing. There were people standing in their yards, staring and waving at them as they passed by. People with bland, shifting features. He looked left and discerned more of the same. "What is this?" Katrina demanded. "What the hell is going on? How can spiders imitate people?"

"I don't know, baby," Evan said. "I don't know. We'll figure it out when we—"

Katrina screamed then. The little brown specks were pouring in through the air vents, leaping onto their laps. Evan flailed in his seat and swerved off the road. The Malibu jumped the curb, massacred a lawn before crashing into the side of the house nearest the end of the street. Somehow the impact did not knock either of them unconscious. The airbags deployed as designed, depriving them of that precious gift.

Evan had just gotten his wits about him when a garbled voice drifted in through the shattered driver's side window. "It won't hurt very much," the voice said. "We promise. Not much."

Evan turned his head and observed a man lingering by the car. The man's face was undulating. Evan attempted to murmur a plea for mercy, but found his mouth full of Fiddlebacks. With a whimper he tried again to gaze at the man, to beseech him with a pleading look. But then specks of brown clotted his vision. The world went dark and silent.

He reached his hand out to find Katrina, his love, but found only a heap of moving, biting things.

W. B. Stickel works on computer systems for the military by day, and reads and writes as much horror as he can by night. He has had stories published in *Abomination Magazine #1* and the Fantastic Horror *Good Vs. Evil* anthology, as well as various online forums. He lives in upstate New York with his wife and three children and is deathly afraid of Teletubbies.

A War on Vets

BY NATHANIEL TOWER

Bernie Hillgerd hated trees and war veterans more than anything else in the world. Trees were always dumping their leaves on his lawn and their branches on his roof and car. Veterans were always demanding rights they didn't deserve expecting a hero's welcome everywhere they went. Unfortunately, it seemed that most people liked trees and veterans. Or at least they tolerated them enough to let them take over the world.

Bernie could hardly go anywhere without seeing at least a dozen of his foes. It was starting to drive him mad. To help solve the problem, he developed on Arbor Day a tradition where he drove around with a trunk full of saws and axes, hacking down one of each type of tree he could find. He even brought a checklist with him. One year, he managed to chop down fifty-two varieties. He laughed as they splintered to the ground with a thunderous crash. Then he sped away, leaving the mess for someone else to clean. He always hoped that a veteran would have to come do it as some sort of service project.

He knew that his Arbor Day routine had little impact on his problem, but he enjoyed doing it nonetheless. It brought him joy knowing he was at least getting a little revenge. Unfortunately, he had no clue what to do about those pesky veterans. At least they weren't as bothersome as the trees, although they were starting to annoy him even more every day as more sprung up from the many wars that were happening all the time.

One Veterans' Day he saw a homeless man begging for money with a sign indicating he was a veteran. The beggar was walking around extra cocky, demanding even more attention and money than on any normal day. Bernie wasn't really sure what the big deal behind Veterans' Day was. People celebrated military men and women every day. There were always wars going on. Yet people clapped, hooted, and hollered every time someone in any type of military uniform walked by. He wasn't sure why they deserved so much admiration. Most of them just couldn't decide what to do with their lives. Before today, Bernie always thought he hated trees more, but now he knew veterans were the bane of his existence. So he decided to start a new tradition in the same vein as his Arbor Day massacres.

Luckily for Bernie, he never took the axes and saws out of his trunk.

The homeless veteran on the corner looked ragged, like he'd been on the battlefield for months.

"Wanna ride, buddy?" Bernie asked.

The man stared at Bernie, squinting through long wisps of dirty hair. He stood up, leaving behind his small American flag and the placard that announced his homelessness then climbed into Bernie's four-door sedan mumbling an awkward, "Thanks."

The men's foul stench almost made Bernie regret his decision, but he knew that he would make the man pay for it.

"Where do you wanna go?" Bernie asked to distract this man from the impending doom.

"I'm so hungry," the man shook.

"I'll take you to a place with food," Bernie told him. "What's your name?"

"Reggie Lanard," the veteran replied.

"What's your favorite kind of tree, Reggie?" Bernie asked without looking at the filthy man. He shuddered at the thought of having to clean up after this guy.

"Tree?" Reggie responded.

"Yeah. What kind of tree do you like?" Bernie persisted.

"Oak," the man finally said.

Figures, thought Bernie.

"Do you prefer axes or saws?" he asked casually, as if this was what normal people talked about.

"Saws," the man said without much hesitation.

"Do you like hamburgers?" he asked next.

"Sure," Reggie responded with a little enthusiasm this time.

"I know just the place," Bernie said.

Bernie took him to a cheap fast food restaurant. After all, he figured Reggie deserved a last meal. Wasn't that what they did for the execution victims?

Reggie gobbled down three hamburgers in a manner of seconds. It was like he'd never eaten before in his life. Bernie ate nothing as they drove to the park. He tried not to watch as Reggie devoured the burgers. Hunks of bread and meat clung to the man's wiry beard. Bernie couldn't believe he was letting this slime eat in his car.

When they arrived at the park, Reggie didn't bother to ask what they were doing.

"Let's go over to that tree," Bernie said after parking in a secluded spot near a forest.

Reggie marched as if under orders while Bernie retrieved from his trunk a large saw and some sturdy rope. The man stunk even from ten feet away.

Bernie fought the stench bravely as he ordered Reggie to sit down. Oddly the homeless veteran didn't ask why or offer any objections. Bernie supposed the man had no reason to question someone who'd been so nice to him.

"Do you recognize this tree?" Bernie asked once they were standing just inches away from it.

"No," Reggie muttered. A piece of hamburger fell from his face.

"It's an oak tree," Bernie said. "Your favorite."

"What's with the rope and saw?" the man finally asked.

"We're going to play a little game," Bernie responded as he set down the saw and started to unravel the rope. "You owe me after that nice meal I gave you." Bernie spoke in jovial tones. The veteran didn't seem alarmed.

"Sit down and close your eyes," Bernie ordered the man, but the order was issued in a friendly way, not at all like a drill sergeant. The man acquiesced without the slightest reservation.

Once Reggie was seated with his back against the oak, Bernie tied the rope tightly around the putrid man and the thick tree trunk. He wrapped the rope around four times before he was satisfied with the tightness of the hold.

"Now keep those eyes closed," Bernie commanded.

The veteran continued to follow orders. It even looked to Bernie like the man had a slight smile underneath the beard.

Bernie shrugged at the smile before taking the saw to the man's chest, cutting just above the taut rope. The veteran was silent at first, as if this were part of the game, but soon he tried to let out a wail he must've learned while fighting in whatever war it was he claimed to fight. Bernie couldn't remember, but he knew they were all the same anyway. He silenced the veteran with a quick blow of a heavy stone to the face. Two teeth shook loose from the man's mouth and slid down the beard before landing at Bernie's feet. Bernie laughed at how easily the teeth had become dislodged then he continued sawing through the veteran's torso until he heard the saw blade tearing at the bones. He found himself laboring a great deal more than he had ever labored cutting down a tree. Still, he pressed on, putting every ounce of strength into slicing the veteran through to the trunk. He laughed again as he watched the top half of the man collapse onto the ground, the bottom half still sitting up tied to the tree. For a moment, Bernie contemplated whether he should chop down the whole tree. He decided it was a must, at the very least to hide the body.

Bernie hacked away at the tree from the opposite side, watching intently as it finally timbered on top of the halved body. The sound of the tree landing on top of the man was no different than the sound of any tree landing on top of the forest ground. Bernie was already back in his car before the echo had died.

Driving home quite satisfied that he had taken care of two enemies with one act, Bernie decided he needed some type of token of remembrance. He drove back to the corner where he had picked up the homeless man to see if the sign and flag were still there. They were. He tossed the two tattered items in his trunk and contemplated where to go next. A sense of unquenchable bloodlust built in him every time he saw a giant waving American flag or a gently swaying tree. He had to find more veterans to dismember. He would make it just like his Arbor Day routine; he would find a veteran from each war he could think of, tie that veteran to what he claimed his favorite tree was, and mutilate the body and the tree until that satisfying echo thundered through his ear drums.

Since it was Veterans' Day, Bernie knew it wouldn't be too hard to find vets. After all, they all wore their war badges so proudly that day, walking around as if the rest of the citizens wouldn't be there if it weren't for them. He hoped more than anything to string up some marines or Navy Seals. They would be so easy to lure to the trees. Hell, they probably would welcome the challenge of withstanding the saw's blade.

Bernie's next stop was the site of the Veterans' Day parade. He knew the parade was over, but there were bound to be loads of proud vets hanging around the area, lingering in the nostalgia of wars they pretended they had won. All he had to do was offer one a beer, something American like a Bud Light, then he would have them under his control for the rest of the day.

True to his suspicion, there were dozens of uniformed and decorated men and women walking up and down the parade route. He decided he would stay away from the women. Although they bothered him, it was for a different reason. They didn't have the same arrogance or sense of entitlement. They were more there just to show that they were empowered women. Killing one of them wouldn't be much different than killing a female construction worker, and that would just be insane. Bernie knew he wasn't insane, so he scoured the streets for unsuspecting males.

After only a few minutes of driving up and down the ticker-taped parade route, Bernie found exactly what he was looking for. Two skin-headed men who looked like jarheads from slightly different eras, were engaged in a friendly shoving match, boasting which war was more important to the overall safety and well-being of the nation. Bernie knew they were both equally worthless as well as the fact that the most beneficial thing to the country and the world would be having these two men sawed in half and impaled by a massive elm or spruce. The type of tree really didn't matter much, as long as its branches were sharp and its trunk was massive.

Bernie slowed his car as he drove by the two marines, shouting, "You guys rock!" at them. They pumped their fists high in the air in acknowledgment of this celebration. That was Bernie's cue. He stopped the car then got out, leaving the engine running. "Let me take you to a bar and buy you guys a drink," he suggested.

The two marines looked at each other briefly then headed for Bernie's car, slapping each other's backs on the way. "Shotgun," called the younger marine.

The men got in Bernie's car. He began to drive, asking them

questions on the way to wherever they were going.

"So where'd you guys fight?" Bernie asked.

"Gulf War," one of them said.

"I did my tour of duty in Italy," the other said.

Bernie scoffed to himself at this second marine. He wondered if he should even bother to kill him. What was the man doing in Italy? He certainly hadn't been protecting this country or any other. But he considered himself a veteran, and that was really all that mattered. In fact, the Italy marine was probably even worse than the real veteran. At least the Gulf War guy had done something to warrant a parade.

"What's your favorite type of tree?" Bernie asked the marines.

The marines hesitated before answering. There was an awkward tension in the car that Bernie realized was the marines' inability to relate to him in any way. The marines exchanged a glance as if to say they needed to humor the guy who was about to buy them booze.

"Oak," the Gulf War guy finally said. This disappointed Bernie. He didn't want to take down another oak.

"Elm," said Italy. This was only slightly more pleasing. While he hated elm trees just as much as any other trees, he had hoped that one of these marines could give him a bit of a challenge or at least a response that wasn't so cliché. Not that he expected marines or any other soldiers to have much knowledge on the subject of trees.

Bernie didn't bother to ask them if they liked the axe or the saw better. He decided to distract them with talk of beer and heroism as he drove to the park.

"What types of beers do you guys like?"

He barely listened as they rattled off the usual list of manly American beers.

Halfway through his list, Italy must've recognized where they were. "What the hell are we doing here?" he asked.

"It's a shortcut to my favorite bar," Bernie quickly said.

"And what bar is that?" asked Italy.

"It's a surprise." Bernie cursed that these men were so observant. This wouldn't be as easy as the homeless veteran, but he would find a way. Then he had it. "Besides, I want to get your pictures in front of some trees first."

The marines looked at each other again and shrugged. A few minutes wasted taking pictures was worth free beers and showers of honor and praise.

When Bernie was satisfied with the location, he pulled the car off the road then told the marines they were at the best trees in town. "I want to take your pictures in front of that big tree," he told them. They walked over to the tree making jokes about what a weirdo Bernie was. Bernie retrieved the rope and an axe from his trunk then followed them over to the tree.

"Tie him up," Bernie said to Italy. "I want to get an action shot."

"Buddy, this is some weird shit," Gulf War said to Bernie.

"I photograph for the *Times*," Bernie said. "This is the kind of stuff that makes the cover."

The two marines seemed pleased with this explanation, so Italy started tying Gulf War to the tree.

"Make it look real," Bernie announced as he started snapping pictures with his cell phone camera.

"Shouldn't you use a better camera?" Gulf War asked.

"Not for this type of shot," Bernie explained. "We want something raw."

Again the marines seemed satisfied.

Italy was finishing up the knot when Bernie planted the axe blade in the man's spine. The marine fell over like a young sapling on top of Gulf War. Gulf War's cries were muffled by the burly man on top of him. Bernie quickly pulled out the axe and swung at Gulf War's neck. The axe penetrated halfway through the thick neck, rendering the marine completely silent. Bernie alternated swings, one at Italy and one at Gulf War, until he had decapitated both and removed several limbs as well. The base of the tree was stained a thick red that looked almost like dyed sap. Before going at the tree, Bernie retrieved a token from each marine. He took a small flag pin from Italy, and he took some type of honorific medal from Gulf War. After pocketing the mementos, he began swinging the axe like a deranged baseball player. Bernie smiled as he chopped at the trunk of the tree until the elm collapsed on top of the two dismembered marines. He marveled at how much more difficult it was to pull an axe out of a tree trunk than it was to pull it out of a man's neck or spine.

Once again, Bernie was back in his car before the echo of the fallen tree had died away. He didn't leave the park this time. On the way to this little forest he'd noticed a party at a pavilion that looked like some celebration of war heroes. There were flags all around the pavilion, and a fair number of the attendees were in patriotic outfits. He knew there had to be some veterans in the group.

Bernie parked at the pavilion site then strolled up to the party. The smell of bratwurst tickled his nose, making him realize how hungry he was. It was interesting that you didn't think about things like eating while you were killing people, but the act of killing people sure built up the appetite.

Rather than make a grand entrance, Bernie approached a small group of what looked like ex-soldiers. A brief conversation told him he was right. The three men in the group had all fought in various wars. One battled in the jungles of Vietnam. One had just gotten back from Iraq. The third had been somewhere Bernie had never heard of. They all tried to outdo the others with their war stories. Bernie just nodded, laughed, and cheered with the rest of them. The three men were all obviously drunk, which only added to the ridiculousness of their stories.

"Can I get a picture of you guys?" Bernie asked during a lull in the bragging.

"Sure," one of them piped up. They all instantly put their arms around each other.

"Not here," said Bernie. "I'd like to take it in a more foresty setting."

The three looked at him with suspicion.

"I'm a photographer for the *Times*," he said. "I'm trying to get some nice raw cover shots of veterans. We're doing this feature where we put vets in war-like settings."

The three men were very interested in such publicity.

"If you just hop in my car," Bernie said, "we'll be there in about two minutes. The spot is in this park."

The three followed Bernie to his car. Iraq sat in the front seat. Bernie wondered if he could smell the homeless man, but the vet didn't say anything.

"Here we are," Bernie said just a few minutes later when they had reached the forest. He wasn't worried that they might stumble upon the dead marines. In the unlikely event that they did see the mess he would just explain that was part of the scene he was creating.

He didn't bother to ask what types of trees they liked. He coaxed them over to a grove of maples and explained he had to tie them up. The drunken vets didn't seem to mind. After tying them up, he retrieved the bloody axe from his car. Now the men were alarmed.

"What the hell is going on?" yelled Iraq.

Bernie responded with a grunt as he swung the axe in a downward fashion at the man's head. The head split in two like a small piece of wood, and it took a moment before the blood began gushing out. The geyser of blood gurgled for several seconds before turning into a steady flow.

The other two men began screaming and squirming, but the knots Bernie had tied were inescapable. Bernie approached Vietnam next, then standing on the man's side, swung the axe downward through the man's head. His face came right off, dropping to the ground like a pile of dead leaves. Bernie thought he heard the face scream when it hit the ground.

By the time Bernie got to the third man, the vet had almost wriggled free of the rope. Bernie's axe cut his flight short. He chopped at the man's legs first before delivering a forceful blow to the sternum. The blade stuck, so Bernie had to place a foot on the man's shoulder to get enough leverage to remove it. Bernie watched as the blood of the three soldiers pooled together. He took a piss in the puddle of blood before taking a few more swings at the dead men. Then he grabbed a token from each and chopped down the trees to bury the bodies. This was his most satisfying kill yet. He waited until the sound of the third tree had finished reverberating through the forest before heading back to his car.

As he drove around the park, he wondered if it would be too risky to just drive back to the same party. He thought it would be and decided instead to visit the nearby veterans' hospital. He imagined it would be easy to get one of the patients to follow him. When he pulled into the parking lot of the hospital, he immediately saw his next victim. A geezer of a man was ambling around the sidewalk in front of the main entrance. The man looked utterly insane. Bernie pulled the car up next to the man and shouted, "Grandpa! Happy Veterans' Day!"

The old man looked at him then flashed a beaming smile that caused Bernie to wonder when this man last had an occasion to be happy. A smile spread across Bernie's face as he realized the irony of the situation. This fogey's happiness would be very short-lived. Actually, Bernie was probably doing this man a favor. Not only would he make him happy for a few minutes, but he would also end the man's miserable existence that was probably haunted by nightmares of war and torture.

"Hop in, Grandpa," Bernie told the man.

The man limped around to the passenger side of the car and

struggled to pull open the door. Once he had it, he collapsed his body into the seat. Bernie sped off before anyone could catch a good glimpse of what had happened.

"Where're we going?" the old man asked Bernie.

"To the park," Bernie told the nearly dying veteran.

"I love the park," the man said.

Bernie found the man somewhat pleasant. He didn't scoff at questions about favorite trees or cutting preferences. This old man was willing to talk about anything. It was a shame that Bernie was going to slaughter him.

Without asking what war he was from, Bernie drove the man to the park stopping in his usual spot. "We're here, Grandpa," Bernie said. Without going to the trunk, Bernie walked around to open the door for the old man. Once the door was open, he offered a hand for the man to lean on. No rope would be necessary here. Bernie would just ask the man to stand next to a tree then chop the shit out of him. He figured the axe would go through this man easier than through a slice of soft cheese. Although the ease of the cut would be welcome, he would miss the crunching sounds of the axe crushing thick bones. This brittle man might actually break before the axe made contact.

"Go over to that tree, Grandpa," Bernie said before heading to the trunk for the axe. Glancing around at all of the cutting tools and war mementos in his trunk, he wondered if maybe he should use something lighter. Then he noticed his favorite axe was missing. He must've left it somewhere in the forest. With a shrug he reached for a saw and decided to find the axe after he took care of this man.

When he turned around, the ancient veteran stood in front of him with a terrifying gleam in his dark eyes. Bernie heard the sharp crack of his skull only briefly before his body collapsed to the ground.

* * *

"Damn Nazis," the old veteran said before tossing the axe on top of Bernie's crumpled body. The man tried to walk away, but the exertion of swinging the axe had been too much for his feeble heart. He collapsed just a few feet from Bernie's bloody carcass, a crooked smile across his heroic face.

Nathaniel Tower writes fiction and teaches high school English in the Midwest. His fiction has appeared in over 100 online and print magazines and has been nominated for several awards. His first novel, A Reason to Kill, was released in July 2011, and his debut novella is coming out in May 2012. Visit him at www.bartlebysnopes.com/ntower.htm.

Jamie's Imaginary Friend

By Laila Murphy

Jamie was an unusual child. Mum said he was imaginative. Matt said he was a liar. Dad used to say he was touched in the head and it was Mum's fault for babying him. So he would give her a kicking. Dad used to beat Mum up for all sorts of things, like his tea wasn't in the right mug or she was making too much noise, that sort of thing. Jamie was glad when he took off.

Jamie lived in the shed at the bottom of the garden. This was a new arrangement, since the night Matt had arrived home completely wasted, bursting through the door, slamming it against the wall, not caring how much noise he made. Mum had been out with her latest boyfriend. Jamie had padded down the stairs in his pyjamas, yelling at him to be quiet. Matt knocked his little brother to the floor, banging his head against the banister.

Screaming, Jamie had sped outside towards the shed at the bottom of the garden. Matt swearing blue murder locked the front door. Yeah, it was a cruel thing to do, but he had been sniffing glue that night so it was hardly his fault.

Jamie stayed in the shed after that.

He was only nine years old, but soon he would be ten then things would be different. He would be bigger, stronger. He would take on Matt and win. Give *him* a black eye. Grab his head and smash it against the wall, push him down the stairs and hear his bones crack, tie him to his bed and set fire to it. He spent hours in the shed quietly plotting his revenge. It was a shame he was only nine. If only he had a friend, someone bigger than Matt, who could do those things.

Just as he was wishing this, *he* appeared. He opened the door to the shed then came in, just like that. Jamie was very surprised though once he got used to the idea he was pleased. For once his wishes had come true. That had never happened before.

That evening, he came indoors to tell Mum about his new friend.

"He lives in the shed and doesn't want to come indoors. He likes the dark."

"Leave it out, Jamie. I'm on the phone." Mum shooed him away. Matt, who was watching TV in the living room laughed, cracking open a can of beer. Jamie pictured smashing Mum's ashtray over Matt's head, splitting it open. This made him feel calmer. He went into the kitchen to make sandwiches for himself and Busby.

Busby was thirsty as well so Jamie sneaked back into the kitchen then brought him a six-pack of beer. They sat together in the shed talking until it grew dark.

"I hate Matt. He's my brother. He hits me."

"Why don't you hit him back?"

"I can't. He's bigger than me. He's nearly eighteen."

"Is this his beer?"

"Yes."

"It tastes good, doesn't it?"

Jamie nodded in agreement, slurping from the can. He liked the way it made him feel dizzy.

"Does he smoke?"

"Yes."

"Why don't you bring us his cigarettes? You know where he keeps them?"

"Yes, in a drawer in his room. He smokes other stuff too. It makes him act weird. He thinks I don't know where he keeps it but I do. It's under his bed."

"Good lad."

Jamie spent most of his time in the shed with Busby, smoking, drinking, and talking. Busby was a great friend. He always listened and gave good advice.

"My mum spends all her time with her stupid boyfriend. He talks about himself a lot. He's a creep. I hate him."

"Next time he comes to the house, slip some bleach into his tea. That'll shut him up."

"Good idea. I know where she keeps it."

"You can do anything you want, kid. Just don't get caught."

"Matt does whatever he wants. He never gets caught. He sells stuff for his mates. I reckon it's robbed."

"Does he now? He earns a lot of money flogging stolen gear, I reckon. I bet a clever lad like you knows where he keeps his dough?"

"He sleeps with it under his pillow."

"Does he now?"

Over the days that followed Jamie stole his mum's jewellery from her room and gave it to a pawnshop that didn't ask questions. He pinched cigarettes from the corner shop. He pick pocketed his mum's boyfriend's wallet as he slept in front of the TV. He gave everything to Busby. Busby said he was a good boy, a clever boy. Jamie glowed with pride.

Until he was caught.

It was bound to happen. That Matt would notice his dwindling supplies of drugs, beer, and money. That he would suspect his little brother; then he would follow him up the stairs when he heard Jamie creep along the landing towards his room. He would burst in catching Jamie red-handed.

He punched Jamie in the face, breaking his nose with a crack, red spurting across the walls. Jamie gurgled as blood filled his mouth. He stumbled down the stairs and outside to the shed, his sanctuary, Matt screaming abuse as he went.

Busby agreed that now was the time to *get Matt.*

***

That night as he lay in bed, Matt was sure he heard a light tread on the stairs. He opened one eye and listened. There it was again, the floorboards outside his room creaked. He sat up but heard nothing more. The house was silent. Jamie had probably sneaked in from the shed. Smirking, Matt lied down then promptly fell into a heavy, boozy sleep. He didn't even hear the rattle as the door handle was turned and slowly opened.

It was the smell that woke him. Matt leapt up wide awake. He stopped abruptly, falling back. He struggled. It took a minute to realise he was strapped down to the bed. Jamie was stood by his side, staring at him with a look in his eyes that Matt didn't recognise. In his hand was an empty plastic can, the remains of which he sloshed over the duvet. It was this liquid that smelt so strongly.

"What are you doing, you little bastard? I'll kill you!" Jamie didn't say a word. Matt thrashed about the bed, eyes bulging, falling silent as Jamie advanced; his empty eyes looming. There was the bright flash and crackle of a match being struck. Matt's yell was engulfed by the *whoosh* of flames.

Coughing, eyes streaming, Jamie ran for the door but it slammed shut with a bang. He rattled the handle. It wouldn't budge. Somewhere in the room came a low throaty chuckle.

"Why don't you stick with me, kiddo?"

As black smoke filled the room, the heat scorching his flesh, Jamie used the last breath in his lungs to scream before he too was swallowed by the inferno.

***

It took the fire brigade hours to put out the blaze. The entire house was gutted. Luckily the woman who lived there managed to stumble out just in time.

No such luck for her boys. They were both charred to the bone. The police suspected foul play.

There was a full investigation, but the fire had destroyed everything - almost. An inspection of the shed at the bottom of the garden proved disturbing. Along with dozens of empty beer cans and cigarette stubs, sniffer dogs detected human remains buried underneath it. A skeleton was dug up and identified as David Bradshaw. It caused a stir among the policemen assigned to watch the site.

"He escaped maximum security ten years ago. We never found him. Always suspected he'd been done in. Don't suppose we'll ever find who bumped him off. He had a lot of enemies. No wonder. Drugs, kidnapping, extortion, murder. Anyone who crossed him got tied up, doused with petrol and set alight."

"Bloody hell."

"Know what else? He always had kids with him. Used to show them the ropes, you know, treat them like apprentices. He said they were only ones he could trust. God knows where he found them. They

were only eight or nine; that kid's age, the one who burned to death."
The policeman shuddered. "Imagine a mass murderer being best mates
with a kid. Creepy, eh?"

His colleague agreed it was.

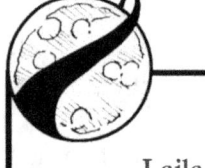

      Laila Murphy: "I am the librarian at The Belvedere Academy
in Liverpool. I was born and bred in the city and while I have travelled
widely I still believe there's no place like home and am a proud
Scouser. I write short fiction and scripts during the evenings
and weekends. I am also part of a small yet supportive
writing group that meets regularly to review and critique
each other's work."

JACKS

BY K. W. SCHROEDER

A leaning shadow fell across a pitted curb sprouted brown and yellow with dead summer grass. Its corporeal form leaned jauntily against a sign post. A shaking hand scratched absentmindedly at something in the crook of the elbow, beneath a business suit of a corporate non-color. In the right pants pocket was a document stamped with a date, time, and scrawled with a physician's chicken scratch. The figure was only one of a dozen or more people to leave the doctor's office that day no better for their trouble. Had any of the group been capable, they might have considered that the most common adverse symptom of an inoculation is fever, not a sudden severe drop in body temperature—certainly not exponential cellular corrosion.

The outline of the hands and head, instead of their usual backlit sharpness, seemed to fade at the edges, like wax paper before to a candle. The bright early afternoon sun passed through the cartilage of the ears refracting into beams of cloudy pink and blue. Words tumbled from the mouth into a bastard jumble of prayer, dismay and resignation. The shadow sat abruptly onto the concrete. A brief word of protest seemed to pass from the lips, just before the shadow slumped to its side there in the beating mid-afternoon sun. Not long after, the collapsed shadow began to bleed.

* * *

"What happened to her?" a small, green-eyed girl in red overalls asked. "Did she fall?"

The children looked upward considering the possibility. Above them, unimpeded for millions of miles, lay the bleak immensity of summer sky.

"No, stupid," came the reply from a tall fair-haired boy in a hushed, not-unkind tone. "There's nothing she coulda fell from."

At their feet—the dozen or more clusters of tennis shoes, flip-flops, and bare soles—the body lay bleeding slowly, imperceptibly from the eyes and nose. This plus the faint pallor of the face were the only visible signs of distress. A moment's work with a tissue, and the woman could very easily have appeared to be asleep.

"What she bleedin' for? Somebody hit her?" The round, mocha-colored face of the speaker convulsed with worry and nervous energy. "I bet it was Roscoe. He a meany."

A loud ripple of agreeable mumbles spread out through the crowd like applause at a political rally.

"Naw, Roscoe's at his grammy's house all summer," said the fair-haired boy with a tinge of leadership coloring his soft, confident voice.

"Oh," came the shy reply.

"Is she alive?" inquired a voice from the back of the crowd.

The realization that the woman might not be alive froze each face into separate but comparable masks of mute confusion. Death, that unwanted visitor, was not something the children had experienced first-hand. Below the still, worried faces, the body slowly lost more blood from the eyes and mouth. A trickle, hidden by her hair, began a slow drain from her ear closest the ground. The ear facing the sky pooled to overflowing with thick cranial blood. Underneath the tailored business suit—now utterly ruined by her rapid physical decline—her flesh began to open apparently on its own, as if quick invisible razors passed over with a feather's weight and a surgeon's touch.

"What's that smell?" asked another voice. "It smells like doo-doo."

Nervous titters all around gave respite from the tension. A hollow sigh escaped the lips of the seeping corpse, not overloud but unheard by the giggling crowd. Down in the moist dark of the lungs, tiny organisms worked diligently to create a new home for themselves. Well they should have, too, for they numbered already in the trillions, and increased with every passing moment. Were an experienced eye to view them, one would liken the organisms to the metal jacks with which so many of the children's parents played when they were children themselves. That single similarity, however, would be where all pleasant nostalgia would cease.

The invaded tissue of the lungs behaved in much the same way as Styrofoam soaked in gasoline: the intricate structures broke down into viscous gels, affecting each neighboring membrane in turn. The creatures, or whatever they were, changed method and purpose as often as needed, with a rapidity and gusto that seemed almost cheerful. Nerve tissue, crystallized bone, fatty cells—the jacks found each as easily usurped as the last, wasting no time in considering the value of their conquered territory. They spilled out of each small pocket of living tissue like a river flood, snatching up new fuel as their legions expanded and divided up duties, leaving behind only a biologically neutral substance devoid of even the slightest tinge of life. Should any learned eye have seen them so merrily at work in the poor woman's form that lay melting on that concrete sidewalk, it would have registered immediately the nature of the jacks. Their name, collectively, would have sprung to the lips as biblical references do to the clergy. That name, spoken in reverent, hushed tones, was Pestilence.

A small, chubby hand reached to touch the quietly seething cyanotic flesh. The jacks recoiled briefly at the pressure and heat upon contact, changing their loose formation into that resembling a phalanx of geometric Roman centurion. Upon the frictionless rupture of the skin's surface, they broke ranks rushing gleefully into the outside air. The pudgy fingers recoiled at the sight of blood—much thicker than human blood, and lighter in hue— were wiped frantically across the knees of a shopworn pair of faded corduroys.

"Owwie!" cried the child, as his fingertips peeled neatly away against the rough cloth. "OWWIE!"

At this, the other children leapt back in horror. Nothing was quite so shocking to a child as the sudden pain of another. The little boy turned on his heel then ran for home, bleeding fingers crammed safely into his mouth. A few others, confused and terrified, followed suit fleeing their own ways home.

A brave, foolhardy toe, wrapped safely in a scuffed sneaker, nudged the woman's shoulder. Beneath the cloth of the jacket, an indentation welled with pinkish syrupy blood yawning widely. It opened down to the bone and beyond in much the same way as a sinkhole rapidly swallows a home. The slack, detached limb sagged out of the cuff of the jacket, exposing unraveled muscle and tendon as well as a small rectangular object in the crook of the soupy elbow.

The curly headed boy—face full of mischief and wonder—stood over the body leaned close to look, then said in a low voice, "It looks like a band-aid."

The tall fair-haired boy pushed him gently to the side. "He's right! It's a Snoopy band-aid!"

The little black child grimaced at the sight of the famous cartoon dog on the bandage. It brought back memories of doctors and nurses as well as being poked in the arms with large needles. She wondered aloud at the absurdity of a fully grown adult needing to get shots just like she and her classmates.

"Is she sick? Why they gave her a shot?"

"Lots of grownups get shots now," said the curly haired boy. "It's 'cause they don't want to get sick like all those people after that place blowed up last year."

"That place," the second floor of a university biochemical laboratory, was destroyed in what was publicly termed an accidental chemical reaction. Privately, among those who tended to know more about such things, it was viewed simply as an uncharacteristically judicious decision by an unscrupulous biological tinkerer. Neither explanation was entirely accurate or took into consideration the absolute absence of the tinkerer in the resulting rubble.

The smaller boy, he of the scuffed sneakers, thought for a moment.

"Everybody, get back," he murmured, a sly grin spread obscenely across his face.

"What?" cried the little green-eyed girl. "My ears hurt! I can't hear you!"

Unfortunately for them all, he couldn't hear her, either. Inside the canals of the children's ears, small tributaries of conquered blood flooded their banks, spilling out into every available space, the tide carrying with it an armada of tiny insatiable marauders. It could be said that this was the point from which there would be no turning back, but that, again, was only half correct. It was certainly a point of no return, inasmuch as is each passing foot of a total free-fall.

With the wild, thoughtless violence of a youth just discovering his strength, the boy leapt forward and brought his sneaker down onto the woman's gaping shoulder with terrific force. Though small and relatively weak, the foot passed easily through the woman's liquefied tissue, in the process shoving the fabric of the woman's suit down into the gaping cavity of her dissolving ribcage. The shock of his action, and the ease with which he passed through the body, combined to sweep his feet from under him. As he fell, his imbedded foot shifted inside the mire of rapid decay. A small pocket of air in the neck ruptured violently under the sudden intense pressure.

A spray of blood misted the faces and brows looking down upon the horrid scene. Thick clots spattered loudly on the attacker's cheeks, mouth, and chest. Though viscous with a copper-scent, the blood was now the faded pink of old carnations. The tacky rivulets seeping from the ruptured neck were almost virginal white.

"Ugh!" came the almost simultaneous cry from the crowd.

Several pairs of hands wiped furiously at brows and cheeks, peeling away crinkled layers of skin against the smooth yellow-white bone exposing through those awful fissures nasal cavities and teeth. Agonized screams rose up from the gaping, tattered mouths. Blinded, bleeding, melting bodies ran haphazardly away from the scene, trailing sprays and chunks behind.

On the ground, the body of the woman spread steadily out into a whitish puddle of roiling biological mush. Above it—and in it—hung two parts of a leg eaten away at the ankle and knee, held together by a dripping pair of new blue jeans. The boy with the scuffed sneaker's whimpers were drowned out by the stuttering scrape of his exposed metacarpals dragging along the blacktop. In their wake lay streaks of active liquefaction.

Up and down his arms, legs, and back, teeming masses of the little jacks happily toiled and multiplied in pink trenches dug into the flesh by the brushed cotton of his button-down shirt. A muddy snap, and the boy fell back onto the street. The back of his head flattened against the blacktop. Small bits of gravel and dirt tore through his flesh like musket shot. Milk-white rivers sloshed inside his open maw. Teeth the texture of old erasers shook loose, falling without resistance through the hard palette and passing into the cavity of the brain. Mercifully, the jacks swarmed immediately there, feasting heartily on the youthful fatty tissue.

Up and down the avenue lay puddled clothing and writhing forms bleating out strangled cries for help. At one doorstep, a long pink streak led to a shapeless mass rapidly disintegrating under the excited attentions of a family dog.

Next door, in the living room, a cordless telephone stood half-sunk into the mire of an open collarbone, the dripping head leaning to one side. A pair of faded corduroys lay slack across the lap.

Back down the road, near the empty, sopping business suit, a small robin danced fitfully at the edge of the white soup. Its bright eye focused on a movement in the middle of the roiling white fluid rapidly evaporating into the hot summer air, the edges frothy and crisp like the perimeter of a pancake. Unable to recognize edible remains—or, indeed, solids of any sort—in the evanescing mass, the robin bounced once, twice, and took to flight.

The Red Death had entered the kingdom of Prospero once before, and lay in wait in his final blackest chamber. There, the prince confronted his own doom, and that of his cloistered revelers. A visitor with a new mask came prancing down the road of that tiny community, and took hold in its youngest revelers—those from whom aid and comfort would be least likely withheld.

The masks that Death wears come in many colors. Red for Prince Prospero, black for Queen Antoinette. The mask that death wore on its final visit was not worn upon its face, however. The attendees of the parties have become too wily to be fooled by such a cheap ruse. Unlike Prospero, the children of that lonely macabre avenue did not glimpse a mask until it was much too late. The tiny rectangular bandage, with its familiar cartoon dog and bright colors, covered the face of Death for just long enough.

Somewhere above us, at any given time, Death floats on spread wings. His tiny head cocked to one side, and his bright robin's eye attached to whatever suits his fancy. Along his tail feathers, and the tips of his wings, is a coating of busy white fluid. It cannot overtake its current carrier, and well it should not. After all, they number in the trillions, and have much better homes to build for themselves once they land.

K. W. Schroeder is a Texas-based writer whose work has been featured in print, online, the stage, and in short films. He lives in the Hill Country with his wife and two terrible dogs.

The Honeymoon's Over

By E. E. King

My brother Chris and his new bride Margaret were as happy, good looking, and nice a couple as you could hope to see. Chris was tall with a slightly muscular frame. He had long, laughing hazel eyes with a wicked lopsided grin. His mop of dark hair was usually unruly, in a cute way. Maggie was a red head with creamy skin. Her wide blue eyes seemed to reflect the sky right back at you.

They weren't altogether practical, but you couldn't really hold them responsible. Fortune had smiled on them and they smiled back. Who cared if they lacked money or jobs?

Chris was a musician and Margaret a writer. They eked together a living, he, by playing bar- mitzvahs and weddings, she, by writing articles for *Good Housekeeping* and *Better Homes and Gardens than Yours*.

Together they were irresistible; a combo of charm, brains, enthusiasm, and cheerfulness that would be right at home in a Disney movie. Oh, they had their moments like anyone else I guess. Chris could be a little lazy, Maggie liked to buy things she couldn't afford, but who could blame them? We all knew they'd work it out.

They had a cute little apartment off Hill Street. It was a quiet neighborhood. Chris could bike to his part time bar job at Frankie's. Maggie stayed up nights writing.

Later, they adopted a puppy. He was a spaniel/retriever mix, with curly golden hair, long ears and huge liquid, soft brown eyes. He was irresistible! They named him Mr. Baggins... Mr. B for short.

Now they had their troubles... sometimes they'd fight a bit, all kids do. I always thought of Chris and Maggie as kids... I mean he was my baby brother.

Well, one day Chris came home from Frankie's a bit late... He always came home late, it was a bar after all, but this time it was later than usual, and he was a tad lit. To make a long fight short, they quarreled. Maggie didn't like him drinking and biking home; Chris, bless his heart was usually not at his most reasonable when drunk. Still, it was nothing, really. I knew it. One of those little squabbles you don't even remember in the course of a year. The next day Chris woke up late with a hangover to discover Maggie and Mr. Baggins were gone. Now I don't mean they'd left or anything, they were just out for a walk. Chris felt grumpy and ashamed. But, he was still angry with Maggie for not leaving a note. By 4:00pm, he was worried. She'd never been gone this long.

He was leaving the house when a neighbor came up, dragging behind him a whimpering, dirty Mr. Baggins. She'd found the dog running, crying hysterically through the streets. Somehow, she'd managed to catch hold of his leash then bring Mr. B home.

Well it didn't take long to find out what had happened. They found her near the dog park, broken and crumpled in the street. It had been a hit and run, not much to go on.

It's still hard to talk about that time. Seemed like we just froze while things moved around us. There was the body... God! To call Maggie "the body," but that's what she was now. We had her cremated and kept her ashes. Chris wanted to take them to Italy with him. He and Maggie had always dreamt of going there...

Chris and Mr. Baggins moved in with me. I knew he shouldn't be alone. Quite frankly, I was rather glad to have his company. I'd hear him weeping in the night, with Mr. Baggins making little soothing sounds. I think that dog comforted him more than I could... and he comforted Mr. B too.

Maybe it sounds strange, but that dog was nearly as heartbroken as Chris was. For a week, I couldn't get him to eat. However, slowly they both began to mend.

The weather was lovely. That warm caress in the air that spring brings. Every morning like clockwork, Mr. Baggins and Chris would jog off to the dog park.

That summer Chris went off to Italy, I got emails daily plus two phone calls. It's a good thing I wasn't the jealous type, 'cause I swear he missed Mr. Baggins more than me.

I took Mr. B on his walks, watched him race around the park like a wild thing. When we'd get home he'd fall asleep at my feet. When I came home from work, it was as though he hadn't seen me for a year. He'd jump up and down, wagging his tail looking at me with eyes full of love. Yet, I swear, since Maggie's death they always held a deep touch of sorrow. I began looping Mr. B's leash around my wrist. I said it was because Chris- and I- would have been heartbroken to lose him. I pretended it was to keep him safe. But, really, it comforted me to feel the leather wrapping me like a bracelet. It was like having a friend hold your hand, feeling Mr. B so close.

Chris was away for only two weeks. He just couldn't stand imagining Maggie there with him. After a month or so, he got his own apartment. I sure did miss him and Mr. Baggins, but I was glad too. I wanted him to get his life back. I had loved Maggie, probably as much as two sisters can love each other... but I didn't want Chris to live in the past.

I still saw him and Mr. Baggins often. Every Saturday we'd meet at the dog park to watch Mr. B have a morning frolic, then spend the day together. Go to a movie. Go for a walk. Or sometimes just have a big long meal, usually ending up drunk.

It was the sweet time of sorrow. The time when the wound has healed enough, so that you can remember, talk, or even laugh about the past.

Then one Saturday, God I'll never forget it, I headed over to the park as usual. About a block away, I heard a noise I'll never forget. If I could sleep, I'm sure it'd be in my dreams. It was a kind of heavy thud, then a wail. A horrible cry, a howl that was more than animal, but sure not human.

I ran, but I wasn't even aware I was moving. I don't know what I thought I'd see. As soon as I got close, I knew. Knew that somewhere inside I had known what I'd see.

There was Chris, my beautiful, sweet baby brother, my only family, my best friend. In the street. His body was bloody and arching at an unnatural angle with Mr. B by his side. I swear to you, that animal was weeping as hard as I was.

We went through the motions. Got a police report. People at the park had heard the squeal of brakes, but no one had seen anything.

I don't know how I got through the next few weeks. If Mr. Baggins hadn't been there, I swear I would have just dried up and died. His big, sad puppy eyes reflected the pain I felt.

They say time heals all wounds; I can't say I think that's true. Some wounds never heal. Life goes on, no matter how you feel.

One day, Mr. B who was watching me bathe, stood up to sniff the water and tumbled in. I laughed. For the first time in forever, I laughed. Mr. Baggins looked embarrassed, but I swear he chuckled a bit too. There are few things as faithful or accepting as a dog.

The next day we went out for our morning walk. The sky was a bright, clear blue. Birds were singing cheerful songs. I felt better than I had since Chris died. Suddenly Mr. Baggins took off, running as hard and fast as he could. I pulled on his leash.

"No, Mr. Baggins, sit." But he did not sit or stop or even slow.

"Mr. B! Heel!" I screamed. He continued to race full on, heading at a dead run toward the street that edged the park in a blind corner. Although I couldn't see around the bend, under the twitter of bird song I could hear the growl of a motor.

You know how they say, that right before the end your whole life flashes before your eyes? Well that wasn't true for me- though time did slow down. Instead, I saw Maggie. Maggie, beautiful alive and laughing… then Maggie, just a crumbled corpse. I saw Chris, my beautiful brother, from burbling baby through carefree boy, handsome man, and loving husband, my Chris.

I dropped the leash, but it kept it hold, still looped round my wrist. Not as a bracelet, but as a noose. It held me fast, cutting into my flesh. Dragging me into the street.

The last thing I saw was Mr. B turning to look at me with detached curiosity out of those big, brown eyes before leaping onto the sidewalk, just clearing the wheels of an the oncoming car.

There was blackness, the grind of breaks, a car door slam, and a high shrill scream.

Mr. B gave a little yelp, like he was crying.

The last sound I heard was an unknown voice saying, "Oh, you poor, sweet dog. Don't worry. I'll take care of you."

E.E. King is the recipient of various international painting, writing and biology grants. Her murals can be seen in downtown Los Angeles and Spain. Her first novel, *Dirk Quigby's Guide to the Afterlife*, came out 2010, released in Spanish in 2/2012. The New Short Fiction Series, Los Angeles' oldest reading series, launched her anthology, *Real Conversations With Imaginary Friends*, 1/2012. Sponsor, Barnes & Noble. All of her books, including her children's book. *The Adventures of Emily Finfeather or The Feathernail and Other Gifts,* are available on Audible.

WHO'S FOR DINNER

BY SARA LUNDBERG

"I had another one of those dreams again last night," I said as I let us into my dingy apartment.

"The ones where you're being cooked for dinner?"

I nodded and dropped the keys on the counter. I offered him a beer from the fridge, but he declined. I took one for myself then flopped down into my recliner.

"What was it this time?"

I took a long pull from my beer. "I was sitting in a pot of boiling water. Like they do in cartoons when they're being cooked, you know?"

"Yeah, sure," my best friend nodded. "You figured out what's causing them yet?"

I shook my head. The reoccurring nightmares of me being turned into a human feast had been going on for months now. About once a week, I dreamed about being cooked, baked, poached, boiled, sautéed – every possible way to cook something, I'd experienced in excruciating detail while still alive.

Because everyone knows you wake up when you die in dreams.

No, these were agonizing dreams I couldn't wake up from where my skin boiled away from my body and my eyeballs melted; where I felt each knife stroke as it cut me to pieces or removed my innards like a fish.

Sometimes I could still smell my hair burning when I woke up.

"Maybe it's because you have a secret dream to go to culinary arts school to become a chef," my friend offered. He began to slowly pace my apartment, distractedly looking at the piles of junk that had accumulated over the years of poor housekeeping.

"Nah, I don't think that's it. I'm abysmal at cooking."

"Maybe that's what's causing it. You're subconsciously worried your lack of culinary skills will be the death of you."

"Ha, ha, very funny."

"Oh, so you are looking for a *serious* dream interpretation, are you?"

"Mock all you want. You're the one who asked," I grumbled, dry-washing my hands.

"True, true. Could be if you figure out what it means, maybe you can figure out a way to make them stop."

I perked up at that. "Yes. Please. Anything to make the dreams stop."

He frowned, becoming serious. "Did you have any traumatic childhood experiences having to do with cooking?"

I felt my face wrinkle as I thought back. Mom had been a terrible cook. Dad had worked long hours and had rarely been around at dinnertime. A lot of nights I had ended up making myself cereal for dinner and eating it in front of the television.

"That could be it, but why would I just now start having dreams because of it?" I scratched my head vigorously. "No, this feels more immediate."

"Ok, look. No offense, man, but it could be because of your job."

I sighed. "It's not because of my job."

"You butcher animals for a living. How does that not leak into your dreams? I'm amazed you haven't had nightmares since you started there, what, a decade ago?"

I had worked at the meat packing plant for a long time. When I first started, it freaked me out somewhat, however I adjusted quickly. Desensitized to the gore.

I stared at my hands. Sometimes the blood just didn't come out all the way, though.

My friend cleared his throat. "Maybe it's because your girlfriend, y'know, stepped out on you last year. Something about sex and being eaten?"

"No, I really don't think this has anything to do with sex."

"Everything has to do with sex, my friend," he said with an eyebrow cocked in my direction, a half smile on his face.

"There's nothing sexual about being blended in a food processor, poured into a pan and popped into the oven, trust me." I involuntarily shivered.

"Sure there is. Haven't you heard the expression 'bun in the oven?'"

"Well, yeah, but I still don't think that's it. No. Besides, that whore did me a favor, leaving me."

My friend shrugged then gave a thoughtful nod. After thinking a moment, he winced.

"Ok, look, don't hate me for bringing this up, but maybe it's because your mom died recently."

I grimaced. We'd been in a horrible car accident awhile back. After screaming for over an hour while they pried us out of the car, she slipped into a coma, and never came out. For years I left her at the hospital on life support, thinking maybe she'd wake up someday.

She never did.

"Could be, I suppose. But the dreams started long after the accident. And it was a good thing, right? To finally unhook her?" I looked away, focusing on the deep scratch on my arm.

"Yeah, it was. You felt a lot of relief, finally letting her go."

"Relief. Yeah."

My friend sighed sharply. "I'm running out of ideas. Maybe you're just messed up."

I frowned. "Am I really all that more messed up than any other average guy, living his life?"

"I dunno, man. Yeah, maybe a little."

"Thanks for that, asshole."

He smiled, but it was a tight smile. Didn't quite reach his eyes.

I tried to light a cigarette but my hands were shaking too badly. I set the lighter and cigarette back on the end table next to my chair.

"It could be because I keep eating right before I go to bed. Indigestion. Bad beef or something."

"Bad beef, indeed. It's probably because you murdered me and turned me into sausage at your meat packing plant. Some kid out there is probably eating a best friend burger as we speak." His grin was just a show of teeth.

I blinked, the image of my best friend blurred around the edges. I rubbed my eyes, and when I looked back, he was completely gone. Of course he was gone. I'd killed him then disposed of his body at work when I found out how badly he'd swindled me. I blamed him for all of it: my unhappy childhood, telling me my girlfriend was cheating on me (with him), his suggestion to take Mom off life support, and getting me the meat packing job in the first place.

Best friend my ass.

"Nope, I don't think that's it, either." I didn't really feel any remorse.

Honest.

Sara Lundberg is a Kansas-grown writer of the urban fantasy and horror persuasions. She is an editor and contributor for The Confabulator Cafe, a website for her writing group that she helped create, where some of her flash fiction is showcased: www.confabulatorcafe.com.

Asleep

By Angela Trumbo

It was the thing he'd always loved about her. His Gayle, in her many different forms, resembled an angel reincarnated. Golden locks of hair fanned out on the navy bed sheet encircling her head like a halo. Her face appeared as delicate as porcelain against the dark fabric. A fading shade of pink tinted her cheeks, a purplish-blue stained her swollen lips. Even in her endless sleep, his Gayle still beckoned for his touch. Henry bent over the bed then kissed her.

Perspiration beaded his forehead trickling down into his eyes, causing them to sting and water. Henry used the bottom of his palms to rub away the irritation, but with little success. Through watery, bloodshot eyes, he stared at the lifeless body tangled in ruffled sheets on the bed. A smoky haze drifted through the air like a light fog. All was quiet in the room except for the faint sound of popping and crackling outside the door.

It is time. We need to go now.

Henry glanced around the room blinking several times to clear his vision before his gaze rested once more on the contents of the bed. "Is she coming with us?"

No.

His mouth opened, ready to argue with the denial of Those who dwelled within. Instead the thickening air caused him to cough.

She's not the one for you.

"But she is my Gayle," Henry choked on the increasing smoke.

She is not your Gayle. She is like the others. We will try again soon. Now go!

A salty breeze and the sound of crashing waves met Henry when he slid the patio door open. With intensifying heat at his back and fluffy sand ahead to silence his footsteps, Henry left the growing inferno that was once a quaint hideaway bungalow nestled in palm trees on a secluded beach.

***

S*top here.*

"Where?" Henry's hands gripped the steering wheel as he slowed the car then rose a little from his seat to peer more closely through the windshield.

The park. On your right.

Henry made an abrupt turn into the paved lot then stopped the car beside a cement sidewalk. Beyond the walkway, a white vinyl banner with black letters stretched out between two trees and read "Annual Community Picnic."

Henry frowned. "Why am I here?"

It is time.

His eyes widened. "No. Not here. Not now."

Yes. It has been too long.

"I... I haven't... had a chance..." Henry swallowed. "I haven't prepared for this."

We have. We will tell you what to say and do.

Henry pulled back onto the main way searching for a parking place, all the while Those living within the shadows of his brain spilled forth words of encouragement to urge him forward. Their chattering remained constant as he walked from the car to the park entrance then stepped up on the sidewalk leading to the front gate.

Excitement fueled Their energy until They became strong enough to force a reluctant Henry forward against his will. A wave of panic rippled through his chest causing his breath to come in short gasps. His vision blurred as dizziness washed over him. Despite the pressure of They behind him, Henry stumbled back off the cement. He placed a hand to his brow then turned away from the entrance.

No! You will not leave. Your need grows for a woman.

His eyes narrowed as his lips thinned. "I am not ready for this."

We will whisper in your ear what to say and what to do.

Henry shook his head. "No. I'm not ready plus she's not even here."

Your Gayle is here. We will find her.

The thought of being with his Gayle again quickened Henry's pulse. He started to take a step toward the entrance, but nerves made his feet immobile. Anxiety rooted Henry to the spot until the air grew thick around him with Their presence.

Come with us.

They guided his footsteps moving him through the gate. Once inside, Henry ventured of his own accord from table to table. He sampled the large spread of food but hungered for none of it. Boredom and restlessness worked to erode his patience as he scanned the crowd, each female face an instant rejection. He had warned Those who dwelled within he wasn't ready. Now he wanted to go home.

Dark shades of orange, much darker than the constant haze that normally shadowed his world, played tag beside a long table of sweet confections. Henry scowled at Their lack of participation in his search when it had been They who had brought him here. Anger narrowed his vision to Their carefree actions until Henry caught sight of golden blonde hair glistening in the sun.

He stared at the woman, eager to view her face willing her to look up. To further his agitation, her head stayed bent slightly downward as she served deserts to the patrons who visited her table. Those within laughed as They continued to play Their games around the woman.

Despite Henry's distaste for sugary treats, he moved closer to her. Determined to catch at least a glimpse of her hidden features, Henry came within a few feet of the table. She glanced up. Those within cried out, Their sudden and extreme outburst made his head throb from the pressure. The dark orange shadows representing Those who dwelled within joined rising into the air to hover above the woman. Henry clasped his ears as a screeching tear ripped Their joined mass in two.

No! Not this one. The left side shouted.

Go to her! The right side countered.

No, don't go to her!

She is the one.

No, she is not the one. Already she is involved in what you do not like.

She will change. You can make her change.

No! She is not the one for you. Remember what has happened many times before.

Henry rubbed his temples as he closed his eyes. Those within continued to war with each other, the force of Their argument so strong Henry thought his head might explode from the battle. Even though he tried hard to suppress any audible show of emotion, a groan escaped his lips.

"Are you okay?"

A gentle female voice followed by a soft touch on his arm caused his body to jerk. He recoiled from the contact as if stung by a bee. His eyes opened to find the subject of his inner dispute now stood in front of him. A look of concern clouded her warm brown eyes surrounded by spiraling blonde curls.

Those within grew quiet as if They, too, waited for his response.

His gaze traveled from her face to her bare shoulder and the multicolored strap pressed against her skin. The variety of colorful designs and how they floated on her dress held him captivated. Like a cat with a ball of yarn, his eyes chased the lines tracing the patterns until he reached the area where her bodice stopped before the ample swell of her breasts began. His eyes remained fixated to the spot. He licked his lips.

"Sir?"

Henry's attention flew back to her face. He gave a sheepish grin.

"Please excuse me, Miss...?"

Her smile accentuated rosy pink cheeks sprinkled with tiny freckles reminding Henry of strawberries. She extended a hand in greeting. "Gayle."

He made no move to accept it. Her cheerful smile began to fade as she started to retract her offering, "Oh. I'm sorry."

Gayle gasped when Henry snatched her hand holding it firmly in his.

"My name is Henry. It's a pleasure to meet you, Miss Gayle."

She patted her chest as she gave a nervous laugh. "Sorry. I thought maybe you had a phobia or something about being touched."

Henry tensed, tightening his hold on her. "Why would you say that?"

Gayle blinked. "Um, when I touched you earlier-"

"Oh. That." Henry laughed, relaxing his grip. "You startled me is all."

He leaned in closer while he looked into her eyes, gently rubbing his thumb in a circular motion on her palm. "I don't mind being touched. In fact, I do quite enjoy it at times."

Gayle flushed crimson. "I need to get back to work. My friends will start to wonder what happened to me."

Henry glanced at their joined hands then squeezed hers before he let go. "Can I see you again sometime?"

She bit her bottom lip before glancing away. He took her reaction as a discouraging sign and braced himself for her eminent rejection. After a moment, to his delightful surprise, her eyes met his as she smiled. "Sure. I'd like that."

Gayle walked back to the table. As Henry watched her leave, a desire to have her, whether she wanted to be taken or not, built inside him. The urge grew stronger as he stood there with her image in his sights, the conditions of her fate in his mind until she glanced up. Henry quickly turned away for fear she might guess his true intentions.

Henry wanted her, had to get her, and keep her. This Gayle made all the others before her pale in comparison. Whatever she wanted to do, he would want to do, too. He would handle his Gayle differently this time and not let Them take her away.

Those who dwelled within remained silent.

***

At the sound of thunder, Henry looked up from his task of weeding the flower garden. He tossed the small pick and shovel onto the ground beside him then stood.

"Storms coming," he said as he stared up at the band of dark gray clouds approaching the sun.

"Hope not," Gayle replied as she remained kneeling on the ground, sat back on her heels. "I don't like storms."

Words formed to defend his love of storms, but the argument died on his tongue as he viewed the cleavage her low neckline revealed. His eyes roamed over the generous mounds of exposed flesh above the maroon camisole. Her perspiration-covered skin plus the damp material clinging to the form of her breasts worked to fuel his imagination of what may lay hidden underneath. He had all but forgotten about the weather until the sky rumbled once more. Henry blinked, ran a tongue over dry lips, and turned away. They had been together for over a year and still he craved her as if for the first time.

"Maybe it will be a nice gentle rain to cool everything off some," Gayle said as she rose from the ground to dust the hay-like grass from her bare knees.

Henry scowled in displeasure of her words before raising his gaze to the sky again. The frown turned into a smirk as the increasing winds pushed the heavy gray clouds toward the blazing hot sun. His laughter rang out as his eyes closed. He tilted his head back to better experience the gusts of wind upon his face.

"Your wish for a gentle rain will be denied. It's a storm that will greet us this day."

"Then I think it might be best if we go inside now."

With half open eyes, he gave her a sideways glance before he shut them again and responded, "No. I haven't heard them yet."

"Heard who?"

He remained silent.

She touched his arm, his eyes flew open.

"There! There they are!"

Henry turned to Gayle. "Do you hear them?"

"Who?"

"The spirits!"

She took a step back.

"No. Don't go." He grabbed her arms. "They want you here."

Her eyes grew wide with confusion. "Who does?"

"I told you." Henry peered out over her head. His lips curved into a smile. "Can you feel them? The air is charged with the electricity of their waking."

Gayle frowned. "What are you talking about?"

Henry's smile widened, barring teeth as he stared down at her. "Tell me you can feel them." His hands began moving up and down her arms.

"Listen." Henry's body went still. He tilted his head as if placing an ear to the wind. "Do hear them now?"

She slowly shook her head.

"They're sharing the secrets only told before a big storm comes," Henry whispered then straightened to stare at Gayle for a long moment. When she shrank away from his intense scrutiny, his brows rose and eyes widened.

"This is your first time, isn't it?" He threw back his head and laughed. "I knew it had to be something!"

Henry lowered his gaze to study her. "Otherwise, why..." he began, frowned and shook his head, then started anew, "You know what spirits are."

When she didn't respond, his eyes narrowed. Gayle swallowed then nodded.

A satisfactory smile spread across Henry's face. "That's better. The spirits," he released one of her arms as he waved his hand in the air. She made to pull away, but he grabbed her arm again.

"The spirits use the storm's wind to move from place to place without being noticed. Only a selected few get to hear them whispering." His hands ran up and down her arms again, this time at a quicker pace.

The fierce wind whipped at their bodies, tore at their hair.

Henry's eyes grew large with excitement. "Surely you felt them right then!"

He moved closer to her. "They love you as I love you."

His lips came within inches of hers as he whispered, "Tell me you love me."

"Henry, you know I do..."

His hands squeezed the upper parts of her arms. "Say it. Say you love me."

Gayle's body trembled. Her voice shook as she responded, "I love you."

His mouth claimed hers, bruising her lips forcing her mouth open as he attempted to transfer the burning energy rushing through his body.

The wind around them increased in its turbulence. Henry raised his head to look out beyond the woman he held. He laughed as his hair blew chaotic around his head.

"Aw, to be snatched up by a spirit and ride along in its clutches!" He turned his head from side to side. "To know what it's like to be tossed about until the storm comes into its own then dispels the spirits as well as all they carry with them."

Henry's gaze came to rest on her face.

"Our journey could lead us anywhere in search of where our spirit had been deposited so the soul and spirit can reunite once more." He released her and raised his arms wide.

"Take us! We are yours for wherever you decide to roam!"

Henry heard her squeal. His arms dropped to his sides, his spirit deflated as he witnessed Gayle's flight into the house. The rain pelted his body from the outside while Those within berated him from the inside. They raged about the way the woman had treated him and how she must pay.

Claps of thunder rumbled as bright streaks of lightning raced across the dark sky. The pounding rain lulled Henry into a deafening state of numbness as several loud snaps followed by hissing and an electrical buzz never registered as odd. The screams, however, broke Henry from his own pain. He stared in disbelief as Gayle's little house erupted in flames. He ran into the burning home with one purpose in mind, to save his Gayle from Those within.

***

Several of the bandages on her burns had been removed and Gayle wanted an outing. The doctor assured them there would be few scars, but even those would be small in nature. Her face had been spared, so she was still his Gayle, still his angel reincarnate.

Henry took her to a park near the hospital. As they entered the path, he placed a bandaged wrist in his palm gently smoothed a piece of tape back into place. Gayle looked up at him then smiled.

"My hero," she said. Henry looked away, the guilt of what Those within tried to do threatened his serene mood.

They walked in silence. Soon Henry became fascinated in how the falling leaves danced around his feet. Skipping, twirling, doing somersaults, and cartwheels, the leaves created their own music with which to move by. Henry listened with a sense of awe as he was serenaded by the leaves when they scraped alongside his shoes and the pavement. A gentle breeze lifted the remains. The fragments rustled in the wind as they drifted from place to place.

"The particles of dry leaves are being disseminated like the ashes of a dead body, free to lie wherever they happen to land – not one resting place, but many. That is how I would like to live after death."

Henry gave Gayle's hand a quick squeeze from excitement. He glanced at her in hopes she shared his enthusiasm. When she showed no emotion, he tugged at their joined hands.

Gayle stopped and turned. "What is it?"

"Didn't you hear me?"

She sighed then nodded. "I heard you."

"What did I say?"

"You said something about death." Gayle sighed again. "You know I don't like to talk about death."

"I wasn't referring to death in general – only to how free the leaves are once separated from the tree." Henry's gaze moved from Gayle to the grass on the side of the path. He envied the freedom of the leaves as they sailed in the air or scooted along the ground. The leaves rested in one place for a brief time only to be picked up and swirled about by another gust of wind.

"They are as light as ashes. I want to be like that when I die."

"You want to be cremated?"

His eyes snapped back to her face. He scowled.

"No! I just want parts of my body to drift in the wind like the particles of dead leaves."

Gayle rolled her eyes. "To have ashes, the body must be cremated. Cremation involves fire. You don't like fire." She disengaged her hand from his. "And I don't like talking about fire or death, either."

Gayle turned from him then continued to walk along the path.

"But the leaves aren't ashes, they float in the air." Henry called after her after taking a few steps in her direction he stopped then looked down at his feet.

A leaf swept by. It tossed and turned as it touched the top of his shoe before it floated on, leaving fragments of itself behind on his toe and the pavement beside his foot. His head jerked up. Spotting her a short distance away, he hurried to her side then took hold of her arm. "I know!"

Henry dragged Gayle around to face him.

"I will have my dead body left above ground. That way when I begin to decay, the pieces will be swept off me by the wind so I can fly with the leaves."

"What?" Her brow furrowed. "You can't do that. No one's going to let a dead body just lay there on the ground." She turned away muttering, "That's just stupid," as she attempted to free herself from his grasp.

Gayle winced as Henry's fingers dug into her flesh until he pinched her bone. He whirled her around to face him, ignoring her grimace and the fear entering her eyes as he grabbed her other arm clamping down. Enraged, he yanked her to him. His face hovered above her. His eyes bore into hers.

"I'm not stupid! Don't you ever call me that!"

Henry shook her, mildly amused as her head bobbled up and down. He flinched when a few drops of water splattered against his cheeks. When he noticed her face covered in tears, he shoved her away from him. His hands clenched into fists at his sides. Damn her. She ruined his moment with nature. No doubt this would be the last day the leaves danced around Gayle's feet or played their music for her with their dead limbs.

The gentle sound of her sobs curbed his anger. Henry wrapped his arms around the trembling body of his Gayle, held her close. He slowly swayed with her from side to side while he worked to soothe and comfort her. Whispered oaths promised of changed ways and better days to come. Those within remained silent, but Their disapproval weighed heavy in his mind.

***

Paranoia kept his visits to Gayle brief while she stayed with friends and healed. Even though no one ever accused Henry in person, he suspected they knew of his true role in Gayle's injuries. Gayle, on the other hand, often expressed her gratitude for him saving her life, yet she politely refused his more intimate advances. The situation with his Gayle grew more precarious each day. He desperately needed to find a way to keep her before Those within decided his time with her had expired.

***

Crisp winter air stung their faces while the blinding snow crunched under their feet as Henry and Gayle left the jeep then walked to the cabin. Henry studied the structure as he made his way through the untracked land. He marveled at the stark contrast of the dark wooden frame against the white covered land surrounding the retreat. Evergreen trees encompassed the cabin and rose above the roof, the limbs still heavy with an icy layer of snowfall from the night before. A sudden gust of wind stirred the branches. To his tickled delight, snow sprinkled down upon the partially hidden shelter.

"We'll both freeze to death if you stand there gawking much

longer."

Henry frowned at the displeasure in her voice. He diverted his attention from the sparkling rooftop to Gayle hugging herself while shivering beside the front door.

Even now she's not happy. Nothing you do will ever satisfy her.

"I'm trying. What more do you want me to do?" Henry mumbled shuffling his feet through her tracks as he trudged his way to the cabin.

You know what to do. She is like the others. It's time.

Startled by Their response, Henry's foot missed one of the steps leading up to the porch and he stumbled forward. He grabbed for the railing, but it slipped from his grasp, the remaining porch steps came quickly into view. His eyes squeezed shut tensing in preparation for the fall. Gayle cried out his name and instead of the hard landing he had expected, he collided into something soft.

Henry opened his eyes, to his surprise saw Gayle, her features etched with a mix of shock and concern. She took his head in her glove-covered hands, peered into his face. "Are you okay?"

He leaned against her, both of their bodies now supported by the top part of the railing which connected to one of the porch's rectangular beams. Still reeling from the experience and irritation by the opinions of Those that dwelled within, he yelled out, "You're wrong!"

Instant regret plagued him as her eyes grew wide then filled with tears. His mind raced in an effort to find the words to explain his sudden outburst without stating the true cause of the anger. She pushed at his chest to free herself. He grabbed her hands.

"About the gawking," Henry said moving his head closer in order to capture her attention. When his eyes locked with hers, he continued in a soft voice, "You're wrong about me gawking. I was merely admiring your beauty from afar."

Gayle huffed. "Sure you were." She tried to turn away, but he released her hands to cup her face.

"It's true." Henry's eyes lowered to her lips. "I love you so much."

Henry bent to kiss her, however Gayle placed a hand over his mouth before he could make contact. "Slow. Remember? You agreed to take things slow?"

His teeth gritted in frustration. He wanted to argue with her in regards to the fact that she had only assumed he agreed. However, hurt still lingered in her eyes from his earlier display of temper. He thought it best to leave her to her assumptions – at least for the moment. As a sign of peace, Henry took her gloved hand and kissed it before he moved away from her. He fished for the key in his coat pocket before he unlocked the front door then motioned for her to lead the way inside. As she passed by, Gayle peered up at him. He grinned.

They spent the next few days exploring the area outside the cabin. Friendly snowball fights and making snow angels entertained Gayle the most, Henry relished in her laughter. However, each time he tried to get close to her in a more intimate way, she always withdrew to a safer distance. Her rejection bruised his ego leaving him vulnerable to Those within who used his lagging confidence to grow stronger. Every time she turned him away, Their voices nagged at him to make her bend to his will. His patience grew thinner as his frustration mounted. The night of the blizzard changed everything.

The sun lay hidden behind gray clouds that grew heavier as the day went on. Delicate flurries gradually became larger snowflakes. Wind whistled through the cracks, lowering the temperature in all the rooms causing the couple to seek comfort closer to the hearth.

Gayle and Henry huddled together under layers of blankets on the couch. Gayle's head lay on his chest while Henry's arm wrapped around her in a protective embrace. As they sat before the crackling fire, he casually observed the flickering of the various flames. Soon he became mesmerized by their movement.

"Look how some sway back and forth while others appear to reach up to the sky."

Gayle raised her head from his chest then asked in a sleepy voice, "What?"

Henry removed a hand from beneath the blankets to point to the fireplace. "Look! See? See what happened when the flames reached too high? They just break in half like that." He snapped his fingers and was puzzled when she flinched. A frown wrinkled his brow as he pondered on her reaction to such a simple noise. The lines smoothed as once more he became engrossed with the blaze.

He scrutinized the progress of the fire, taking in every detail of how it glided along the wood until it sparked and branched upward. Henry's eyes widened in astonishment to discover what resembled a pattern in the flames. His laughter pierced the silence. "Now I get it!"

Gayle jolted then sat up straight. She twisted on the couch to stare at him. "What in the world?"

He stared back at her with mouth agape, eyes round and large.

"Not again," Gayle said, shaking her head, scooting across the cushions. Henry followed, pinning her to other side of the couch where she could go no further.

"Don't you want to know why they break apart?" Henry hovered above her.

"What?"

"The flames!"

"What...what about the flames?"

"Don't you want to know why they break apart?" Henry asked again, his face reddening with anger.

"Why?" Gayle whispered.

He turned his head to look at the fire. "Part of them wishes to be free while the other part wants to remain attached to the burning wood." He turned back to her leaning in closer to her face. "When the one part is freed, it shoots up the chimney to fly away while the pathetic other half slithers to its death."

"Oh! Why must you always talk about death?" She pushed at his chest. "You told me things would be different this time."

When he made no attempt to move, she pushed harder. "I want to get up."

"Where are you going?"

"What does it matter? Somewhere, anywhere, as long as it's away from you."

He pressed against her. When she started to speak, he placed a hand over her mouth. "Don't."

She squirmed under him struggling to talk through his hand, but he clamped down around her mouth then gave her head a hard shake. "You will be quiet. For once you will listen to me."

His breath came in fast spurts against her face, his facial features contorted with fury. She trembled beneath him, her eyes wide with fear as she met his gaze.

Outside the storm attempted to compress them within the cabin. Tree limbs banged against the sides of the cabin as the blizzard raged. The door rattled on its hinges with the force of the gusts. Behind him, the wind tried to force its way down the chimney. It hissed when it met with a blast of fiery air from the flames below.

Henry's pulse quickened as he imagined how the scene unfolded outside. The frozen particles of water whipped and whirled through space, hurled against objects to disintegrate or mate with the existing snow left clinging for life. Through that copulation, the ice became stronger, its hold on any surface more unbreakable. Visualization of the winter storm left his emotions in turmoil. His loins tightened at the thought. He grew feverish.

There are other ways to experience nature. The woman can provide what you seek.

Henry looked down at Gayle while he considered Their suggestion. Those who dwelled within picked that time to taunt him with seductive images of a passionate Gayle who wantonly displayed her desire for him which matched his to have her. He nodded once.

"I have been patient. I have waited as you had asked of me. I will wait no more."

Henry removed his hand from Gayle's mouth then got up from the couch, tugged at the blankets wrapped around her body hauling her up.

She grabbed his shirt collar with both hands pleading, "Henry, no. You promised you wouldn't do this."

Rigid as stone, he clutched the blankets surrounding her body and stared into eyes sparkling with unshed tears. A small twinge of guilt weeded its way into his mind causing him to pause.

Don't listen to her. She plays games teasing you day and night then denies you anything asked of her.

Henry pulled away from her grasp. He ducked a shoulder into her midsection, lifting her off the floor as he carried her to the bed. He dumped her on top of the quilts then covered her body with his.

"No! Stop this now!"

Henry's head spun to the right from the force of Gayle's open-handed slap. He blinked then turned with eyes narrowed.

"This has gone on long enough. Now get off of me." She made to rise, but he held her down. "Did you hear me?"

He continued to glare at her without making a move or saying a word.

"Henry, get up!"

Do you hear her? Telling you what to do as though you were a child? Show her you are not a child, but a man.

Wind whistled through the crevices of the windows and baseboards. Bare wooden branches thumped and scrapped against the exterior wood. The door rattled in its frame. Ice pecked against the glass panes. The sounds assaulted his ears jumbling his senses in a way that energized him as though he had been touched by a live wire.

Yes! Show her. Show her now!

Henry looked to the ceiling and wailed, "I want to fly!"

Teach her to fly with you! Do it now!

The more she struggled, the more excited he became. He tore at the blankets and her clothes. Sounds of ripped seams, tearing fabric mingled with her screams and cries of protest as well as his animalistic grunts and growls.

That's it. Make her feel the man you are. It's what she wants. It's what they all want.

Henry slowly opened his eyes, yawned. They widened in surprise as he found himself kneeling beside what appeared to be a still sleeping Gayle. His gaze traveled from her face to the pillow held firmly in his grasp. With a faint cry, he hurled the item over the side of the bed.

His hands ached from clinching the pillow. He flexed his fingers, repeatedly curling them in to make fists then releasing them. He avoided looking at Gayle preferring the sight of his hands in motion to her unsettling stillness.

A flash of memory invaded his mind. He tightened his hands into fists with enough force to have his nails cut into his palms. His eyes closed he welcomed the sharp pain radiating from fingertips to wrist seeping into his arms. He gritted his teeth until his jaw shook from the pressure.

You know what needs to be done.

Their presence surrounded his body. Henry relaxed then opened his eyes. With a given purpose, he rose from the bed, walked into the kitchen and squatted beside the cabinet below the sink. He hesitated but a moment before he placed his hands upon the knobs then pulled. At first sight of the red gas cans, he felt both excited and afraid. His fingers closed over the handle of one of the tanks then he lifted the item from its hiding place. With eyes no longer his own, his gaze swept the cabin interior.

You know what you must do.

Sitting on the couch with an empty red container resting on his thigh, Henry stared at the liquid spilled out on the scratched hardwood floor. He followed the haphazard trail to the edge of the fireplace. An over abundance of logs rose high above the cast iron barrier. The fire popped and crackled while burnt embers flew up the chimney. A few rebellious deserters tested the security of the rigid grate meant to contain them. Despite the intense heat which radiated from the roaring fire, a sudden chill filled the air. He shivered.

You know what comes next. Be done with this then we can go home.

"Not yet."

Why do you wait? It is time. She is nothing to you now.

The hollow gas tank fell to the floor as Henry rose from the couch and went to stand beside the bed. His Gayle laid motionless upon the ruffled sheets.

Do it! Send her away from here.

"No!"

She is no different than all the others.

"Yes, she is! I love her. Why can't you see that?'

You cannot save her.

"Don't say that!" His gaze roamed over the tranquil features of her face. "See how she looks like an angel when she is asleep? I love her best this way."

Henry climbed onto the bed and snuggled close to Gayle. He put an arm around her pulling her stone cold body against him. With a gentle hand, he moved her head to lie on his chest just beneath his chin. Gasoline fumes invaded his nostrils. Instead of being repelled by the poignant fragrance as he had many times before, he now found the aroma intoxicating.

Dark orange shadows circled the bed.

No Henry! She is not for you!

The erratic beat of his heart slowed as an overwhelming sense of fatigue gripped his body. His eyes burned as his head sunk deeper into the pillow. Through the light orange haze he watched Those who once dwelled within grow darker and darker.

No Henry! Get up! We won't let you do this.

Henry shifted so the side of his face rested against the damp hair on top of her head. He pulled the box of matches from his front pocket then selected a stick. One strike against the side and the flame came to life. He tossed the lit match toward the end of the bed and closed his eyes.

Angela Trumbo is a resident of Nashville, Tennessee and enjoys writing in the paranormal, horror, and thriller genres. She has one short story published, "Folly of Youth", in the anthology *Soundtrack Not Included*. Another short story, "What Happened to the Girl?", is scheduled to be published in the anthology *Nashville Noir* in September 2012. Check her website, angelatrumbo.com, for more information about the author and a link to her blog: Angela's Visions.

Doll's House

by LJ Gastineau

The old house gave her the creeps. Ashley Fairfield stared at the splintering wood and peeling paint. Eerie willow trees flanked both ends, their tendrils of Spanish moss dripped from brittle branches like cobwebs. "Why did Aunt Mary have to leave us her ugly house? It looks like it hasn't been cleaned in years."

"That's the funny thing about wills; they can bring about unexpected surprises to the next of kin." Elizabeth shook her head, tossing back her dark ponytail. "Let's get this over with."

"Wow, talk about in dire need of maid service." Ashley wrinkled her nose in disgust following her sister inside. "There's got to be at least ten layers of dust on everything. How gross!"

"I'm sure your dorm room is in worse shape."

She snorted at her sister's comment, but said nothing. Despite the dust, the living room was rather homey in a strange outdated sort of way. Graying dollies covered old wooded furniture that at first glance seemed to be well cared for. Pale pink pillows were placed in a tidy fashion on what was once white sofa covers. Everything seemed to have an almost romantic feminine style to it. Lots of pink and lace, both of which neither she nor her sister cared much for.

"It's almost like some sort of a Victorian dollhouse." Ashley remarked tucking an auburn strand of hair behind an ear. "Way too girly though. No wonder she never married. No guy would ever want to live here."

"Ashley!" Elizabeth scolded in almost outrage.

"What? She's dead. It's not like she's going to come back and haunt me."

"It's rude and disrespectful."

Ashley narrowed her eyes in annoyance. Her older sister could be bossy, but nothing like this. She however was too stubborn to put any real thought into it. "She was just a crazy old bat who died in her sleep. Like anyone is going to give a rat's-"

"That's enough!" Elizabeth cut her sister off. "You don't know anything about her therefore you have no right to insult her."

She drew back as though slapped. "What's your problem? You didn't know her either and now you're defending her like she was your best friend."

"I—Sorry." She touched her head then sighed. "Let's look at the rest of the house."

They wandered in each room, unimpressed with anything in particular. Elizabeth guessed that the furniture might go for a pretty penny at an antiques dealer, but like everything else it would need to be cleaned. Ashley suggested dumping everything on one of their other relatives until her sister reminded her that the money they would make if they were to sell everything off would not only pay for the rest of her education, but also finance the boutique and café they wanted to open. Nowhere on Ashley's life plan was 'starting a minimum wage job immediately after college.' She also knew that Elizabeth didn't want to work at the tiny diner forever.

Just when they decided that the house couldn't be any spookier, they encountered the stairs to the attic.

Ashley shivered. There was just something about attics, especially in old houses that gave her the heebie-jeebies. A flash of lightning appeared through the lone grimy window followed by an angry roar of thunder. "Great. Now it's storming."

Elizabeth said nothing. She brushed past her sister as though in a trance, her footsteps making loud creaks as she walked deeper into the room.

"Be careful, Lizzy. You don't want to fall through the floor." She let out a shriek when another loud boom shook the house then scampered after her sibling.

If she thought the downstairs was dirty, compared to the attic, it was clean enough to do surgery in. Ashley coughed, trying not to choke on the musty odor as she stumbled past old lamps, broken toys, and battered books. A bright flash filled everything with light before plunging it into pitch black. Ashley swore, cursing their luck to be in the attic of all places when the power decided to go out. Now she would really have to watch where she stepped or else risk breaking something; possibly her own neck. "Lizzy, we should go back downstairs. It's way too dark in here."

Ashley cried out as she tripped over something, barely catching herself before she crashed into some boxes. "Lizzy? Are you okay?"

Lightning struck again, illuminating her sister's back as she knelt over something that Ashley couldn't see. "What did you find?" She stepped closer, her curiosity overruled her fear.

Elizabeth didn't react. She remained crouched in the corner of the cramped room.

Ashley angled herself to the other side then froze. Leaned against a tarnished mirror was a porcelain doll. Her golden curls framed a face painted with a rosy blush and petal pink lips. Her dress, also in a shade of pink was covered with a lacy apron that was once white. Matching stockings and shoes covered her feet. What took Ashley's breath away were the doll's eyes. Framed with dark lashes, the big blue eyes seemed to see right through her.

She dropped her hand on her sister's shoulder. "We should go."
"Why?"

The question was lifeless and empty. Ashley grabbed Elizabeth's hand trying to pull her to her feet, fear quickly creeping up her spine. "Please, come on, Lizzy. I want to go home."

The door slammed shut, the house groaned as though it were alive. Ashley bit her lip, struggling against tears. Her sister only continued to stare at the doll as though it were the only thing that existed. Her anxiety continued to build as the storm outside worsened.

She didn't even want to go to the spooky old house to begin with. It was all Elizabeth's idea. Now, she was trapped there because her older sister thought a stupid old doll was more important than she was. Enraged, she bent over to grab it so she could smash it to pieces when Elizabeth screamed like a banshee, striking her little sister across the face.

Stunned, Ashley backed away. She brought her hand up to her

stinging cheek; drew back in shock as her fingertips smeared against something warm and slick. "Liz—"

"Don't touch."

The words came out in an almost unearthly hiss. The single light bulb in the room blazed to blinding life. Ashley covered her eyes in pain then gaped at her sister.

Elizabeth's raven locks had become golden ringlets. "How—"

"Run," a cool breeze seemed to whisper.

She screamed more in fear of the phantom voice than her own sister as she bolted to the door.

"Foolish, sister. You think you can stop me? You kept me imprisoned for twenty-five years," Elizabeth sneered. The temperature of the room continued to drop; her eyes seemed to glow an arctic sapphire; as hot as a flame. Loose papers flew around the room as books fell off the shelves.

"I—I don't know what you are talking about… Please don't hurt me!"

Her only response was a cruel laugh.

Ashley whimpered, slowly backing away. Just as she took another step, a loud groan erased all thoughts as she fell through the floor.

* * *

"Wake up."

Green eyes fluttered open as Ashley moaned in pain. What happened? Where was she? Was she still dreaming?

"You must get up," someone urged.

"Lizzy? Is that you?" She rolled over, biting back a cry as a sharp pain stabbed into her left shoulder. There was dust and debris all around her. Her head was pounding to the point that she could almost see stars. A sick sensation stirred in her stomach. Fighting not to vomit, she rolled over; narrowly missing the plunging blade.

Head screaming, she pushed herself to her knees in time to dodge another slash of the butcher's knife clenched in Elizabeth's hand.

Windows shattered, the air around them shrieked. Books and knick knacks flew from the shelves pummeling the murderous sibling as through trying to save the other one.

"Stop trying to meddle, you worthless ingrate!" Elizabeth bared her teeth like a savage animal as she growled at the wind.

Ashley used the distraction to make her escape. Her mind struggled to comprehend what was going on. Her sister had never tried to harm her before so why now? She wished they sold the house as it was rather than set foot inside.

"Through the kitchen."

"Where other sharp objects that can be used to kill me are? Forget it!"

"If you value your life, you must listen to me." The voice warned in an urgent yet impatient tone. *"There is no time to argue."*

"Just who the hell are you?"

"Your crazy old bat of an aunt."

"You—"

"I should have known she would have latched onto your elder sister. She was named after her despite your mother's better judgment."

Ashley found herself at a loss. "I don't understand."

"Go into the pantry. Quickly. Then I'll explain."

"If you say so." She grabbed a kitchen knife for protection, even though she didn't think she'd have the heart to use it against her older sister. Reluctantly, she did as the ghost bid. The pantry, she realized was a small closet with a tiny door in the back. Without any further arguments she crawled through the threshold.

Her shoulder throbbed in protest, but she ignored it. Her mind was too distracted with unanswered questions to allow the pain to hinder her descent. One in particular seemed to haunt her; why was Lizzy trying to kill her?

Ashley froze at the sight of another small door. With a deep breath she pushed it open. She frowned at the tiny cavernous room. Something felt very off about it. Along the wall rickety wooden shelves held what looked like ancient books covered in grime. In the corner was a large equally dirty mirror. On the opposite side of the wall, several other shelves held bottles of multiples shapes and sizes. In the center of the room sat a large rusted over kettle; cauldron her mind corrected.

"You were a witch. You cursed Lizzy!" She spun around, anger radiating off her like rays of the sun. The only thing that kept her from pummeling the ghost was the fact that she couldn't see her.

"Not precisely, child. Though I do have to inquire, how badly do you wish to save your sister? Could you end her life?"

Ashley choked, her fury melting into complete horror at the concept. "How could you even ask such a thing? I could never kill

Lizzy."

"Then you will die."

The reply was said in such a matter of fact tone that she felt as though she had been punched. "You can't be serious…"

"History is repeating. Part of it is my fault. Part is destiny."

"Destiny is for fantasy novels."

"You are here for a reason; to put an end to what had begun twenty-five years ago." The ghost paused as though collecting her thoughts. *"My sister dabbled in witchcraft. During her careless adventures she unleashed a vengeful spirit that took over her soul. I was less practiced but managed to seal her into a doll; the doll that your sister was drawn to. My sister's name was also Elizabeth."*

"But if you're Aunt Mary… I never heard about her- I mean you having a sister…"

"Hazel to be exact. I had a strong dislike to my first name, but that's beside the point. After her disappearance it was decided that she was dead. Because of what happened I asked that she never be mentioned. Not everyone heeded my wishes however."

"Why did you leave this place to us in your will? Did you know this was going to happen?"

"I was not certain how long the spell would last."

Ashley rubbed her shoulder. "Now what?"

"Now, you die."

Ashley turned reflexively, then gasped more in terror than agony as the blade of her elder sister's knife sank into her left arm. Blood seeped from the wound in a light drizzle then gushed like a geyser as the weapon was ripped away.

"Binding me to that pathetic doll only delayed your suffering, sister. If only I could have found a spell to prolong your miserable life so I could torture you for eternity." Elizabeth smirked. She licked the blood from the knife and snorted. "You taste foul, but will have to do. Perhaps bleeding you out like a sacrificial goat would be the most enjoyable method of revenge."

"Lizzy," Ashley cringed, clutching at the cut, her arm screaming in pain. There had to be some way to reach her sister. "Listen to me. I know you're still in there somewhere. Fight her off! I know you can do it. You have to."

Elizabeth only laughed. "Fool. That poor excuse of a girl is dead. She will never hear your voice ever again."

"I told you. You must kill her."

"Shut up!" Ashley rushed to the shelves of books, tore them down in a heated rage. Elizabeth shouted at her, but she ignored her words. Instead Ashley picked up one of the boards then smashed it into the bottles and the mirror. Glass shattered, fire erupted as smoke filled the air.

"You whore!" Elizabeth shrieked, racing to plunge the butcher's knife into her sister.

Ashley merely stood there, then at the last second, threw herself to the floor, rolled, and scrambled to her feet, bolting to the door that would lead her back through the pantry.

Just as the door began to close, she dove inside crawling like her life depended on it.

She didn't know what she was doing. She only knew that she didn't want to kill her sister despite how much her mind tried to convince her it was the only way. Her only other option was to go back to the attic.

"What are you doing? You have to kill her."

"I told you to shut up. Leave me alone. I don't want to hear anymore. If something has to be finished then I'm doing it my own way." Ashley hissed, bursting out of the pantry. She raced up the stairs, the ghost still trailing behind.

"But—"

"You're already dead," she snapped, sprinting up the stairs. "Go away."

Ashley shoved her way into the attic. Everything in the room seemed to come to life as though they were some sort of guardians of their queen's chambers. That confirmed her suspicions; the doll had to be destroyed.

Books launched themselves at her head. Wires snaked out, lashing towards her limbs. She nearly got yanked back down through the hole in the floor that had formed when Elizabeth had attacked her the first time, but managed to escape from the attacking fan by smashing her foot into it.

She gasped for breath as a lamp cord wrapped itself around her throat. She wrenched her hand in between it then sliced her knife through nicking her neck in the process. Once she freed herself, what felt like an entire box of toys, rained down upon her. Ashley grabbed at them, tearing them off her clothes and hair. She could feel the bite of several cuts as sharp pieces scraped against her skin, but wouldn't let that prevent her from continuing her mission.

"Stop!"

Ashley swore under her breath at the sound of her sister's voice. Apparently trashing the secret room was not enough to keep her at bay for too long. She narrowed her eyes. "I'm bleeding, my shoulder is probably dislocated. Do you really think I'm going to listen to you? Think again."

She drew a breath and leapt over a pile of books, clothes, and other junk stacked up like a barricade. Her foot caught on a shirt sleeve, causing her to trip, landing hard on the odds and ends. The breath knocked out of her, she pushed herself up, and over the rest of the barrier.

Limping, she reached for the doll, them screamed as a large amore fell over, attempting to crush her. In a flash, her sister was on top of her. Ashley blinked pondering how Elizabeth could have moved so fast as the blade plunged into her chest.

"I told you, you shouldn't meddle, little sister."

"Go…to hell." Ashley threw her fist into Elizabeth's face, kicked her off, then with all her strength dove for the doll.

Elizabeth and the ghost yelled as Ashley crashed into the mirror, shards rained down upon her, slicing her skin and clothes. Just as she felt the blade pierce into her back, she smashed the doll's fragile body into the floor. She glared at the broken porcelain littering the wooden floor as she struggled for breath. Gritting her teeth, fighting against the pain, she slammed it repeatedly until the remains were too small to piece back together.

It was then she could smell smoke. It seemed that Elizabeth was too bent on murder to bother putting out the flames which were probably going to swallow them whole. A chill crept over her body but she ignored it.

Pushing herself to her knees she turned around then cried out. Sprawled under the amore was her sister. A large puddle of blood surrounded her from a gash in her head. Her body looked lifeless.

"Lizzy?"

There was no answer. Ashley collapsed to the floor as she coughed several times, grimacing at the blood then everything went black.

* * *

Nancy Fairfield stared in disbelief at the still smoking remains of her ex-husband's great aunt's house; the last known whereabouts of her daughters. Her eyes filled as they fell upon the scorched license plate of her eldest's car. They were just supposed to look at the house, not disappear. Where could they have gone? Were they dead or by some miracle still alive somewhere?

A firefighter approached her, wiping sweat from his brow. "Sorry Ma'am. There's still no sign of your daughters. Did they or the late Miss Fairfield by any chance collect dolls?"

"Not that I know of, why do you ask?"

He signaled for her to wait a moment then walked off. He appeared a minute later with a slightly burnt metal box containing two porcelain dolls. One had long dark hair pulled back into a ponytail, while the other had shoulder length auburn hair and striking green eyes. Both were clad in white dresses. "The crazy thing is, they kind of resemble the pictures of your daughters."

LJ Gastineau lives in Saint Augustine, Florida and is a graduate of the University of Central Florida. She is one of three founding authors Trinity Gateways LLC (www.TrinityGateways.net). She is also the author of *Frozen Reflection,* her first published young adult fantasy novel for the series, *The Crystal Garden Saga.*

BLACKSPOT

BY TIM JEFFREYS

The boy came out of nowhere.

Laura shouldn't even have been driving on that road. She'd taken a wrong turn somewhere leaving Halifax – no surprise considering her state of mind – and instead of following her usual route had ended up on this lonely road over the moors. The bleak landscape made her uneasy. To the right was a valley of greenish brown moorland patched with snow. Low hills made a bank on the left side. Laura checked her fuel gage and groaned. She'd planned to fill up before leaving Halifax, but then this afternoon she and Dan had argued again. She'd left in such a state of agitation she'd forgotten to stop at the petrol station. With one hand she reached across to her handbag in the passenger seat then rummaged inside for her mobile phone. When she saw it she groaned again. Something else she'd forgotten to do: charge it. She dropped it back into her bag. As she stared down the long road ahead, her eyes flicked repeatedly to the fuel gage. She had checked it before she left. She could remember doing that at least. To her eyes now it looked dangerously close to empty.

There'll be other cars, she told herself. *Even if I do run out of gas, there'll be other cars passing along this road.* But then she heard Dan's voice in her mind saying, in that patronising tone he sometimes had: *Yeah, and you never know who might be in them.*

"Jesus fuck."

Thinking of Dan, she began to run the argument over in her mind again. She had left work on Friday and driven all the way to his university halls in Halifax, only to find – when she arrived - that he had another girl in his room. She was some pretty little thing in glasses who had looked at Laura as if *she* were the one who shouldn't have been there. Dan later claimed they were revising together, but Laura knew him better than that. They had argued all weekend. Laura hadn't even had a chance to tell him the news; the main reason she had driven all that way in the first place.

She saw a house on her right, a lonely stone-built structure set back from the road. She was thinking: *Jesus, what a place to live*, when something darted out into the road in front of her car. She had time to see that it was a boy. He came up from the moor on the right and ran straight into the road. He looked pale and ashen, as if he were a part of the surrounding landscape. Reaching the left side of the road he halted then turned towards the oncoming car. Laura felt that he was staring straight at her. She had no choice: swerve or hit him.

She swerved.

There was an almighty crash. She felt herself being jolted forward, then flung about. The moment seemed drawn out, as if time had slowed down. She felt her head strike the steering wheel, then the window at her side. Bits of glass were flying all around her.

Then there was only silence.

She opened her eyes.

She was still strapped in her seat. The car windscreen was gone. In front of her she could see the car she had collided with; a red sports car, crumpled now in the middle. She could see a man slumped in the driver's seat.

Next came the pain: in her head, her face, and in her leg. She tried to scream, but only a strangled breath left her throat. She fell still, for what seemed a long time, staring at the wreck in front of her, feeling the cold filling the car through the space where the windshield had once been.

What happened? She tried hard to remember. She imagined an accusatory voice questioning her, as if the police were there already, standing over her.

What happened, Miss?

There must have been a bend in the road. I didn't see the car coming towards me. And that boy. He just stopped right in front of me. I had to swerve or…

Seeing something moving before her face, she blinked. There was an old man walking amongst the wreckage, tall and broad, wearing a wax jacket and flat cap. She saw him crouch, his back to her, to examine the slumped driver in the sports car. He seemed to crouch there for a long time, looking, until Laura got her voice to work.

"Help! Help me!"

The old man stood, startled. Reeling around, he turned his head to the side to look at her. He had a ruddy face, and small black eyes.

"You alive?"

"Help me! Get me out!"

He simply stood, looking at her; as if he were frozen to the spot.

"It might be better for you to stay where you are, young miss."

Laura wanted to scream at him. "No! No! I need to get out!"

She began to panic, jabbing a hand at the seat belt lock to free herself. It came loose suddenly. She fell to the side against the driver's door. Determined, now, to get out of the car, and still panicking, she sought the door release with her head – moaning –then fell sideways into the road. Before her face she saw tiny pieces of glass twinkling in the sunlight. She could feel it coarse under her hands and knees as she crawled away from the car.

The old man was bending now, trying to help her. "Can you stand up?"

"I don't know. My leg…"

As he helped her to her feet, she found she was shaking. Pain shot along her left leg when she tried to put weight on it. She looked down. One leg of her jeans was torn and bloody.

"That car…I didn't see it…there was…there was…someone…I had to…otherwise…I didn't see the car…"

"You just sit over here," the old man said, ushering her to the grassy bank at the side of the road. With his help she limped there, wincing, and perched on a low wall. The old man took off his jacket then draped it over her shoulders.

"That was quite a crash."

"That…that man…the other driver…"

"He's a goner, I reckon," he said, solemnly. "This is a bad spot. Cars are crashing here all the time. We had a bad smash up here five months ago. Absolute carnage."

"We have to call an ambulance. He might still be breathing."

"Now you just rest a minute. Don't get yourself in a state."

"But we have to do something! There...there's a house back there. They might have a phone."

"That's my house, young miss, and I don't have no telephone."

Laura glared at him. "You don't have a phone? How can you not have a phone? You live all the way out here, but you don't have a phone." There was a rising note of hysteria in her voice.

"Never wanted one," the man said. He seemed strangely calm. "I like silence."

"But...?"

The old man had turned away from her, glancing back along the road. She followed his gaze. Her teeth were chattering. She reached up and pulled the jacket tighter around herself.

"Looks like you swerved over from the left. Didn't you see the bend?"

"N-no. There was...there was a boy. He ran out into the road then stopped there. I had to swerve or I'd have...have hit him."

The man glanced at from under his bushy grey eyebrows. "Boy?"

"Y-yes. He ran out into the road in front of me. I would have gone straight into him if I hadn't..."

"Where would a boy come from around here?"

"I'm telling you there was a boy!"

The old man looked thoughtful a moment.

"Him that walks the moors."

"What? What're you saying?"

"There's been talk of a boy. From time to time. Not a real boy. A spirit that walks the moors. Murdered and dumped here he was. Long ago. Doomed to wander."

"Look..."

"Him that walks the moors."

"We need to do something," Laura snapped. "The man in that car might still be alive. We need to get an ambulance here. Somehow."

He glanced down at her injured leg.

"Bleeding a lot, that. You wait here. I'll go up to the house, see if I can find some bandages."

"Bandages?" She felt wild laughter rise in her now. "You've got bandages but you haven't got a phone?"

"I'll be back in a jiffy."

Without another word, the old man left her then began to walk quickly back along the road. Laura called after him but he didn't look back.

Great, she thought. Again, she wanted to laugh. *I crash my car and the only person around is that senile old bugger.*

Her eyes drifted towards the wrecked sports car. All the laughter, however hysterical, left her. The man in the driver's seat was just a dark shape against the backdrop of sky. Then she had a thought: *Maybe that man had a mobile phone.* If she could find that she could use it to call the police and an ambulance. She started up from her seat, but at once felt pain shoot along her leg again. She looked around for the old man, but he was gone from sight. Her hands were still shaking. She would wait for the old man to return then tell him to search in the sports car for a phone. She knew she couldn't do it herself. She couldn't look. She could imagine the man's face, smashed and bloody. She had never seen a dead body before. No, she would just have to wait for the old man. Resolved to this, she began to think about what he'd said after she mentioned the boy. *Him that walks the moors.* Shivering, she looked around at the desolate landscape. *Silly old bugger.* Nevertheless she was unnerved. She recalled the way the boy had come up from the moor then turned to face the oncoming car. She shuddered now as she stood up from the wall, wincing at the pain in her leg. Where had that old man got to? He seemed to have been gone ages. Long minutes passed yet there was no sign of him. Feeling obliged, suddenly, to act if there was a chance the other driver was still alive, Laura raised herself from the wall then began to hobble along the road in the direction of the house. The pain in her leg was terrible, but she put it to the back of her mind.

When the house came into sight, she shouted at it: "Hey! Hey! Hello? Mister?"

There was no reply. She struggled up a few steps then along the path. Seeing that the front door was ajar she pressed it open, pausing for a moment before entering the narrow hallway. There were framed pictures on the wall, faded black and white photographs of people dressed in old-fashioned clothes. She limped towards an open doorway just ahead then looked inside. It was a lounge, full of ugly, outmoded furniture. A large bay window flooded the room with light. There was no television. The wallpaper and carpet hadn't been changed since the 1960s or 70s. The garish patterns made Laura feel dizzy. She was about to turn then move further into the house when her attention was caught by a wingbacked chair set in front of the window. Next to the chair, on a low table, sat a pair of binoculars, a walkie-talkie style radio, and a notebook, and pen. Something about these items, and their arrangement next to the chair, struck Laura as odd. She moved into the room then, pausing for a moment to listen for any sounds from elsewhere in the house, she picked up the notepad. The top sheet was covered with spidery, almost illegible writing. She stared at it, trying to make it out. At the top of the page was written today's date then under this what looked like: *16:12 green from west, red sports from east. Position by road sign. Smash-up! Fatalities...?*

Baffled, but with a dreadful thought dawning in the back of her mind, Laura picked up the binoculars and turned them to the window. She saw that they gave her a clear view of the road for some distance as it approached the house before the bend. The approach to the bend from the other direction was hidden from view, but she could see it further along where the road began to rise. Then she realised – the old man had been watching. *Green from the west.* That was her car – her green Romero. *Red sports from the east.* He had sat in this chair watching with his binoculars as the two cars approached each other.

What sort of a sick...?

Picking up the notepad again, she flicked through the pages and saw more scribblings.

12th December. 10:51 Lorry from the east. Small blue from west. Another following. Position close to house. Near miss.

23rd November. 23:05 Motorbike from east. Van from west. Position close to bend. Motorcyclist hit, but uninjured. Disappointing.

Disappointing? Laura felt a cold fury rise within her. Hearing a noise from somewhere further along the hall, she turned and left the lounge still carrying the notebook. She was going to present it to the old man. She was going to throw it in his face and ask him just what the fuck he thought he was doing.

At the end of the hall was another open door leading into a gloomy kitchen. Entering, Laura gave a start. Sat at the table in the centre of the room was a boy. He started himself on seeing her. In one hand he had a large glass of milk. In the other a sandwich was half-raised to his mouth. He put the sandwich down and stared at her in alarm. It had taken Laura a second to recognise him.

"You?"

"You shouldn't be in here," he said in a small, accusatory voice.

"You ran out in front of me." The anger surged inside her. *"What the hell did you think you were doing?"*

"You shouldn't have come here, Miss. He won't like it. You should have stayed with your car."

"He said there was no boy. He tried to make me think you were a ghost. What the hell are you two...?" Laura's anger trailed off. She had noticed something on the table by the boy's hand. It was another walkie-talkie style radio, like the one she'd seen in the other room.

"He's...he's not just watching the accidents, is he? He's...he's *causing* them. And you're helping him." She lifted the notebook in her hand waving it at the boy so violently that he drew back in his seat. "Position by the road sign! That's where you ran out from, isn't it! He watches and you time it so that you'll cause a crash. You sick fucking bastards!"

"You shouldn't have looked at that," the boy said. "He won't let you go now."

"Won't...what are you talking about?"

"Now you've seen that, he won't let you walk away. He'll make it look like it happened in the crash. No one will know."

"What?" Laura felt as if the floor were opening up underneath her. In a small, blank voice she said: "I'm having a baby."

"You better put that back and get out. Maybe he won't notice."

"Where is he?"

"Downstairs. In the basement. He's looking for something."

Laura turned then, moving as quickly as she could on her damaged leg, returned to the lounge. The awful colours and patterns there seemed to swim about her more violently now, making her feel sick. Moving towards the chair by the window she halted, spying a row of box files lined up against the wall behind the door. Uncertain why she was doing it, she crouched and grabbed one. She opened it, flicked through what the contents as she moaned quietly to herself. Inside, amongst newspaper cuttings with headlines that cried out at her – CRASH! BLACKSPOT! THREE KILLED IN PILE UP! – were what appeared to be driver's licences, car registration certificates, other oddments. *Things he collected*, she thought wildly. *Things he stole from the crashes, the victims. Souvenirs!* Hearing a noise, she closed the file abruptly then pushed it back in place with the others. Standing, she moved to the chair and table by the window. She threw the notebook back onto the table, but saw as he did that she had smeared it with her own blood. Perhaps he wouldn't notice. No, he would. He would. She took it up again and tore off the top page. Then she arranged it carefully on the table, trying to remember how it had been when she found it. On the way back to her car, she tore up the bloodstained page, tossing it into the wind.

He'll notice, she thought. *He will notice. Have to get that phone. That's if there is one! Have to find it. Have to find it for my baby's sake. For my baby.*

The pain in her leg was almost unbearable now. She moved slowly towards the smashed up sports car then popped open the driver's side door. The driver was still strapped in his seat, with his head slumped forward. Blood splattered the window at his side. From the small glances Laura gave him, she noticed that he looked young. *Where would he keep his phone?* Squirming, she felt at his breast pockets, then at his trousers pockets. Nothing. She glanced around inside the car, noticing the glove compartment. She opened it and scrabbled inside. Her hand felt something. Yes, phone! Standing, she looked back towards the house and saw the old man approaching. He was a dark figure against the glare of the sky. In one hand, he was carrying something, swinging it as he walked. It looked like a hammer.

With jittering fingers, Laura dialled and put the phone to her ear. The old man had stopped a moment, noticing her stand beside the sports car. Then he continued at a quicker pace.

There was a voice in her ear.

"Police! Ambulance!" Laura barked. "Quickly. Oh, quickly. Please!"

"What's your location?" the voice asked, Laura – looking anxiously around - felt her heart drop.

The old man had now reached the wreck of her car. He stopped then stood there gazing at her, his face flat and remorseless. Alarmed, Laura saw that he was in fact holding a hammer in one of his hands.

"It's...it's the police," she said to him, her voice quaking. "They're asking for our location. They'll send an ambulance for...for..."

"Turn that telephone off, Miss. There ain't going to be no ambulance."

"W-what? But I need help. My leg. And that man...that man in the..."

Without thinking, she had lowered the phone from her ear, but she could still hear the voice of the emergency operator, small and tinny:

"Miss? Miss? Your location?"

"Put the phone off," the old man said. "I've talked with the boy."

"The boy?" she said, with a sudden flare of anger. "You mean the boy you tried to tell me was a ghost? Who is he anyway? Where're his parents?"

"Gone. Turn the telephone off."

"You make him run out into the road, don't you? You make him run out so the cars swerve and crash. That's…"

"Aye. He's quick, that lad."

"But why? Why do you do it?"

Just briefly, she thought she saw the flicker of a smile on the old man's face.

"Ain't no other entertainment round here. Ain't got no TV. Now, give me that."

He began walking towards her, his free hand stretched out towards the mobile phone. Backing away from him, she put the phone to her ear and began pleading with the person on the other end of the line. But then she stopped. She had spied something over the old man's shoulder: a glint on the road. A car. There was a car coming. Pushing the old man away as he made a grab for the phone, she lurched sideways into the middle of the road frantically waving her arms.

"Help! Stop! Help me! Help!"

Casting a look at the old man, she saw that he too had glanced back along the road, his face darkening.

The oncoming car roared around the bend in the road screeching to a halt before Laura. To her bewilderment, she found herself looking through the windscreen into the face of her boyfriend.

"Dan!"

The car door opened as Dan half climbed out, his face stricken.

"Laura? What the fuck…?"

"No!" she shouted, moving as fast as she could around to the passenger side of the car, though her leg screamed with pain. "Get in! Get in!"

He ducked back into the car as she fell into the passenger seat beside him. She looked for the old man. He was moving towards the car.

"Drive! Drive!"

"What the fuck's going on?"

"Just go! Get moving!"

"Did you crash your…? Are you all right?"

"Dan! Drive the fucking car! Drive!"

The old man had reached the car. Laura saw him swing back him arm and the windscreen splintered in front of her face. She screamed. She was jerked back in her seat as Dan hit the accelerator shooting the car forward, curling around the wrecked sports car and on down the road. Laura turned, glancing out of the rear window. The old man stood amidst the wreckage, staring after them. She let out a huge breath of relief then started to laugh. Dan, trying hard to see through the shattered windscreen, glanced at her as if she were crazy.

"Who was that crazy old bastard? "Why did he...? What the hell happened? You were so angry when you left that I got in my car and followed you. Then you pulled ahead of me at a red light and I lost sight of your car. When I couldn't find you, I realised you must have taken this road. What were you doing on this road, Laura? What the fuck happened back there?"

"Dan," Laura said, calmly. "Drive carefully. We're going to have a baby."

"*What?*"

She glanced down, hearing the tiny voice coming out of the phone that was still in her hand.

"What the hell's going on, Laura?"

"I'll explain in a minute," Laura said. She lifted the phone to her ear. "Hello? You still there? Yes, there's been an accident."

Tim Jeffreys is a UK-based writer of horror and fantasy fiction. He has self-published several books of short stories. His work has appeared on-line and in print anthologies such as the recent "What Fears Become" from Imajin Books and "Night Terrors" published by Kayelle Press. Visit his website: http://www.timjeffreyswriter.webs.com/

DADDY

BY JASMINE FAHMY

Jack already knew which one she'd choose. There, at the very end of the left aisle, a scraggly mutt with haunted eyes. She loved the broken ones most.

She pattered forward, her little black shoes *click-clicking* on the tiles, to the dog he'd predicted. She knelt before the cage, black dress pooling around her, and pressed her hand against the bars— of the cage beside it. The puppy padded forward then eventually worked up the courage to lick at her hand, while the scraggly mutt looked on forlornly.

"Him."

"Emily," he said past the lump in his throat. He crouched beside her. "Em, look there, isn't he cute?"

But the old mutt didn't interest her. She was already whispering to her new puppy, saying she loved him, binding him under her spell. She named the pup Leon. Her smile, when she looked up, seemed suddenly devilish.

***

Leon ruined the couch within five minutes of being in the house. Emily came to apologize sweetly, wide blue eyes beneath long lashes, promising that she'd keep her puppy under control.

155

"It's alright." Jack tucked a lock of hair behind her ear. "We won't be staying here much longer anyway."

Right? Please say yes. Please.

Emily went back to playing with her puppy, leaving him in the cold.

The doorbell rang. He checked that the switchblade was in his pocket before answering. A boy with too many freckles gave him an awkward, crooked smile.

"Uh, Mr. Ambrose?"

"Can I help you?"

"I'm Neil Carter. Is Emily in?" He had the audacity to try and peer inside. "I heard about her dog at school. I thought I'd—"

"Yeah, tragic. She's really too distraught to see anyone right now, so..."

The boy stopped him from closing the door. Jack's jaw clenched. He was hardly anything. Jack bet he could easily snap the kid's neck.

"She shouldn't be on her own," Neil said, tugging something from his backpack. He produced a bunch of papers. "And I have all the class work she missed."

"I'll be sure to give it to her."

Neil held the papers back before he could take them.

"I thought I could explain all the new stuff to her."

"I'm more than capable."

A heartbeat of silence. Neil didn't look so awkward and nervous now. The boy looked him straight in the eye. Challenging. Unseen behind the door, Jack reached into his pocket, felt for the comforting blade.

"Daddy?"

Emily was at his side before he had a chance to slam the door. Now she wouldn't let him. Instead, she smiled at the brat then said a sweet tone, "Thank you," and invited him inside.

"With your permission of course, Daddy?"

Devilish again. She knew he hated it when she said that. She also knew he hated bringing humans into their house. But he had no choice, not against that gaze, that voice...

The worst thing about it, he thought, watching her lead Neil to the living room, was that she hadn't even been using *the voice*. He did have a choice about it. There was no tingle, no all-consuming need to obey her every word. Just to please. He lived to please her, after all. He had for years.

The worst thing about it, she didn't even need to use *the voice* on him. Not anymore.

He watched them for too long. They turned their heads to him almost as one. Neil, in Emily's presence, was playing the awkward boy and dropped his gaze, fidgeting in his seat.

"Hey, Daddy? Could you feed Leon, please?"

In other words: Leave. Go. She didn't need him right now.

Or ever?

No. No, this wasn't forever, not over his dead body. Not for this Neil boy.

Leon the puppy was waiting obediently in the too-large bed that used to belong to Hector, her old dog, and yipped to see him. He sat up wagging his tail. His big brown puppy eyes were glazed over, of course, because Emily had said she *loved him.*

Neil stayed for lunch. Emily told him not to bring her 'cranberry juice' (fresh from the hobo he had killed yesterday, for her). Jack was relieved, until he saw how Neil made her laugh. How their conversation was not scripted, they held no pauses, but flowed easily in a way that couldn't be explained by just *the voice.*

Secrets had been shared. Maybe Neil knew. Maybe Emily was only pretending, for her poor old 'Daddy,' her poor Jack. Hadn't they pretended as well, for the 'Daddy' before him?

Richard. His name was Richard and he had sat at the head of the table (just like Jack was now), watching them both with haunted eyes. Jack had laughed inwardly and thought, when their gazes met, that Emily laughed too. It seemed so funny, an old man like Richard thinking he could keep her.

But Richard had been graying. Richard had been *old.* Jack wasn't old. He was just barely—why would she—it hadn't been that long and surely—he'd done everything he could to...

Jack slammed his hands on the table then stood up. To Emily's bewildered gaze, he forced a smile as he said he was tired and heading inside.

His lips twisted into a wry smile. "Not as young as I used to be, darling."

Had Richard left that day?

He couldn't remember.

***

Neil's parents were all smiles when they met him. The smiles faded a little when he began to explain why he was there—the father, especially, sat up straighter and began shifting into a more defensive stance. Jack was quick to assure them. Young Neil had the best of intentions, he was sure, but his 'daughter' was in too fragile a mindset right now and—

"Then she needs her friends around her, now more than ever," the Father said, frowning beneath his moustache.

"I think I understand my own daughter's"—the word left a bad taste in his mouth—"needs, Mr. Carter."

The mother gave a nervous titter. She assured him they weren't trying to imply anything. The father did not agree, evidently, but Jack refused to leave before he'd made it perfectly clear that their brat was to stay away from his Emily.

Said brat came in just as he was about to leave and faced him with wide eyes. Jack smirked inwardly as he shouldered past Neil, bidding him a good night.

Didn't think he would be so quick on the uptake, huh? Thought old Jack would just lie down and die?

Glancing back at the door, he found it open just a crack, the brat looking through.

Jack fingered the blade in his pocket, barely kept himself from grinning. After a few moments, the door slammed shut.

***

For once, she let him choose their next town.

"To put you at ease, darling," she said, her small hand cupping his cheek. "This place seems to have troubled you."

So Jack spent the next two days packing bags, gathering enough money and blood to keep them going for a week, then pored over maps. He wanted to get as far away from Neil, school, and quaint suburbia as he could.

It was three a.m., then he'd found it.

"Emily!" He gulped down the remainder of his cold coffee before he got up, a printout of the town brochure in his hand. "Emily, I found it!"

Down the hall to the door painted white. Jack opened it to find her awake, of course, sitting on her futon by the open window, her nightgown pooled around her folded legs.

"I found it." He wore a breathless smile. "You'll love it. It's called Belleview and— "

What was that?

"Jack? Something wrong?"

"I thought I saw something move..."

"Probably just a squirrel." She shook her head, smiling that patronizing smile, then patted the space beside her. "Come. Belleview, you said?"

Rather than sit down, he leaned over the futon to peer out of the window. One beat, then another, then Jack saw him. Nestled among the branches, looking up with wide eyes, there was Neil.

Their eyes met.

Neil dropped from his hiding place. Jack tore out of the room.

Emily did nothing.

***

Neil's parents were much easier to tolerate when they were dead. No tittering, no strained smiles, no gushing about how he was really such a good boy, so well mannered, polite, friendly, and so, so *stupid*, or else he'd have stayed away. He couldn't even blame it on *the voice*. As powerful as it was, it lasted for a very limited time unless Emily was there to reinforce it.

"Don't look at me like that," Jack muttered, closing the Mother's eyes. "It's your own son's fault."

If he'd found the brat here, maybe his parents wouldn't have had to suffer.

He straightened up, sighing, and brought the blood stained covers over Mr. and Mrs. Carter's heads. So messy. Such a waste. Emily had taught him better.

Well, that wasn't his fault either, was it? He hadn't been in his right mind. She would understand, wouldn't she? She had to.

Jack tugged his gloves off and turned away.

Then paused.

Turned back.

Put his gloves on.

It didn't have to be a complete waste, did it?

***

Jack was careful this time, meticulous, as she'd taught him. Every slash of the knife had purpose, and he tried not to waste a drop.

He collected the blood in plastic bowls from the Carters' kitchen. Five, so far. Now she had to forgive him. She needed him. Neil couldn't bring her what she needed. He couldn't take care of her. She'd see, surely.

Hearing a sound, he paused, knife poised over the Father's left shoulder. Strange sound. Not ticking, not creaking, not thudding, not breathing. He couldn't pinpoint what it was, even. But it was there. It made his stomach clench, because he knew what that meant.

Neil was back, and he wasn't alone.

Jack held his breath then took a careful step backwards, facing the door. The knife would be useless if what he was thinking was true, but he held it up anyway.

A heartbeat. Two. Three. Four. He exhaled slowly. Five. Six. Seveneightnine.

Footsteps.

Only one pair. Sneakers slapping on the floor, not dainty little black shoes.

He grinned. She'd brought Neil to him. She had chosen. She'd brought the brat to his death.

The door was flung open then there he was, wide-eyed, red-faced, and panting, like a raging bull. He lunged for Jack with a cry, hands grappling for his neck.

Then Neil caught sight of his parents. This threw him, just for a moment.

A moment was all he needed.

Jack jabbed the knife into his side, only to have it glance away and fly across the room.

"You're not playing fair, Jack," she said from the doorway. "If you can't play fair, then maybe you shouldn't play at all."

Emily moved her hand in a smooth arc in the air that lifted Neil from his grasp, setting him down beside his parents' bed. Then she was before Jack. Her smile wasn't devilish, but sad. She lifted a hand and he, obedient as always, dipped his head to meet it, allowing her to cup his cheek.

"Why do you do this, darling? Why must you make things so

difficult?"

"Look." He pointed with a trembling hand at the bowls. "Look what I got you."

She tutted. "Did I tell you to get that?"

Jack swallowed as he gave a small shake of his head. "But I thought... If we were leaving, we'd need—"

"I'm not leaving, Jack."

No. No, no, no...

She was shaking her head. Smiling that sad little smile. Bringing him down, down, down, because he couldn't do anything else.

On his knees, she stroked his hair back.

"Oh Jack," she murmured. The cold fingers ghosted over his cheeks, his nose, his lips—and then his neck. "I always loved you, you know."

She kissed him, like she used to when he was young.

Then her lips found his neck. And her teeth.

Alone on the floor, with darkness at the edges of his eyes, he watched Emily dab her mouth clean and fix her hair. Then, in a blink, she was at Neil's side. A smile, not so sad now. She pulled his head to her chest whispering, over and over, that she'd always be there for him.

That she loved him.

The darkness crept in, swallowing Jack whole.

Jasmine Fahmy lives in Egypt, where she spends her time hiding from the sun, ignoring her homework, and staring at a page until the muse strikes. She likes to pretend she's a writer and appreciates it when people play along. She has had a short-story accepted by Daily Science-Fiction.

GOD PILL

BY MARJEV FINNEGAN, ERIE MATRIARCH

I am dreaming that I lost my baby in the sea, even though she is still in the ocean of my womb. The moon is full, pulling on the tides. I become aware that I am dreaming. Immediately, I am in control of the dream. Like God. I grasp my baby's—Zina's—tiny hands in mine, pulling her into my embrace... She is safe in my arms.

I awake to a tightening, as if a big hand is squeezing my uterus; my water has broken. I'm a nurse; I know that my baby is going to be born, too soon.

Silence. The room is shadowed by moonlight. Panicked, I reach for my husband, John. I am alone. John is not there beside me in bed. I cup my swollen belly, as if I can keep my baby safe inside me with the protection of my love. Another cramp, more intense than the last.

Awkwardly I stumble to the light switch. No lights. I hit the button on the TV. No TV. I pick up the phone to call 911. No dial tone.

I stumble downstairs as the sun lends a pale light to my surroundings. There is John, the fireman who risks his life to save others, who has put his hand on my swollen belly and felt the baby kicking, and opened a savings account for her. John, who goes to work each day, even when no one else does; who mows the lawn, eats, and sleeps. And loves. Even if no one else does.

John is sprawled on the sofa in the living room. His lips are parted, his eyes half open and glassy. I go to him shaking him as I scream, "John. John, wake up! The baby is coming!"

His eyes remain blank. He is seeing another reality; one of his own choosing.

As another labor pain grips my small frame, I damn the pharmaceutical companies, those greedy bastards, who came up with the God pill. The pill to relieve all pain, to cure both addiction and depression. Cure everything. Everyone is depressed living in a world of greed. Everyone is addicted to ego. Except for death-- And the God pill--.there is no cure for the self. The God pill induces a state of universal elation by blocking all physical sensation to the brain allowing pure consciousness. Allowing the ego to create its own blissful reality. To be God.

A hit of God in pill form takes one into a virtual reality of their own making. Like lucid dreaming, which I achieve naturally... I realize life is just a dream. I don't need artificial means to enlightenment. I know!

I can't believe this!

John, my John, my husband, my rock... John has taken a hit of God. He's in heaven.

I'm in hell.

As the pain subsides, I pick up a vase then crack him in the head with it. No response, just a vacant stare. I look at the trickle of blood running down his forehead. I'm dreaming, I tell myself. Become aware that you are the dreamer and the dream, as well.

* * *

The first time I saw God prescribed was to a rich and famous woman, an idol, a star, with six kids, and two cats, a dog. I read the leaflet that came with the God pill. I wondered, then, if the world should be left to crazy people-- If, perhaps, I might be crazy-- and maybe it would be for the best if schizophrenia became the norm.

Important information about God, the leaflet read: God may also be used for other purposes not listed in this medication guide. This medication may be habit-forming and should be used only by the person it is prescribed for. God should never be given to another person, especially someone who has a history of mental illness, such as schizophrenia. Keep this medication in a secure place where others cannot get to it. You may have withdrawal symptoms when you stop using God. Do not stop using God suddenly without first talking to your doctor. God can cause side effects that may impair your thinking or reactions. Be careful if you drive or do anything that requires you to be awake.

The next time I saw this famous star, she was in a wheelchair. She had lost her children, her cats, even her dog. I wheeled her into the examination room where she'd come to renew her prescription. She was trembling, tears flowing. She clawed at my white uniform with skeletal hands. "Understand," she begged me, seeing the judgment in my eyes, "This pill allows me to leave my body. When our soul is free of the body, nothing is impossible!"

"It is an artificial trigger to the leaving of the physical," I told her. "The same thing can be done through meditation."

"That takes years," she moaned.

"LSD. Once you've opened the gates of consciousness, you don't necessarily need to constantly repeat the process!"

"You don't understand!" she whined. "*I am God!*"

"I do understand," I told her. "I become aware when I am asleep and dreaming. I can control my dreams. Lucid dreaming. I am God in my dreams."

The doctor entered the room then renewed her prescription. The next time I saw her, she arrived at the hospital in an ambulance called by her bodyguard. I witnessed the doctor telling the guard, "Leave her alone. She is being cured."

"Cured of what?" the guard screamed. "The body? Reality?"

I ran to her lying on a stretcher then grabbed her by both shoulders. I shook her. "Wake up!" I screamed. I was pushed aside. She was admitted to the hospital, hooked to IVs to feed her and tubes to eliminate her waste.

Her doctor treated her with God until she died.

* * *

The first to get hooked on God were the rich, but that's what they do-- get rich, get famous, die of a drug overdose. Actually, in reality, it was nice, no rich people thinking they were God. No government. The heads of state all slumbered in peace in their own perfect heaven.

Everyone got along pretty good without them. As a nurse, I cared for the sick and injured. When the cops started going into a peaceful state on prescription God, my husband John, a fireman, took care of emergencies. He saved lives; so did I. Someone ran off with someone's money or possessions-- let them. We cared for those who needed help surviving in reality. We cared for the children, the elderly, and dogs-- the cats took care of themselves.

One day I was driving by the Rite Aid drugstore and saw a pile of bodies spilled through the electronic doors. About twenty people had run over each other in a wild stampede to get God in pill form. John and other rescuers were there pulling bodies out of the pile trying to revive them. As I approached, John pointed at several bodies already extracted. "Over there!"

Shocked, I discovered my own mother lying on the sidewalk. My mother was using God! I cleared her airway of several blue pills, gave her resuscitation, breathed into her lungs, pounded on her heart until she gave a low moan. "Mom!" I held her in my arms and wept with relief.

"God," she begged. "Give me some God."

John and I brought her home with us, but she snuck off in the night, taking my engagement ring with her to exchange for the drug. By then, the FDA had passed a law against God, and most of the doctors, writers of prescriptions, were addicted. But God had been duplicated by chemists. Millions were hooked on the street drug, a stronger version of the original. Its effects last for months. Users enter their own virtual reality, where eventually they remain until they die, starved to death or suffocated in their own waste.

Why would anyone take a drug that they knew would eventually kill them? Such was the power of God.

* * *

Pain grips me in a world all its own. There is nothing but pain. As it slowly subsides, I reason that this reality is much too detailed to be dream. This is real! My baby-- Zina,-- that is what John and I are going to name her-- although we don't know if the baby is a girl. I'd gone for an ultrasound, at the hospital where I work, but by then all the technicians were using God. So we never got an ultrasound.

As the pain subsides I realize I have to get to my sister, Ruth, who watched with me, the decline of civilization.

I'm not depressed. I'm not insane! I'm not dreaming! I'm giving life in reality! Ruth, my dear Ruth, is a midwife who uses hypnotism for pain free deliveries. I'm going to give birth to Zina naturally, in a hot tub, so the baby will calmly enter warm water, the same environment as the womb.

On my front porch I discover a small body, alive, yet, for all purposes, dead wrapped in a worn blanket. A note attached to the boy, age 8 or 9, reads: PLEASE TAKE CARE OF MY LITTLE BOY. HIS NAME IS BOBBY.

I step over Bobby. Mercifully, he is under the influence of God.

On the drive to my sister's, my body wracked with labor pains and sorrow like violent grief. I see the physical remains of many God addicts lying scattered across the landscape. Some are in cars, sitting upright, some still have their hands on the wheel, as if they were going someplace and were raptured. Or couldn't wait for God.

I find Ruth slumped at her kitchen table, her head resting on her arms, long hair sprayed around her head, tiny blue pills spilled out of a prescription bottle on the table.

I squat, brace my legs between the stove and refrigerator then give birth. My baby is covered in mucus and blood. I clear her mouth. Breathe into her. Zina gives a breath.

Zina.

I can see her beating heart through her veined skin; it is beating slower and slower. She purses her red lips then gasps for air.

I tell myself, I am the dreamer and the dream. I tell myself I must become aware that I am the vision and like God, I can take control.

But I am not God.

Zina isn't going to live, I know. I take up a God pill, crunch it with my teeth, mix it with my saliva then press my lips to hers. Like a bird feeds its young, I use my tongue to force it down her throat. I'm aware of my own breathing. For one second, her eyes seem to focus on me. I am God. I gave her life, now I give her heaven. Her tiny body shudders; my baby, Zina, dies.

Then I take a God pill too.

Mariev Finnegan: "I'm Matriarch of the Erie — and everyone is Erie — and the writer of *SORROWS BRIDGE* (available for the Nook at Barnes & Noble) who lives in upstate NY with my grandson, Jacob Stump, an owl called Who? and a three-legged dog named Bloody Stump. I can be followed at www.marievfinnegan.yola.com and yinarchy@yahoo.com."

Thieves Don't Scream

by Janett L. Grady

She was not your average, run-of-the mill ghoul lurking in the shadows on dark and stormy nights, nor was she the blood -thirsty vampire you read about in horror magazines. No. Amy was something else. A bit weird, yes, but a careful, well-educated woman who thought of herself as being a decent person, a hardworking law clerk who just happened to have an obsession, an uncontrollable hunger for the occasional crunch of human bone, marrow soft and gummy with a touch of crisp.

How Amy acquired such a taste was a mystery even to her, but it might have had something to do with being born of a wicked, cannibalistic old hag who had finally been caught and lynched. Amy was born having a full set of permanent teeth, no growing and discarding of the usual baby-teeth. Two of her teeth just happened to be set one inch apart and a bit longer than her other teeth. However it happened didn't matter. Amy had never thought much about it, but had simply enjoyed the quirk of her off-the-wall appetite. She did, however, live in fear of being caught and hanged.

"Get right with God," she said. "I think you're dying."

She then left the bleeding drunk behind a dumpster. Amy half-walked, half-ran out of the alley and into the street, homeward bound, eyes scanning for cops.

Approaching her building, she smiled prettily at the old bum on the stoop, walked inside then hurried the four flights to her apartment. Only after she was inside, the battery of locks in place, did she lean against the wall and take a deep breath.

But there was still work to be done. Amy hurried into her bedroom, stripped, examined her skirt and blouse for traces of blood. Stains, still damp, were on her blouse. She stuffed her soiled clothing into a laundry bag for the cleaners. She walked into her bathroom, brushed her teeth, paying particular attention to the gum line. Blood and something gray swirled into the drain. Amy then pulled on a robe, moseyed into her living room, poured herself a glass of brandy, plopped onto the couch and started sipping her drink. Now she allowed herself to remember.

She saw herself strolling through the alley toward her prey. Her skirt was short, slit to the hip. Was her blouse unbuttoned? It might have been. The smile. The nod. The feeling of power when she spun around and struck, slamming her fist to the back of his head, kicking at his groin as he fell, tearing open his shirt, stabbing her fist into his gut to rip out a bottom rib.

Well, then, how did she feel? She felt a sense of power. But that was basic. It was, after all, easy to subdue a drunk. What amazed her, what completely amazed her, was the texture of gum-like flesh on her tongue, the scratch and break of crisp against her teeth, all somewhat rancid but thrilling. Now, recalling what she had done, she felt that sense of heightened intimacy. Captured in passion, Amy closed her eyes, drifted into a long and peaceful sleep, dreaming the sweetest of dreams.

Morning light awakened her. She glanced at the clock on the mantel. 7:10 A.M.

"Damn, I'm going to be late."

Dashing into her bedroom, Amy tore off the robe. Rummaging through her closet, she stepped into a pair of black slacks, buttoned a white blouse all the way up then pulled on a jacket, which matched her slacks. She checked herself in the mirror. The slacks were a bit wrinkled, so she quickly kicked them off, stepped into a pair of panties and pulled on an ankle-length skirt, which matched her jacket. She rechecked herself. She looked neat and well-groomed.

Amy raced out of the apartment carrying her bag of dirty clothes.

After dropping her laundry at the cleaners, Amy stood anxiously at the bus stop waiting for the bus that would take her to her job at the courthouse. There was no sign of the bus. If it was late, she'd be late. The old judge would then put on his sour face and say, "Late again, huh?" It was the same old monologue, day in and day out. Abruptly she crossed the street before she could change her mind. She hurried to a drugstore, fishing for the cell phone in her purse then found a secluded spot near the pharmacy.

"Carter? Amy. Listen tell the judge I'm not coming in. I'm going to the clinic. No, Carl, it's a female problem. You wouldn't understand. Yes, I'll do that. Thank you. Goodbye."

Carter had sounded pissed. For one brief moment, she had second thoughts. But it was too late now to reconsider.

She walked out of the drugstore, staying on the same side of the street. For the rest of her day off, Amy strolled, watching people and window shopping, her mind mostly on the drunk of the previous night. A-a-ah, the thrill. By three o'clock, Amy felt terribly anxious, hungered for the crunch of bone, the texture of marrow on her tongue.

She walked into a department store then wandered around. She turned right at Gloves and Purses, then paused, scanning the aisles for a potential victim. A bum with a hangover? A guy who looked lonely? That's when Amy saw the young girl, about twenty, shoulder-length hair, kitten-cute in a short white dress and shorter brown coat. The girl was at the jewelry counter, eyes darting warily about. Amy knew what the girl was going to do even before seeing the small white hand close over the necklace, then slide quickly into the coat pocket.

Amy followed her through the doors and into the street. "Hold it right there," Amy said. "You forgot to pay for that necklace." The girl stopped in front of a window filled with naked mannequins. She turned to face Amy, eyes downcast, pretty little jaw trembling. "I saw you take it," Amy told her.

"Oh, please," said the girl through quivering lips. "Please let me go."

"Can't do it," said Amy. "You're a thief."

"Here," said the girl, reaching into her pocket. "Take it."

Amy raised a protesting hand. "Can't do it," she said. "If you get away with it once, you'll do it again."

The girl fumbled through a small brown purse then brought forth a fifty-dollar bill. "I'll pay for it," she whined. "Please...please take it and let me go."

"Well..." There was hesitation in Amy's voice, yet the hand that snatched the fifty showed not the slightest pause. "...all right, but there's more to it," she said, tucking the bill into the pocket of her skirt. "We're going back to the store," she said. "I want to see the clerk ring it up."

"But..."

"No buts," Amy cut in. "Let's go." She latched onto the girl's arm and dragged her along, walking swiftly until coming to the alleyway of the previous night. "Through here," Amy insisted, pulling the girl into the shadows.

A setting sun to the west kept the shadows from becoming too dark in most of the alley. However, on a short stretch of it, tall buildings screened off the light. When they reached the darker stretch of the alleyway, it was like walking into the ladies room of a rundown bar. Dim light. Eyes slow to adjust. Steps cautious. As they made their way through the shadows, stepping around barrels of garbage, something scurried in the trash behind them.

"What was that?" the girl asked.

"Rats," Amy answered. "They live here."

"I don't like rats," the girl whined. "They're scary."

Amy almost felt sorry for her, but not quite. Her arm felt warm and vibrant in Amy's hand. She gave it a final, sudden squeeze. Then she struck, punching the girl in the gut, an uppercut to the chin. The girl fell back. Amy pounced, yanking hair, grabbing a wrist and chomping down on a pair of fingers. Squirming and flailing her other arm, the girl was moaning and groaning but not screeching or screaming. Amy thanked God for that. After one long chewing on bone, Amy climbed off.

"You're one tough chick." Amy grinned. "Forget about going back to the store," she added. "I want you to squeeze off the bleeding then make your way to the street, find help then head for the nearest emergency room."

Amy felt proud of herself. She hadn't hurt the girl too bad, or at least there was little chance of the girl bleeding to death. Amy thought of herself as a good person.

Leaving the girl whimpering behind a trash bin, Amy felt somewhat satisfied but still a bit hungry. She walked out of the alley and into the street. She hailed a cab. The yellow sedan slid to a halt at the curb. Amy ordered the driver to drive her around. She had some serious thinking to do. She reached into her pocket then pulled out the fifty. She stared at it, amazed that her victim had actually paid her. Amy toyed with a new idea. Unlike the bums and drunks, her usual prey, shoplifters couldn't afford to be screaming for the cops. There'd be less danger of getting caught. She brought the fifty up to her lips and kissed it. Her day off had progressed amazingly well. Plus there were reasons to believe the rest of her day held promise. She ordered the driver to take her back to the store.

Janett L. Grady lives and writes with her husband in Palmer, Alaska. Her stories have appeared in magazines, anthologies, and on websites all over the country, and in a few magazines based in the United Kingdom.

GERÜCHT

BY S. L. CORTÉS

The guns stopped firing right as the rain did at two pm. Private Muller lit a cigarette scavenged from a nearby body—a boy, couldn't be a day older than seventeen. Muller appreciated a moment of relative silence. Somewhere far down the line, he could still hear the big guns going, the gray horizon lit with bursts of red and orange glow. Here it was quiet.

The other soldiers hunched in the trench with him, ignoring the ankle high slop of mud and piss, taking Muller's lead and enjoying the moment. Even if they had not been jammed in close quarters, they would have huddled together for warmth. Some spoke in low voices, afraid to disturb the quiet, their mumbled conversations barely registering to Muller.

"It's going to rain again." Kruger had set his gun across his knees as he crouched and leaned back against a sandbag.

Muller nodded in silent agreement. There were three certainties in this war: artillery fire, death, and rain. He offered the fag to Kruger. The older private took a deep drag from it, letting it out with a sigh.

"I thought we'd run out of tobacco," he said, smoke pluming from his nose in a blue mist.

"Got it from the kid. He also had a blade," Muller said, holding up a small pocket knife. There was an engraving set in delicate silver on the handle. *'The Lord is my light and my salvation; whom shall I fear? Psalm 27:1'*. It had to be a present from the boy's parents; a saying meant to give him strength in this place. The blade was too small to use in combat, but it would be good for trade.

Something scurried by his foot, disturbing the sewage. Muller kicked out at it reflexively, grimly satisfied when his boot connected with something solid. Goddamn rats.

"Look alert, boys!" The command cut through the air, disturbing the moment. Both men looked up, irritated. 'Herr Junger', a beefy young man with a shock of blonde hair and ruddy cheeks stood straight, staring at them with his arms folded over his chest. His real name was Lieutenant Otto Schmidt. Compared to soldiers like Muller and Kruger in their late thirties, he was an infant. Junger continued speaking.

"We move out in an hour. Eat some food, get back your strength."

"Hear that, Muller?" Kruger said cheerfully, "We get to have a fine meal. Which would you prefer: roasted or braised?"

Muller snorted, snatching back his cigarette before Kruger could finish it off. They had run out of rations days ago, Junger knew that. These same sullen looking soldiers had given up on the possibility of getting resupplied and taken to eating rats. The rodents were plentiful and fat from gorging on the dead. Muller often sat at night picturing the other side having trenches filled with food; sausage, cabbage, his mother's strudel, chocolate, and barrels of beer, the enemy happily feasting and waiting for their next useless attack with not a damn rat in sight.

"We'll take those bastards today, I swear it," Junger continued on. Damn if the man didn't manage to sound confident in the face of hopelessness. "Artillery fire's been ordered to start at fifteen hundred; we'll charge while they're cowering in their shitholes over there."

Junger stood for a moment, mouth opening and closing as he struggled to find more words to inspire and encourage his men. But there was nothing to say. Any battle determination had disappeared weeks ago, each new body count ensuring it would stay away. The young officer closed his mouth with a snap then spun on his heel, stalking away through the mud to his own little cave scratched out of the side of the trench.

Kruger was already up hunting for his meal, but Muller wasn't hungry. He hadn't been hungry for days now, only taking water sparingly. Sometimes he simply turned his face upwards, catching rainwater in his mouth and that was all he needed for the day.

So, he sat, puffing the bare remnants of the cigarette until the paper had burned down to his fingertips, waiting for the orders to move out.

It started as all advances did, with a round of artillery fire to keep the enemy's head down allowing the Germans to rush the field. Muller ran as fast as the thick mud allowed him to, focused more on avoiding shells from the other side than actually reaching French lines.

Even experienced soldiers could not dodge the endless barrage forever. A shell slammed into the earth, the impact sending out a deep shock that rattled his bones, nearly deafening him. Muller struggled to focus, to keep a clear head, but everything was sluggish and muffled as though all was underwater. He did not hear the whistler coming in until it landed, mere yards from him. The gun was ripped from his hands as he toppled back landing hard at the bottom of a muddy fox hole.

Blackness engulfed him.

When Muller's eyes opened and stared blankly at the gray sky, he could not guess how long he had been unconscious. A small eternity passed before he remembered where he was, what happened, even who he was. He eventually recalled he had a body when pain sliced through him, snapping him out of the haze.

Muller sat up, a sucking noise sounding from where he pulled free of the mud. The pain grew sharper. He looked down, trying to find the source. A piece of metal jutted from his leg, just where calf met knee, the fabric of his pants was stained dark from the rain and mud.

He touched it. Lightning lanced up his spine. He let out a cry, hand falling away immediately.

"Fuck," he moaned, "*Fuck*."

The soldier sucked in shuddering breaths, looking around for another person, but he was alone, save for a French officer lying on his face in the muck near him. It didn't take a hardened veteran to see the man was dead. It was difficult to stay alive with your legs and most of your back gone.

"Medic. Medic!" Muller shouted, not caring if the other side heard him. If they found him and killed him, well, it would be better than dying alone in this shithole. "For the love of God, *medic*! I'm down here!"

Silence met his shouts, the eerie silence that hung between skirmishes. Before it had been a welcomed respite, but right now it rolled over him like a thick woolen blanket, making it hard to breathe.

He fell back on his elbows, eyes shut tight against the rain, the mud, the dead soldier. They had not taught him in basic how to survive something like this. They had not taught him about the whistlers, the trenches, the barbed wire, the gas, and infection, all of the things that could kill him in grisly ways.

There was no one coming for him. Not now. Sucking in shallow breaths, he opened his eyes again, straightening slowly. He gritted his teeth, reaching out again. This time holding onto the shard of metal until the pain became a sharp ache then gave a forceful tug. It ripped free, tearing out of flesh and fabric. He screamed long and hard. He screamed at the sky, the mud, the damn war. He screamed until his voice gave out and his chest heaved with the effort.

Shifting as best he could, he dragged himself through the mud to the body, hands scrabbling at the wet wool of the brown uniform as he scavenged until he found a handkerchief. It worked as a temporary bandage, tied tightly around the wound.

Something shifted in the mud near him. He instinctively kicked out with his uninjured leg. The movement stopped. Standing was not an option. Muller started dragging his body by his elbows towards the steep side of the hole.

Every motion made his nerves scream in agony. However he continued on gamely until he could reach up, fingers clawing at the soft earth, trying to find purchase. If he could only get out of the hole, he would be able to take stock of everything then get back to the German line.

There was something moving again by the French officer's body, but his concentration was on the slow process of hauling his wounded body up the embankment. If crawling through the mud had been difficult, climbing was nearly impossible. It seemed that with every foot gained, he slipped back three. Little grunts escaped him as he used his arms and uninjured leg to push and pull himself slowly to the top.

Minutes could have past, or it could have been hours. Sweat soaked his entire body as he panted and strained. The pain grew worse with each movement. He pushed it to the back of his mind until his hand reached over the top of the hole, finding somewhat solid ground. With one last heave, he hoisted himself up until he could rest on his torso, half in and out of the pit.

The battle ground was empty of life, littered with shells, bodies, and barbed wire. Muller felt a drop of water hit his head. He looked up at the darkening sky. Sure enough, the rain started, a slow heavy drizzle, drowning out the silence.

As Muller began to pull his body the rest of the way free, something caught the corner of his eye. Twenty yards away a man crouched over the body of a fallen horse. Muller blinked water from his eyes, wondering how he had missed that before. Maybe because the soldier was hunched near the horse's belly, the rest of the animal blocking a clear view of him. Raising a hand, Muller called out to him above the rush of the rain.

"Hey! Hey you there! I need help!"

The man did not look up.

"Help me out of this damn hole!"

Finally, the man moved, slowly lifting his head to stare at Muller. He had blood smeared slickly over his mouth and nose. Before Muller could tell if he had been injured, the man stood, something falling from his hands. In a sickening moment, he realized it was the horse's intestines as they flopped over its body.

The man stumbled around the carcass, walking towards the hole. He moved like a drunk, swaying and stumbling, arms hanging limply at his sides. His eyes were fixed on Muller, the skin on his chest flapping around a gaping wound as he shambled closer. He hobbled on a stumped leg, where the foot was completely gone past the ankle.

Muller reeled back in terror, losing his grip on the ground and rolled right down the hole's embankment, landing with a squelching sound at the bottom.

"Oh god, oh god, oh god," he gasped. He had seen so much in this war. Men exploding into sprays of pink mist, men cut wide open, moaning piteously while trying to push their spilled bowels back in, men caught on the barbed wire lines like ragged, torn dolls. But they had been dead. Not wandering around gutting horses. He choked back acid bile.

His head snapped around when something stirred in the pit, splashing water. The French officer was moving. His hand reached out towards Muller as he lifted his head out of the mud, turning in that same slow motion towards the German. Half of his face had been ripped off.

"Sweet god!"

Muller scrambled away until his back hit the wet earth of the wall.

The officer continued reaching out to him, purple tongue hanging free from the side of his mangled mouth. A sound like a groan and wail escaped the moving corpse—a sound so terrible Muller covered his ears to block it out.

Dirt hit Muller's shoulder. He looked up to see the other dead man standing at the edge of the hole, staring down at him, expression as blank as the French soldier's. It stepped out into empty space and fell straight into the pit. There was a sickening crack when it hit the mud. Muller could swear it had been the spine from the way it landed. The world seemed to hold its breath as he waited to see what would happen next. Surely the thing would not be able to recover from a fall like that.

He almost allowed relief to sink in when the body moved, sluggishly pushing itself out of the sticky floor of the hole, looking at him with its head hanging at an odd angle now, neck broken from the impact. The thing moved again, taking a stumbling step towards him. Muller stared at its face, gaze locked on the eyes clouded with death. There was nothing there. Yet it came towards him, inexorably urged on by something.

Muller pushed back against the wall again, fingers scrabbling at the soft dirt as though he could dig right through the ground away from it. It would pause, then step, pause again, as though trying to sniff out its prey. Or perhaps it knew he wouldn't be able to go anywhere and was taking its time. The dead Frenchman was making guttural noises. Muller realized with mounting terror that it was actually pulling its mutilated body along with its hands, intent on reaching its goal.

He had to get out of there, Muller knew that, but how could he get away from these things when it had taken so long for him to pull himself out of the bloody hole before?

Muller could smell the putridity rolling off the dead body in waves as it approached. In a flash, he felt anger start to rise in him. The man had been killed already—he should have *stayed* dead. He had no right to be walking around while Muller struggled to survive.

His hand closed around the pocket knife in his trousers. He fell forward, and the blade of the knife buried itself deep in the dead man's eye. The thing stood for a moment, swaying drunkenly on the spot before it crumpled to the earth, a marionette with its strings cut.

Muller stared at it, the breath whistling in and out of his lungs in hoarse gusts. It wasn't moving. He reached down, wrenched the knife free and turned to the other dead man in the pit.

It was closer, but not by much. It was completely unfazed by its companions' recent demise, one clouded eye staring at Muller with dull intent, thick purple tongue lolling about uselessly. Maybe it was the adrenaline, the pain, the anger, or a combination of all three, but Muller found himself standing and hobbling the last few steps between them, kicking away the hands when they reached for him. One boot pinned its head to the mud, holding it in place while the knife rose in the air and slammed into the exposed skull, right in the soft spot behind the ear. Not even a gurgling noise sounded as its limbs stopped moving.

Muller waited the rain a shroud around him and the two corpses.

A noise caught his attention, but it wasn't a noise coming from the bodies. It sounded across the battleground. Muller shouted back at it. Any live person, even the enemy, was better than the recent company he had been keeping.

The noise came again, this time closer. Muller yelled in response, calling for help. A moment later yet another person was standing at the edge of the hole, looking down at him. He was wrapped in a gray woolen overcoat that had seen better days. But he was most definitely alive.

Muller waved up at him frantically, pointed at his bloodied leg. The stranger gave one nod then disappeared. A moment later, he was back, and a rope of some sort fell just within reaching distance against the wall. Muller stumbled to it, hands groping at it until they closed around it, gripping it tight. It wasn't until he was being pulled half-way out of the hole that he realized the rope was actually the undone leathers of a horse's bridle. His stomach churned, but he held onto the strap gamely.

He pushed at the wall with his good foot, trying to speed the process along, until he felt someone grab the back of his coat, hauling him over the edge of the hole, back into the world. Muller collapsed on the ground, panting. His savior stood nearby, looking around anxiously. Another Frenchman, this one whole. He was tall and reedy even with the bulk of his uniform. Muller could scarce believe he had been able to pull him out on his own.

"Thank you," he said, breaking the silence. The tall man looked at him, nodded. It was just this man and him now sitting on the blasted and torn field.

"God, I have to get back to my line," Muller muttered, pressing a hand to his knee when he saw there was fresh blood seeping out. "Need a medic."

France stared at him uncomprehendingly.

"I need to get a doctor," Muller said louder, pointing towards the German line, then back at him. Something clicked and France's face cleared. He nodded understandingly. He spoke, but Muller could not make out a damn word. He did not have the energy or patience to try and work through the muddled memory of vocabulary.

"Take *me*," pointing, "*There*." Pointing.

The tall man finally shut up and leaned down, hauling Muller to his feet. The German bit his lip to stop from crying out then swung an arm around the narrow shoulders. It was slow going, as the Frenchman tried to walk them across a shredded landscape. The ground was slick with mud. Pieces of shrapnel and body parts made walking difficult.

Muller was determined to not thinking about what happened back in the pit, focusing as much as he could on stumbling along with one leg. France's deceptively thin frame provided most of the support. Time ticked by as ponderously as Muller's steps, the landscape around them barren of life.

They were still hundreds of yards from anywhere when France halted abruptly, startling Muller out of an almost trance-like state.

"What are you doing?"

France was staring straight ahead, lean face tense. Muller realized it had been growing steadily darker—night was coming. The dull shadows were stretching across the field, and it was in one that Muller saw what the Frenchman had spotted. By the wheel of an abandoned cart a figure was huddled. It wasn't until it moved that Muller realized it was a person.

The two soldiers looked at each other warily then his companion drew his pistol out, cocking it. Muller could feel him shaking as he raised it and called out.

The person jumped, head lifting immediately and looking their way. Muller nearly sagged in relief. That shock of blond hair was recognizable from anywhere.

"Herr...Schmidt!" Herr Junger had almost rolled off his tongue, but he had caught himself just in time. He raised his hand in greeting. France was still trembling and had not put his gun away.

The lieutenant stood slowly then started to approach them. It wasn't the drunken stumble of the dead. He continuously looked about as though expecting an ambush at any moment.

"Lieutenant," Muller called as he drew closer. "Lieutenant, by god it's good to see you." 'Alive' hung unsaid in the sodden air.

"Muller? Muller, is that you?" Herr Junger's normally robust voice was dry and seemed to crack with the effort of speaking.

"Yes, Lieutenant."

"Who's this?"

Muller glanced up at his new companion.

"A Frenchman. He got me out of a hole and was taking me back to our lines." He was not about to go into what had happened in the hole. Junger stared at the tall foreigner as though he were some sort of ghost.

"And you've...you haven't...seen anyone else?" the lieutenant ventured hesitantly. There was something there behind the blue eyes that Muller recognized as the gnawing fear he had known since first seeing the dead man with the horse. It was far more insidious than the fear of battle. At least one could understand war.

"Not since the hole."

"They didn't do that to you, did they?"

"No," Muller shook his head, "Got thrown by a whistler and landed on some shrapnel. Went straight through my leg. We need to get back to our lines, Lieutenant."

He wasn't going to ask why the other man had been hiding behind a wheel when he seemed perfectly uninjured and able to move on his own. He thought he knew the reason.

Junger seemed to finally snap to, woken from his haze.

"Yes. Yes, of course. Come, Private. Lean on me as well—we'll carry you."

France accepted the help and addition of Junger to their group without a word. They moved faster with an extra set of hands. It was only then that Muller wondered what would happen if the Frenchman were to come with them into the German trenches. Well, they couldn't very well send him back across No Man's Land with those things out there, could they?

Junger talked as they went, describing what happened to him during the skirmish. Like Muller, he had been knocked out by a shell. When he had come to, he was alone in the field in silence. It was only minutes before he first encountered one of the dead, a German corporal shambling along with no arms.

Muller listened in silence to Junger's description of how he dealt with the corpses that came his way. Young men needed to be able to tell their stories. But it did not take long before he was out of bullets, and his knife had disappeared somewhere in the muck. Which was when they had found him crouched by the cart.

"How did you survive?" Junger asked when he was done. "Injured and alone."

Muller opened his mouth. But something stopped him from telling the story. He had never been one to shy from violence or gore, but there was some part of him that wanted to put that memory away until it was erased by time. He shook his head. Junger allowed them to fall back into silence.

"By god, it's Kruger!" The shout made Muller jump. Junger released him, taking off, running in the direction of something moving through the rain.

It wasn't Kruger. Although his eyesight was not the sharpest, Muller saw that the second Junger started towards the former lieutenant. He shouted a warning, but it was too late; Junger was within arm's reach before Kruger almost fell onto him. Its mouth opened wide, and Muller saw teeth flash in the dull light before sinking into his neck. Junger screamed in agony. It was a terrible sound, like the shriek of a gutted pig.

Junger's scream became a wet gurgle when the thing jerked its head back, a chunk of the man's throat in its maw. Muller stared in horror as blood spurted from the torn veins in Junger's neck. Kruger's corpse let out a grunt as it swallowed its mouthful then went in for another bite. Junger wasn't struggling anymore. He hung limp in the creature's grasping hands.

France released Muller and the German all but fell from the sudden lack of support. He struggled to remain upright, putting his weight on one leg, watching the tall men stride towards the feasting Kruger. It did not even bother to look up as the Frenchman took his pistol out, held it against its head and pulled the trigger.

Muller stared in the silence following the gunshot, staring at the bodies of two men he had fought side by side with. France holstered his pistol and stepped back. He turned his head towards Muller when there was a soft click of metal. Muller saw the brief moment of realization in the other man's eyes before the explosion. The shock of it threw the German soldier onto his back, leaving him stunned as bits and pieces of what remained of the Frenchman rained down on him.

They spattered over him wetly, the warmth an odd contrast to the cold rain. Muller closed his eyes, not wanting to see more death when it surrounded him on all sides. It was a silent night on the field of blood, save for the steady thump of rain as he was once again alone. As his mind teetered towards despair, Muller heard something, something barely there. It was an odd crackling, like a radio. When he lifted his head, he saw a reddish light glowing from near the German lines.

A fire was being kept lit even in this downpour. A big fire, at that. With a low moan, he pulled himself up, forcing himself to his feet. The pain had become a steady ache. He was almost used to it by now, although he was certain he would be losing this leg once he found a medic. But that did not matter so long as he survived. So long as he escaped death this time.

He grabbed a discarded rifle, using it to support his weight, and started hauling himself towards the fire.

As he neared, he could see figures standing around the blaze. The wind changed direction and sent the smoke billowing in his face. He nearly gagged from the smell. Rotten, burning flesh. He had smelled something like that once before when they had burned a pile of rats before they started using the rodents for food.

Moving through pure tenacity now, Muller stumbled forward, reaching out with a free hand towards the soldiers by the fire. One turned his head shouting something lost to Muller under the loud crackle of the fire.

Blinded by the glare of the flame, Muller did not see the soldier raise his rifle and aim it. The shot hit him square between the eyes. Muller toppled to the ground, eyes open to the rain pouring down on him. When they dragged him to the pit and rolled him onto the pile of burning bodies, they did not see the penknife fall from his pocket, silver words glinting dully in the orange light until the wash of rain and mud had swallowed it whole.

A transplant from the north to Savannah, GA, **S. L. Cortes** spends her days among books as a librarian for Savannah Technical College. She is currently pursuing a Master's in Library & Information Science, and spends the little free time she has writing short stories and coming up with bizarre ideas for more stories.

Spread The Insanity

by Trevor Firetog

aggots were festering on the rancid meat, each one squirming their way in and out of every pore. Mold conjugated around stale pieces of bread and old, discarded pastries. Not one thing was edible. Nor was anything sanitary. This kitchen is a chef's nightmare and a maid's worst enemy. It looked to be the aftermath of some food induced crime scene.

"It's a damn mess!" Leon shouted. There was some acknowledgment from the next room, but no direct answer.

"I mean, look at this!" He continued. "How long as it been?" He said as he was resisting the temptation to poke at the maggots.

"Like a week or something." The voice in the other room said.

Leon finally gave into his temptation as he started to scrape the maggots off the steak with a dirty butter knife. They were disgusting creatures. The ones that didn't fall onto the counter held onto the knife coiling themselves around the blade. Leon didn't even want to think how he would begin to clean this mess up.

"How come you didn't call me sooner?" Said Leon, tossing the maggot covered knife into the sink. It made a large clatter as it collided with the other dishes.

"I didn't want to upset you."

Leon turned on the faucet to the highest temperature then let it run onto the dishes.

"You should have called me sooner." He said under his breath.

"What?"

"Nothing," He shouted over his shoulder.

"Leon, I can't here you!"

Leon twisted the faucet off then walked a couple steps closer to the next room.

"I said it's nothing."

There was a brief moment of silence, followed by a frustrated shout.

"Can you just please come in here?"

Leon surveyed the filthy kitchen one last time before leaving the room. He felt the least he could do was open a window. He finally decided against it; He wouldn't want to let any more flies in here.

In the next room, lying on a queen size bed was Kayla, as beautiful as ever. Lavender sheets wrapped tightly around her half naked body. The sheets were taut enough that Leon could see a general outline of her nipples. Immediately, he knew it was already worth it to come over.

"You rang?" He said with a smirk.

She pulled the sheet tighter around her body.

"Can you help prop my legs up?" She asked, appearing to be in pain.

Leon did what she asked, exhilarated to be a part of her world. He tried his best not to steal glances at her bare shoulders, or the curvy treasures beneath the purple sheets. It was not easy. Not when a girl as beautiful as her is laying in front of you.

About three weeks ago, Kayla was involved in a car accident. Aside from cuts and bruises, she broke both her legs and received a hairline fracture in her lower spine. She would be able to walk again. That was not an issue. The issue was her training to walk again. The doctors want to keep her at the hospital and enroll her in a rehab program. However, Kayla's loving, caring, and now ex-boyfriend Brian, wouldn't allow it. He insisted on keeping her home with the intent of taking care of her. Which is what he did, for exactly two weeks. One day he went out to pick up dinner, but never came back. The odd part is Kayla always suspected he would do something like that. It was just like Brian to run away and hide when things got to stressful.

Since then, Kayla asked for a friend to come over and bring her some food. The essentials: a pizza pie, a bag of pretzels, and a case of beer. An old wheelchair sat beside her bed. Although, she just didn't have the strength or endurance to climb in and use it. Instead, she decided to stay bedridden. She told lies to her friends, saying that Brian had a family emergency. She also didn't get to see the kitchen. She made it through almost an entire week on cold pizza and warm beer. Soon, even her friends started to ignore Kayla's calls. She started to consider that all the people around her were unreliable. That's when she finally decided to call Leon. He was always there for her, ever since their high school days. He would understand this situation.

When Leon discovered her, she was drenched in her own sweat and blitzed drunk. She was laughing and giggling about how terrible her situation is, while Leon thumbed through a medical book to see if the alcohol would react with any of the medication she was taking.

He spent the whole night through, cleaning her up. Changing her out of her filthy clothes, cleaning up the spilt cans of beer and the stray slices of pepperoni clung to the bed sheets. Despite her current condition, Leon still finds her attractive. How could he not be in love with that beautiful and innocent face? She would never know, would she? She would never know the way he felt about her.

"Thank you for being here for me." She said making herself comfortable.

"I'm always here for you. You should know that by now." He replied, caught up in his emotions.

He cleared away a few strands of her yellow blonde hair from her face, tucking them behind her ear. She smiled in return. A long uncomfortable silence passed before Leon felt obliged to say something.

"I think I'll get started with the kitchen now."

"Is it really that bad?"

"It's pretty unbearable. Lots of maggots and mold."

"Maggots?" She said with quizzical disgust.

"Yes."

"How many?"

"Lots."

"Bastard. I hate Brian. I hate him for leaving me like this. I can't even go to the damn bathroom by myself!"

"It's fine. I'm here now. If things get out of hand, we can always go back to the hospital. You shouldn't worry about it." Leon said, trying to be as comforting as he can.

"Thank you."

"I'm going to clean up now. Okay?"

"Can't it wait? Are you hungry?"

"A little. Why? Are you?" He said sitting at the foot of her bed.

"I haven't eaten anything today. Can you go pick something up?"

Leon took a breath of frustration. "Sure. You want me to stop by the deli and pick up some sandwiches or bagels or something?"

"That would be amazing." She said with a beautiful, soft sigh. He couldn't say no.

"So you want to just let the maggots stay?"

"Just for now."

"Okay, but you better start charging them rent." He joked getting up from the bed.

Kayla let out a loud almost certainly fake laugh. Leon regretted making that joke wishing he had thought of something better. Something she could really laugh at.

Leon picked up his long black coat from the chair in the corner of the room.

"Do you need to go to the bathroom before I go?" He asked.

"No, no. I'm fine. Please hurry back."

"I'll see you in a bit." Leon said as he closed the door behind him.

On his way out, Leon tried his best to ignore the filthy kitchen. If he so much as glanced at it, he knew that he would lose his appetite.

Outside, the sun was making an attempt to shine through the dismal, gray clouds. Dew frosted the tips of the long grass on Kayla's lawn. When Leon reached his pickup truck, he struggled to open the door from the frost that clung to the handle. Soon enough, the door flung open and Leon sprung backwards. He stood himself straight then quickly jumped into the truck, hoping that Kayla wasn't watching through the window.

As he drove through the town, the vehicle's heat on full blast, a dark, cold feeling sank into the pit of his stomach. He felt a mix of nausea and despair. Still, he kept driving, but at some point; whether it was as he was driving, or it had always been this way, he was greeted by a terrifying realization. This town was empty. Storefronts had been boarded up, cars with their doors ajar were abandoned in the middle of the street, grocery bags and personal belongings from the town's people were spread around the sidewalk. Not even a single bird flew in the sky.

Leon brought the pickup truck to a slow stop. When he turned the key, the truck's engine powered down, he was greeted by an overpowering silence. Confused and scared, he got out of the truck.

"Hello?" He shouted.

Only his echo answered him. He shut his eyes tight then began to wonder if he was over tired. He could have easily been stressed out. Maybe the mold in the kitchen was making him hallucinate. Maybe he was just dreaming. Maybe it was a mix of all three. He prayed it would be so. When he opened his eyes, his prayers had gone unanswered. He shouted a few more times at the vacant town before returning back into his truck. The red color of the vehicle was the most colorful thing in this empty town. Everything else was coated with a shade of gray as an early morning storm color filled the skies. A light layer of fog billowed around him.

He got into his truck then quickly closed the door before any fog could enter. Leon took a moment to himself before putting the key back into the ignition. He turned it once, but heard a loud clicking sound. He turned it again, the clicking turned into a grinding.

"Perfect." He said, grinding his teeth. "Just fucking great."

Leon was about to slam his fist against the steering wheel when he stopped, his fist in mid-air. He heard a noise that came from outside. He held his fist in the air, staying as still as possible, not even allowing himself to take a breath. His eyes scanned every inch of the outside world. It was impossible to describe the sound he heard, but he didn't hear it again. Once satisfied that everything was all right, Leon searched his pockets. A sigh of aggravation came over him.

His phone was not with him. It was in Kayla's room, sitting on her nightstand. The realization of this came slow and painfully. He was stranded in what seemed to be everywhere and nowhere at the same time, plus he had no way of communicating with anyone, not to mention his transportation broke down. In this moment of helplessness, for a brief second, he felt like a child again, crying in his mother's arms.

After pulling himself back together, he did the only thing he could think of. He got out of his pickup truck, and started walking. Luckily, he had only been driving for two minutes or so before he found himself stranded in a state of nonexistence. It should only be a five-minute walk back. As he was walking, he thought of Kayla. He felt so bad not achieving the task she set him out to do. Would she believe him when he tells her that this is what happened? Or would she simply shrug it off? She already thinks of him as just a friend, he doesn't need her thinking of him as a bad friend. She is so complicated, Leon thought. Why can't she just realize the way he feels about her?

He walked in complete silence through the once bustling residential neighborhoods. He walked past houses that appeared to be long deserted, evidenced by signs of vegetation growing within them. He tried to ignore his surroundings and concentrate on his goal: '*Getting back to Kayla*'. With only his racing thoughts to keep him company, he finally was on the final stretch back to Kayla's house. For a moment, he let this enjoyment get to him. Leon was so caught up in his elation that he almost missed it. That noise. The same one he heard before. He immediately put his joy on hold to listen for the sound. He replayed it over and over in his head. It was a *crunch* sound, he was sure of that. The noise sounded like porcelain cracking, or rocks smashing against each other, or maybe the sound of bones snapping.

Leon looked all around him. His body ached, his eyes were heavy, and his legs were weak with exhaustion. He wanted nothing more than to be back with Kayla, but for Leon's mental sake, this mystery needed be solved.

Something caught his eye. It was something that seemed to be small. It was gray; therefore it blended in with everything else but it was there all right. Something, about three houses down from where he was standing, sitting in the grass. Blocking Leon's way to Kayla's home.

It was alive. Leon walked towards it hesitantly. He didn't want to call out to whatever it was before he had gotten a closer look first.

After walking a few more feet, Leon got the closest look he could ever want. This pallid creature sat in the tall grass. Its eyes glowed yellow, its nose was pigged. He appeared to be naked. What lay next to him was even more disturbing than the creature itself; a pile of heads sat in a pyramid like fashion. Flesh peeled off their faces. Their eyes glistened, wide opened. They appeared to be in pain. Leon clutched his hand over his mouth and gagged, smelling their rancid flesh from where he stood.

The creature snapped to life, hearing Leon's gag. It looked up at him then gave a little smirk. Without breaking eye contact, the monster picked up a head, fresh off the top of the pyramid and brought it towards his mouth. The thing's mouth stretched open as wide as it could, almost as if its jaws separated off from the face. The creature placed the entire human head in there with extraordinary ease. Then... *Crunch!* Blood dribbled down the monster's chin-like juice from a rare cooked steak.

Leon slowly started to back away as he watched the beast pick little bits of skull and strands of human hair out of its jagged teeth. He knew it would only be a short run to Kayla's house. Could he out run this thing? With little warning, the creature got up with effortless ease. It stared at Leon, grinning, running its blood red tongue up and down the length of its lips. The monster was evidently a lot taller standing than it was sitting. Its height appeared to top at over eight feet. Its body was thin, showing a malnourished set of ribs through its shark-like skin. Leon couldn't keep his legs from shaking. His body was ready to sprint away at any moment.

The monster took a step forward; its skinny legs resembling that of a lamb. With that, Leon set off. His aim was to race through the backyards of residential houses until he finally reached Kayla's house where he would call the police, or army, or whoever could handle a situation like this. Needless to say, even best laid plans may go astray. The creature, giggling with enthusiasm for the chase, sprouted wings of demonic, gargoyle appearance. The wings appeared to have come from within the body itself, tearing through flesh as they birthed. The beast took to the skies, circling around Leon like a vulture waiting for its food to finally die.

When Leon was finished weaving his way through both the front and back yards of the houses, he finally arrived at the stoop to Kayla's house. That's when the vulture went in for a merciless attack. Leon was out of breath, and was trying to contain his vomit from rising any further up his gullet. With one hand on the doorknob, he felt the pain of razor sharp talons clutching onto his shoulder, pulling him back. He landed on the sidewalk, a few feet away from Kayla's door. He prayed the Kayla could summon the strength to come to his rescue, however, deep down, he knew better.

The beast landed right on top of him. Its landing shattered the pavement around him. Leon was too terrified to move. He closed his eyes to what happened next.

The creature placed its bony hand lightly onto Leon's chest. He stopped for a second listening closely. Once satisfied, it raised its hand back up then leaned in closer to Leon. He whispered in his ear. His voice was coarse, yet proper.

"Soon," It said softly. "Very soon..."

The creature rose back up and took off. After a few moments, Leon finally gathered the courage to open his eyes. He could still hear the beast's wings flapping in the distance.

Once Leon was back on his feet, he gave himself a quick check just to make sure that everything was all right. There was nothing wrong, other than the stinging pulse of a headache brewing deep inside his skull. It has been building up since the start of this dreadful day. Now, Leon was about the breakdown, but he still maintained some form of a clear head.

The door to Kayla's house creaked and splintered. It seemed as though the damn thing was about to fall off right then and there. Once inside, Leon took a deep breath then closed his eyes. He nearly let out a cry. The interior of Kayla's house was entirely populated by plant life. Her living room had turned into a forest. The kitchen became a garden. The hallway was a thick brush of small trees and shrubs. Poison ivy grew from underneath the carpet. Vines crawled up and gripped onto the walls. An utterly large tree stood in the center of the parlor. This was absurd, he thought. This was horrifying.

Leon thought -and hoped- that maybe later he would have the time to further observe and study these surroundings, but right now there were only two things on his mind; finding Kayla, and obtaining a phone.

It took Leon some talent to be able to navigate through the twisted trees and hanging vines. He found it easy to get lost in the greenery on the way to Kayla's room. Leon leaped over one of the giant roots of the tree. He thought he had cleared the jump, but was wrong. His foot got snagged. He went tumbling to the ground, slamming his ribs on the trunk and thick roots of the tree.

Hunching over in pain, clutching his ribs, his mind fell into a daze. He felt as if he was in a movie. It was as if every word he would speak was already planned out for him, like lines in a script.

Once his body recovered from the pain, he slowly sat himself up. It took a moment for his eyes to adjust back to normal. When they did, he saw what he tripped on wasn't a root at all. It was a body, Kayla's body.

Twisted roots and shrubbery grew within her and cascaded out. Plant life filled her oral cavity, and crawled down to her breasts. A small shrub protruded out from within her belly button. These greens around her seemed to be continuously growing, spreading throughout her body. Leon leaned over then wrapped his arms around her, holding her tight. He couldn't contain his emotions anymore. He broke down and cried, rocking Kayla back and forth as he did.

As he rocked her, praying that she would come back, his wish was fulfilled. Whether it was by some sort of magic, or someone was really listening to his prayers, Kayla came to life with a sharp inhale. Her eyes were bloodshot. She was bleeding continuously, but it was still his darling.

"Am I dreaming?" She whispered.

"No, sweetie, you're not dreaming." Leon said, tears rolling down his cheeks.

"Sweetie? You called me sweetie. I've waited so long for you to call me that." She said, joining in on his crying. "Are you sure I'm not dreaming?"

"I'm sure. I love you Kayla. I always have."

"I love you too, Leon." Her voice was getting softer.

"Please stay with me." Leon sobbed.

"Hold me tighter."

He held her tighter bringing her closer.

"Tighter. I can't feel you." She said.

He held her tighter still.

"Tighte-" She exhaled as she slipped back into death.

Leon cried. He kissed her lips for the first and last time as he lay her body back down amongst the greenery. The shrubs devoured what was the rest of her body. Soon, the love of his life was turned into nothing more than a twisted mass of brilliant, green vines and plants.

Just when he thought he could finally have a moment of peace. Just when he thought it was safe to let his guard down. He was wrong. All at once, clangs and booms were heard from all corners of the house. The creature was back, and was entreating entrance. It sounded as if he was clumsily hurling himself into the walls of the house. Leon's heart skipped a beat, his head pulsed harder, and his body seemed to shut down for a split second of paralyzing fear.

He gripped his chest trying to control his breathing. It was impossibly hard to do when the most terrifying creature he had ever had seen was banging on the walls. After a few seconds, Leon heard a window shatter accompanied by a hoard of frightful giggling. That was all the encouragement Leon needed to take cover elsewhere. He couldn't go back outside. The creature was a master of the skies. It would be like a hawk preying on a field mouse. The most logical option that Leon needed was to retreat to Kayla's room.

Once inside, he discovered her room had somehow been transformed into something similar to a rain forest. Large trees stood all around. Water drops fell from the ceiling, smacking against the thick leaves before dripping down into the soggy carpet.

Leon slammed the door shut, locking it, and lobed a chair at it for good measure. He sat down on a grass-covered bed then tried thinking to himself. What did the thing mean when he said, "Soon"? What was it waiting for? For Kayla to die, and now it's back? These questions made Leon's brain feel several sizes too big for his skull.

Soon enough, it had dawned upon him. The creature was trying to make him go insane. It was trying to break him down mentally so he would be more susceptible to the creature's will. Or was he already insane for thinking up such a wild thing? He would find out right now.

He shut his eyes, clamping them as hard as he could. He cleared his mind of all things stressful, trying to focus on his breathing, or the light pulse of his blood flowing through his body. It seemed to work. He no longer heard the creature searching through the house. He felt the bed rid itself of all plant life and be restored of its lavender sheets. With his eyes closed, he heard the trees descend, and the house creaking back into its original shape.

When he opened one eye, he was amazed to see everything in the house had returned to normal. It was all back just the way he had remembered it. When he opened his other eye, he was greeted by the sound of a familiar voice.

"Hey there." Kayla said, lying on the bed next to him.

He was overcome with joy. To see his love lying there with her legs broken and the sheets covering her bare chest was more of a dream come true than he could have ever imagined. He leaped over then hugged her tight.

"I love you, Kayla. I'm never letting you go ever again!" He shouted.

After a brief silence she replied with, "What the hell are you talking about?"

"I love you. I always have. I've always wanted to tell you that. Now that I did, I just feel so damn great!" He said.

"Oh," She responded with a smirk. "I love you too."

"You do? Truly?"

"Yes, of course. I think I always have."

Leon felt the most joy that anybody on earth could have ever felt. For the next two hours, Leon and Kayla talked. Nothing more. He told her about his silly vision and the winged beast. She laughed in his face about it.

They talked about the first time they met, and how much he liked her. They talked about how their past lovers were not as good as they were together. They talked about sweet things.

Finally after a healthy amount of conversations, Leon felt it was time to convert back to his original job, cleaning, and taking care of her as she recovered.

He staggered outside the room, drunk on his own love then went straight to the kitchen. There, he cleaned the maggoty food and moldy dishes as he slowly nursed his headache. He was feeling better already. In a matter of minutes, he simply forgot about the horrible nightmare that he was forced to endure. Leon simply whistled a happy tune as he continued to clean.

"Leon?" Kayla's voice called. "Can you come here please?"

Never had he been so happy to answer that call. He walked through the hallway and into her room.

"Yes?" He said entering.

"I'm not feeling very good," She said then her nose slipped off her face.

Leon gasped then ran towards her.

"Baby!" He said. "Talk to me! Stay with me!"

Other appendages started to crawl down her face. Her mouth dripped past her chin, dropping down onto her lavender bed sheets. Her ears and eyes shortly followed.

She sat there, grabbing for help, looking like an unfinished wax sculpture. No blood was on her skin. It melted off like a candle. She couldn't communicate. He couldn't understand her.

Leon frantically grabbed her nose and mouth from the bed sheets struggling to place them back on her face, but they didn't latch.

After a few seconds, he gave up on her then dashed out of the room leaving her in there begging for help.

He ran into the bathroom then shut the door. His head was pounding. His heart was burning. He fell into the bathtub and tried to catch a breath. Everything seemed to be somewhat normal in the bathroom. However upon on a closer look, something was strange.

Something was in the drain, something yellow. Leon tried to ignore it, but it beckoned to him. He settled on taking a quick peek. He leaned over the grated drain and saw two yellow eyes staring at him. Leon's jaw dropped. He didn't bother to question what he saw. All he knew was that two eyes looked deeply at him.

"Now you're ready," A voice said.

A hand emerged, breaking through the grated metal of the drain gripping a hold onto Leon's face. Leon flew back and watched the events unfold. He sat on the bathroom floor, as the creature yank a body into the drain. The body looked like Leon's, but how could it be? Leon was the one watching it. Whether he was a ghost or simply insane, he was witnessing the death of himself. He let out a yelp as the creature pulled him through, into the drain. Squeezing, crushing, reshaping his body and bones to fit down the pipes. As Leon stared in shock he felt the devastating pain of all the blood, muscle, and fat in his body burst through his lower appendages as though he were a tube of toothpaste.

As his feet were about to be swallowed into the drain, Leon cries out. Kayla -the *real* Kayla- is forced to get into the rickety old chair and wheel her way into the bathroom, just in time to witness the shower drain consume her new love.

Leon sat in the corner, watching the tears roll down Kayla's face. With a frantic struggle, Leon searches to find his voice to guide her out of the room to look for a phone to call the police. Once out of the bathroom, simultaneously they notice something outside the window. The outside world was dark and gloomy. The gray winged creature with the yellow eyes stood at the window, staring inside. Fresh blood was dribbling down his chin.

In his bony gray hand, was Leon's head. A look of terror was forever imprinted on his face. Leon's lips formed the shape of a scream, but it was Kayla's voice that filled it with sound.

The creature devoured Leon's head. His skull gave way with a satisfying *crunch*. Then, just as quickly as it appeared, the creature was gone. The world outside was back to normal.

Kayla couldn't seem to take this anymore. She looked as though she was ready to simply give up. Leon pleaded for her to stay with him; to keep her eyes open. But he could not speak or communicate in anyway. With nothing preventing her, she closed her eyes and fell into the madness that would embrace her.

Trevor Firetog is a writer/filmmaker that lives on Long Island. He spends his time watching movies, reading books, and writing dark fantasy and horror fiction.